Praise for Jenny Hale

"Jenny Hale writes touching, beautiful stories."—*New York Times* **bestselling author RaeAnne Thayne**

"I can always count on Jenny Hale to sweep me away with her heartwarming romantic tales."—**Denise Hunter, bestselling author** on *Butterfly Sisters*

One of "19 Dreamy Summer Romances to Whisk you Away" in *Oprah Magazine* on *The Summer House*

One of "24 Dreamy Books about Romance" in *Oprah Daily* on *The Summer House*

Included in "Christmas Novels to Start Reading Now" in *Southern Living Magazine* on *The Christmas Letters*

"Touching, fun-filled, and redolent with salt air and the fragrance of summer, this seaside tale is a perfect volume for most romance collections."—*Library Journal* on *The Summer House*

Books By Jenny Hale

The Magic of Sea Glass

Butterfly Sisters

The Memory Keeper

An Island Summer

The Beach House

The House on Firefly Beach

Summer at Firefly Beach

The Summer Hideaway

The Summer House

Summer at Oyster Bay

Summer by the Sea

A Barefoot Summer

Meet Me at Christmas

The Christmas Letters

A Lighthouse Christmas

Christmas at Fireside Cabins

Christmas at Silver Falls

It Started with Christmas

We'll Always Have Christmas

All I Want for Christmas

Christmas Wishes and Mistletoe Kisses

A Christmas to Remember

Coming Home for Christmas

The
Golden
Hour

The
Golden
Hour

JENNY HALE
USA TODAY BESTSELLING AUTHOR

HARPETH ROAD
PRESS
Nashville

HARPETH ROAD PRESS

Published by Harpeth Road Press (USA)
P.O. Box 158184
Nashville, TN 37215

Paperback: 979-8-9887744-3-3
eBook: 979-8-9887744-2-6

The Golden Hour: A Powerful, Heartwarming Summer Love Story

Cover design by Kristen Ingebretson
Cover Images © Shutterstock

First printing: April 2024

CHAPTER ONE
LOX CREEK, TENNESSEE

Growing up, Josie Wills thought she'd had so many choices available to her. But when it came down to it, she'd really only had one.

She didn't want to think about the options she'd let go. What was the point? Surrendering to the uniformity of everyday living was much easier. The security of consistency outweighed the thrill of surprises. Or at least that was what she told herself.

She turned off the bathroom light and felt her way down the hall. When she arrived at the kitchen she blinked to adjust to the brightness, where—to her surprise—her teenage brother, Nick, was already awake before the sun. His head was down as he worked on a math problem in his spiral notebook over his breakfast of eggs and toast.

"I have to go in early today," she said. "You going to be okay?"

"Yeah."

When his attention didn't leave his notebook, she knew better than to take his response personally.

"All right, love you."

"Okay," he replied, evidently too fixated on his page to think about being cordial.

At eighteen, his face was starting to appear less youthful and more chiseled, his mature legs stretching out and filling the space under the small kitchen table. Josie tried not to focus on how old he was getting. She treasured her younger brother, and she wanted to hold on to this time together forever.

While they were bound by family and shared the same green eyes their father had, the siblings couldn't be more different. Nick's hair was a much lighter brown than hers, and he'd gotten lankier limbs like the rest of the family, while she was petite and solid. Nick had exceptional skills in math, but she'd been more interested in literature and history. Yet, despite their differences, they got along incredibly well.

She grabbed her purse and rushed out the door, climbed into her car, and sat for a moment in the silence.

Nick had been having trouble in school again. Because of that, he'd become withdrawn. None of the teachers or his counselor seemed to know the best way to reach him, and he didn't have many friends to offer support. Graduation was in a few weeks. He'd asked if he could skip the ceremony, which had broken her heart. The event would probably be a sensory overload for him, but she was willing to bet his reluctance to go was due more to the fact that he was tired of dealing with no one understanding his unique gifts.

Talking to him about how he felt was difficult, and she feared he'd have little opportunity to shine in their town. She needed to get him out, show him what life could be like, but she didn't have the means or the free hours. She had to work just to pay the bills and put aside inadequate savings.

Her hands on the steering wheel, she stared out at the late spring darkness. She wanted to do better for her and her brother. She just wasn't sure how.

Josie started the car and headed to the diner, her mind full.

Whenever she faced hard times, which was a lot these days, recollections of her youth came back to her, as if her mind were stacking up all the experiences that had led to where she was now. It didn't help. Remembering only made her more exhausted.

One memory floated to the surface without warning. She tried to push it away as she drove, but the thought was relentless. Five years old and barefoot—the way she had spent every summer as a child—she'd taken the shortcut from her friend Ruth's through the thicket to get back to the house nestled in the mountains where Josie lived with her parents.

"Head home when the lightning bugs come out," her mother had always told her.

With only her father at home that night, Josie had gotten an early start so she wouldn't worry him. Mama was at the hospital for some tests for her blood pressure and to check on her headaches, and she would soon bring home Josie's new baby brother.

For weeks, up until the day Mama had gone to the hospital, she'd practiced taking care of babies with Josie. They'd worked on pinning cloth diapers correctly using Josie's dolls, and Mama had shown her just how to hold the baby's head to support its neck. Josie couldn't wait to have a younger brother to look after. Mama had told her she'd make a wonderful mother one day, which was good because that was exactly what Josie had wanted to be.

On her way home that evening the sun was barely visible, its pink-and-orange light outlining the valleys before it disappeared behind the mountains—the time of day Mama called "the golden hour." Josie had stopped at a nearby creek to sink her feet in the cool stream, then bent down to pick up a rock with a silver stripe that had caught her eye. Deciding to take it home to draw it, she'd washed off the rock then dried it on her tattered sundress. The cicadas had started croaking, so she'd quickly dropped the rock in her pocket and hopped onto the bank. Careful of loose gravel, she'd continued down the path toward home, thinking about what she could try to make for herself and Daddy for dinner. Being only five, Josie wasn't allowed to use the stove, and she'd wondered how she would fry the tomatoes she was planning to cook.

She'd made it past the thicket, across the meadow, and all the way to the edge of the yard before Mama's golden hour had ended. Proud of herself for getting home so quickly, she'd bounded through the grass as fast as her bare feet could take her and stopped when she reached her father sitting hunched on the steps leading to the door.

"Hi, Daddy," she'd said.

But something wasn't the same about Daddy. When he lifted his head from his hands, his eyes were swollen and red, and Josie wondered if he was having an allergic reaction like she had once when she'd eaten peanuts. He reached out for her and drew her into a tight embrace, and she decided she could comfort him the way Mama had comforted her when she'd had the allergy.

That hour had been anything but golden. It had been the first step toward the life Josie was now living as an adult. She'd had no idea back then how much everything would change. At a very young age, she'd had to learn about conditions like eclampsia and cerebral hemorrhage. She'd also had to understand how to live without her mother.

Now, one hand on the wheel, the other in her pocket as she drove, she ran her fingers over the jagged hinges of her father's old compass, which she carried with her everywhere. The brass cover had been lost, leaving the two broken hinges on the edge. He'd told her he wasn't given permission by his parents to follow his dreams, so he wanted the compass to be a reminder for her to follow her heart and to let it lead her to her brightest future.

But she didn't believe anything could lead her there anymore. She doubted the magnetic needle would point anywhere but the place she was now. However, the compass was the only token she had of her dad's, besides the old mountain house he'd left behind, so she carried the circular object around to feel closer to him. She let it fall to the bottom of her wide shirt pocket and made the final turn to work.

Every day Josie made the same six-minute drive through the Tennessee mountains from her house in Lox Creek to the diner on the edge of town. When she arrived for the breakfast shift, she parked next to the trash bins around back.

Josie went in through the single door to the kitchen and said hello to the cooks before she put her lunch bag in the refrigerator next to the collection of salad dressing jars, then headed to the break room. She liked going in there early to skirt around having to chat with the other waitresses when they came in. She used to know most of them in school, and a few years ago she probably would have fallen right into their chatter, but now it seemed unnecessary. She stole a few extra minutes for herself and tied up her long brown hair using the cloudy mirror on the wall. Then she put on her apron—a thin, denim smock with her name in simple black type pinned above her left breast.

The rest of the day was spent taking orders, putting on her most pleasant smile, and pretending everything was easy and fine, which it certainly wasn't. But she didn't allow her troubles to permeate her work.

When she was only twenty, she'd been tasked with this life; Nick depended on her—and would for a few more years at least—so she'd done everything she could to make the best of the situation. Forced optimism was what got her through. She told herself she was lucky in a lot of ways: she was healthy, she had a job that generally paid the bills, and she had her tiny family of two—just her and Nick. They had each other.

"Hey there," fellow waitress Ruth Swanson said in her usual detached tone as she came into the break room like a whirlwind. Her body language and disheveled appearance gave away the fact that she'd probably overslept. Again.

Josie finished tying her apron behind her back. "Morning."

Ruth gave her a side-eyed glance while putting her own apron on in a flash. It was a far cry from their giggles on the teeter-totter at school when they were girls. Ruth had been one of Josie's friends growing up, but now they barely spoke. Ever since Josie had returned home after quitting college, Ruth had been distant, and Josie wasn't sure why. She guessed maybe Ruth thought Josie had gone off in search of something better, and left her behind. But she'd just been trying to do the best she could for herself and follow her dad's advice to go wherever her inner compass led her. She'd never imagined this job would be the height of her career.

Josie went over to her morning station and set in rolling silverware in paper napkins and dropping the bundled cutlery into the large bin the waitresses used to set the tables quickly between groups.

"It goes knife, fork, then spoon," Helen had told Josie on her first day there. "The knife should be on the bottom because it's the longest." Helen's instructions had faded away as the days went by and Josie plunged into her thoughts, something she did a lot.

Ruth passed her and headed into the dining area. She didn't know what Josie was dealing with these days because Josie hadn't had time to tell her—or anyone for that matter. Sure, there were whispers around town about "that poor girl and her brother who'd lost everything," but none of them really knew entirely what she'd lost. She didn't let herself indulge in the memory of it too often because the what-if was more than she could bear.

CHAPTER TWO
THREE YEARS AGO

The static *whoosh* of the waterfall danced around Josie as she followed Julian Russel down the narrow dirt trail, unaware at the time that the moment would become one of the memories she'd lock away because she'd miss it too much to recall.

She dipped under the shady foliage searching for the source of the sound, but her view of the cascading water was still obstructed. The faint noise had been with them the entire hike, rising to a crescendo as if leading them, only to reveal itself as some sort of grand finale.

Julian trod along with his usual energy, two brightly colored beach towels around his neck and a worn backpack bouncing against his back. Josie tried not to focus on the gold flecks in his sandy-brown hair or the roundness of his biceps peeking out of his short sleeves. He was incredibly handsome, but his kindness and compassion for others was what had drawn her to him. They'd first connected through their interest in what the world had to offer and the classic songs he'd played while they were making dinner one night in the house they shared with other students. Before long, their conversations could go anywhere, and she'd stop everything to have one of their discussions. But she'd only recently admitted to herself that she'd fallen head over heels for him.

The humidity wrapped them in its embrace, and she wiped a bead of sweat from her forehead as her hiking boots crunched against the brush beneath them. For the fourth time she looked behind her for Brit and Maisy, who'd stopped at the restroom along the trail and were still catching up to them.

Now in her second year at the University of Tennessee, Josie could afford to be picky when it came to the people she chose to spend time with. Most students had settled in with their social groups, and Maisy Jacobson and Brit Newsome were the perfect housemates and friends. When their rent went up unexpectedly at the beginning of Josie's sophomore year, they'd needed to squeeze in one more person at the last minute to lighten the financial load. Julian had been Josie's last choice on a short list of options—his striking smile and overly friendly nature an obvious distraction. She also hadn't been keen on a co-ed living arrangement. She'd expressed her concerns to her housemates about living with a guy and all that entailed around privacy and, in some cases, cleanliness, but she knew right away it was a lost battle. His good looks, impeccable manners, and boyish charm had already won over her housemates.

Julian had assured them that with three against one, he didn't stand a chance if he did anything to upset them, and he'd promised to stay on his side of the apartment. Then he'd given them a sob story about how they were his last option because his other rental had fallen through and if he didn't live with them he'd be on the streets. Josie was nearly certain that, with his appeal and charisma, he'd have no problem finding a place to stay. Then he'd told them he'd probably barely be around and offered to pay for the utilities, and she'd relented.

Turned out, while he did keep to his room from late

evening until dawn, he was there all the time. To complicate matters, he'd taken a liking to Josie and always approached her with a brotherly type of affection that Maisy and Brit were convinced would turn into more. They went so far as to give Josie and Julian a nickname of "J Squared." But Josie was too focused on her future in the beginning to allow anything to develop.

The compass her father had given her when she was ten reminded her every day to focus on her future. She was the first of her family to go to college, and she had bigger things to do in life than flirt with Julian, even if she had become smitten with him. But the more time she spent with him, the more her perspective changed. Being around him was a delicious diversion she struggled to avoid as the weeks went on. Loving him was as natural as taking a breath, his mere presence a light in her day. Instead of studying, she found herself thinking about things he'd said or looks he'd given her, and she'd had to force herself to focus. She began to see a future with Julian and dreamed about what it would be like if they had each other to lean on as they moved through life.

Leaving him for any length of time over the summer would be difficult. Josie was glad they'd planned a trip together with Brit and Maisy. For now, they still had a couple weeks of school left, and she spent every minute she could with him.

The southern heat had come in like a lion, before it was officially summer. The sound of the waterfall grew closer and its cool spray beckoned her. Roasting, Josie slipped off her T-shirt to finish the hike in her bathing suit top. She rolled the shirt and stuffed it through the belt loops of her cut-offs.

"How much farther?" she asked.

"Not much."

Julian paused, and she caught up to him. The corner of his mouth turned up, and that familiar affection showed in his eyes, making her stomach flip. She wrinkled her nose at him playfully and drank in his presence as they walked side by side.

With the waterfall a busy excursion for many, they'd agreed to make the hike early in the afternoon on a weekday to avoid any crowds, which meant that, until Maisy and Brit reached them, it was just her and Julian on the path. Josie didn't mind the solitude at all.

"Thirsty?" He held out his water bottle, that sparkle in his blue eyes still as thrilling as if it were the first time he'd looked at her that way.

"No, thanks. I'm good."

A few minutes later she tripped over a root and he caught her.

"Thank you." She swallowed against her dry mouth and strode next to him, wondering if she should tell him she was in love with him. He probably knew already, but they hadn't actually said the words. She hadn't felt this way about anyone before, and navigating her feelings was proving difficult.

He side-eyed her with that subtle grin still playing at the corner of his lips, the same way it did when he sat across the aisle from her in their botany class. That was how they'd ended up on the trail. She'd needed one more science class to meet the requirements for undergrad, and Julian had said he'd take the class with her. As a final project, they'd had several excursions to choose from, the assignment being to research their hypothesis for the question: Does tourism pose a threat to plant life? Julian had asked her to be his partner, and when their roommates had found out they were going to spend the day at the popular waterfall, they'd asked to come along.

Josie had tried not to fall for Julian. Being in close proximity had been so challenging that she didn't trust herself alone with him now, and although she was completely crazy about him, the question often surfaced of whether starting something was a good idea. She had so much on her plate, both at school and back home.

But that was her head talking; her heart had a different opinion.

"Look." He put his hand on her arm and pointed to the right.

Josie didn't have time to register the softness in his touch. She gasped at the stunning sight in front of her and bounded down the wooden steps, off the path, to the small clearing just in front of the spectacle. The vegetation had opened up to reveal a beautiful turquoise pool with a gushing waterfall that seemed to stretch up to the heavens. Water droplets sparkled on every surface of the lush, green vegetation as the sunlight found its way through the canopy of trees. Birds flapped their wings, and the snap of twigs in the distance signaled that they'd probably disturbed an animal and it had scampered off, looking for cover.

She quickly unpacked her sketchpad and took it to a nearby tree, where she pressed it against the trunk, her dark pencil moving a mile a minute. Whenever she focused on drawing, it was as if her sense of sight heightened. She noticed the shades of dark and light green on every leaf, the dips in the rocky soil, the shimmy of the water as it left the waterfall and moved toward the edges of the pool. She couldn't draw the scene fast enough. It was as if her talent consumed her body and she was no longer in control of it.

Art had been one of her escapes as a child. Her father had suggested she be an art major when she went to college. But drawing was sacred to her, and she didn't want the views of her professors or classmates to change the absolute joy she felt when she sat on the cold ground with her sketchpad opened to a blank page, her pencil ready to absorb her surroundings, so she'd settled on a marketing degree instead.

Julian's breath tickled her neck, sending a bolt of electricity down her arm, slowing the movement of her pencil.

"That's incredible," he whispered in her ear. He'd always been supportive of her art, and he said whatever she completed in college wouldn't matter because she'd end up doing something with her talent.

She'd drawn the basic layout of the waterfall and would return to the page later. She closed her sketchpad and pushed it back into her backpack for safekeeping.

Julian dropped his bag filled with their textbooks and a couple binders before stripping off his T-shirt. His bare olive chest had already tanned with the change of season. She slid off her boots and shorts while he hung their towels on a nearby branch. When she'd gotten down to the yellow bikini Brit had convinced her to buy for their summer trip together, she took a step onto the cool rock on the edge of the pool, just above the surface of the water. Julian stepped up behind her and started counting out of nowhere.

"One..."

Standing there barefoot, her pink toenails out of place against the natural terrain, she tried to figure out what he was doing.

"Two..."

He stepped toward her, and before she could process the situation, he yelled, "Three!" and wrapped his strong arms around her. They plunged into the cold, refreshing water, surfacing in the center of the watering hole. Until then he'd never held her, and she hadn't experienced the feeling of a protective yet tender embrace. Coupled with his woodsy scent, it nearly took her breath away.

The water was deeper than she'd imagined, but she didn't have to swim. Julian had a good hold on her, the swirling current no match for his strength. She willed her heart to slow. He let her go and they kicked to the side near the waterfall.

Soon her feet found the smooth rock, and she wobbled before finding her balance. She stared at him, the words *I'm in love with you* working their way through her mind, unable to emerge.

Instead, she put her head under the far edge of the waterfall, allowing the fresh spray to cool her overheated body. Julian ducked behind the thick cascade, leaving her alone. She tried to see behind the spray, but couldn't find him. Waiting for him to return, she let the amazing surroundings sink in once more. The sunlight wound through the brush, landing on the foliage that showed off its varying shades of green. Ferns and vines swept across the rocky soil, right up to the threshold as if they, too, would like a dip in the pool.

The area was just as her father had told her it would be when she'd mentioned their excursion, and she couldn't wait to get back to the apartment to tell him about it on the phone. Would she have anything else to divulge? Anything about Julian? She eyed her shorts draped on a tree branch next to their towels, the compass her dad had given her still in the pocket.

"If you follow your heart, you'll never lose your way," he'd said when he pressed it into her ten-year-old hand.

Surfacing from the memory, she noticed that Julian hadn't come back. She pushed through the sheeting water searching for him.

"Julian?"

No one was there. She peered around for a cave or some-place he could be hiding.

"Julian?" she said again, her voice echoing against the solid rock of the hill.

She swam back to the front of the waterfall, and he erupted from under the surface, grabbing her and making her squeal.

"You scared me to death!" She playfully smacked his arm, her pulse in her ears.

He laughed. "I wondered how long it would take you to look for me."

She loved the sound of his laugh. Then the playfulness in his gaze died down until his fondness for her came through. Gently, he tightened his embrace, the water splashing as if it were confetti celebrating, the cold droplets tingling against her skin. He leaned in, then hesitated as if asking permission, and while everything in her body said yes, the impulsivity she felt made her pause for a split second to deliberate taking this step that would inevitably change things for them.

"We made it!" Brit called as she burst through the trees.

Caught in the act, Josie sucked in a breath, her eyes on Julian. His lips parted and she thought he was going to say something, his fingers giving her a squeeze as if to say, *"Don't go."* Thoughts flashed through her mind of what it would be like to have Julian by her side, his lips on hers, his hand gripping her fingers, going through life together. She'd never felt as if anyone else could fit that role, and she could definitely see Julian in her picture of the future.

Not wanting to cause awkwardness in the house or between them by taking a step toward something more with him, she let her good sense win out over her flipping stomach for now. She slipped away from Julian and swam to her friends.

Maisy joined Brit and put her hand on her hip, her dark braids swinging behind her shoulders.

"We got lost," she said, clearly unaware that Josie was mentally scrambling to move on from what had just happened.

Julian dove under the surface and swam to the rocky edge, where he climbed out and shook the water from his hair. She didn't dare make eye contact with him or she'd give away how much she adored him.

Brit, who was already stripping down to her swimsuit, added, "Apparently there are two trails that lead here from the bathrooms."

"Well, I'm glad you made it," Josie said, but she wondered what might have happened if they'd taken just a few minutes longer.

———

The next evening she was on her belly, textbooks sprawled across the bed around her, tapping on the laptop she'd gotten as a gift from her father when she went away to school. She'd been trying not to let the lure of warmth and late afternoon sunshine outside disturb her studies while she got an early start preparing for final exams.

A knock pulled her attention away from her notes.

"You coming to dinner?" Julian asked from her doorway, his gaze full of unsaid words.

She tried not to permit her fondness for him to sidetrack her, a skill she'd worked on mastering over the last few months. After that moment at the waterfall yesterday, he seemed more affectionate toward her, as if he felt the same shift she had, but he hadn't pressed her. Was he waiting for the right time to address it? Maybe they could move past being friends once the pressure of school subsided and they went to Florida together. She'd played through so many scenarios about how it would happen, and she couldn't wait.

"Come on, Josie-Boo. It's pizza night," Julian added when she hadn't answered.

"I hate it when you call me Josie-Boo." She always told him that, but secretly she found it endearing; she just wouldn't admit it to him.

He grinned at her playfully as if he knew.

"I'll have to pass," Josie replied, his puppy-dog eyes almost making her waver. "My hardest exam is in a week and I'm studying. I need to finish planning our trip too." She waved a finger at her computer.

She was excited about the eight-and-a-half-hour drive with Julian, Maisy, and Brit to the coast of Florida at the start of summer break. She hadn't been before, and she'd never indulged in anything like a vacation. She knew she'd be spending her meager savings on something she couldn't take home with her, but the memories would be enough to carry her through all the late night waitressing shifts the next school year.

She was lucky to have the opportunity to spend time at the beach with good friends—a luxury her upbringing hadn't allowed. Over the last few years, her father had been enamored with the Gulf Coast, often scrolling through images of it on his phone. The photos were like something out of a dream. White sand beaches with blue water lapping over them, rows of colorful beach chairs and matching umbrellas, small tables awaiting an orange, pink, or yellow cocktail spilling with fresh fruit.

"It can't wait until after a Bruno's woodfired, mixed veggie, thick crust with olive oil drizzle? It's your favorite."

Julian remembered every detail she'd told him, and she couldn't deny the way his attention sent a fizz of happiness through her chest.

"I'm saving money too," she admitted.

He rolled his eyes. "Four bucks a slice? You can swing it." He lunged into her room and playfully shook her by the shoulders. "Come oooon," he whined. "I'll pay."

She almost relented, but her work came first. College was important to her, and she and her father worked hard to scrape up the money for her to go. Plus, she didn't know the material for the exam inside and out yet, and she didn't want to let down her dad. She eyed the compass on her dresser, her reminder to follow her heart. She wasn't sure if her heart wanted school or Julian. There was something magical about him that had her considering whether she could find the extra time, give in, and have a few laughs with him and their friends.

"Next time," she said, sticking to her guns. The many months she'd put in at school won out.

He let out a disappointed huff. "Suit yourself." Then he leaned in and kissed her cheek, taking her breath with him. "I'll try to bring you a slice," he said with a loaded wink before their housemates pulled him out the door.

She tried to rationalize away the disappointment of watching him go. No matter what happened in the rest of her life, she needed a degree. It had to be her first priority. Most of her college friends came from privileged backgrounds, not having to worry about how they'd cover their next semester's tuition. Many were running off to the beach after exams for one final hurrah as a group before splitting up and heading to their hometowns until the fall. Josie had waitressed the whole year and saved up for school and she'd planned to do the same again this summer, but her dad had insisted that for her hard work she treat herself to a vacation somewhere tropical with her friends. He'd even suggested the location—Rosemary Beach. He said he wouldn't take no for an answer.

"If anything, go for me," he'd said. "I've always wanted to visit the Gulf Coast…"

There'd been a longing in his voice she couldn't shake. He hadn't taken a vacation in her lifetime, yet he was always looking up the Gulf Coast. He seemed drawn to that area specifically. She'd decided she *should* do it. For him.

"Follow your heart, not your wallet," he'd urged. "And you need to give that Julian guy a chance. He likes you."

"Daaaad," she'd said, her cheeks burning.

Besides her father and Nick, Julian was the only other man Josie had adored. She often thought about how he seemed to fit in with her family. The few times he'd been around when she was on a video chat with her dad, he'd popped in and made jokes that actually made her father laugh. He always spent a few minutes chatting with her dad and they got along famously.

Could Julian be "the one?" Maybe she'd find out in Florida.

She'd had no idea that the moment in her doorway with Julian was her last shot at becoming something more with him. It was the final scene in that chapter of her life.

CHAPTER THREE
PRESENT DAY

"Good morning, Josie," said her boss, Helen, patting Josie on the shoulder on her way past. "Ready to start the day?"

"As ready as I always am," Josie replied, tugging her apron straight in the front. She looked at her reflection in the break-room mirror and ran her finger over the dark circles under her eyes, her mind drifting back involuntarily to the time when her forward movement in life had stopped.

When her mother died after giving birth, five-year-old Josie had watched her father trying to be everything to everyone—changing diapers and preparing bottles, working as an electrician by day and parenting by night. At bedtime, after her dad crashed, she'd cry herself to sleep, missing her mother. Tucked under her covers in the dark silence of her room, she wondered if her father still had the same unmanageable ache in his heart he'd had the day she found him on the porch.

While she did all the things kids did—playing at school, going to birthday parties, and visiting her friends in the after-noons—she'd grown up quickly, having been thrust into the burden of adulthood. She'd learned how to cook and clean by age ten because she'd known that after a full day of work, her father wasn't able to manage it. She enjoyed being helpful. In the evenings, she packed lunches, changed sheets, and washed clothes, folding each person's items in piles and setting them in the respective bedrooms. And she'd always helped Nick put his away.

On the rare days when her father wasn't working, he'd scrape up enough money to take Josie and Nick for ice cream, and then they'd fly kites in the field near their house. If she closed her eyes, she could still see Nick covering his ears while Josie ran through the buttercups squealing as her dad chased her with his fingers in the shape of claws, pretending to be a monster.

Josie yawned while she piled the rolls of silverware she was working on. She had no idea how her dad had had enough energy back then to be such a great father, given how much he worked. She often talked to her father at night, and now she was working full-time, barely able to keep her eyes open after her shifts, she had a new appreciation for what he'd done for them and wished he could show her how he did it. Especially regarding Nick. She often fell into bed, wishing she'd had more time with him in the evenings.

She and her brother had a way of understanding each other and she knew how helpful it was for him when she was there to listen. Nick sometimes struggled in social situations and with some of his school subjects. The school had implemented an Individualized Educational Plan—an "IEP" they called it—with accommodations in the classroom to help him. But where he was unique, and had inherited the interests of their father, was in mathematics—particularly theoretical mathematics. But while their dad had enjoyed the subject, Nick's skills were stronger than even the adults'. Right away, his gifts were clear, testing years above level.

While school-level math and science came easily to Nick,

he had a hard time in other classes, often not understanding how to distinguish the nuances of language. He didn't recognize sarcasm and he grappled with how to make friends since his understanding of the world was so black and white. At five and a half years old, after a battery of testing to try to understand his struggles, he was diagnosed with autism spectrum disorder.

The small, rural school had a hard time meeting his academic needs. When they determined that the best course of action was to pull him out of regular classes for math instruction in a gifted education room, the change in routine was more than Nick could handle. They quickly went back to keeping him in the classroom and tried to supplement their instruction, but they still weren't prepared for his high-level understanding of his favorite subject, so he became bored and either got in trouble or tuned out.

When he was in elementary school, Josie had spent every afternoon digging into her middle-school math books to teach Nick topics like fractions and mixed numbers, percentages, and decimals. She'd been his actual teacher, and every day he'd confided that he didn't want to go back to school.

"You know the information I need," he'd said one afternoon when he was nine. "What's the point of school if it doesn't teach me?"

"You need their help in reading and language arts," she'd pointed out.

"You can teach those to me. It's easy for you."

"Yes, but I'm not a certified teacher, and it's the law that you attend school."

"It's a dumb law." He'd pouted. "I have to sit in a room all day when the teachers don't understand math at all. Their lessons are so easy. They're stupid."

"They're not stupid. They're trying to teach the other kids who don't know."

"But I *do* know. It's a waste of time."

"Your life will be full of these sorts of experiences, Nick. At the very least, you should practice your coping strategies and try to see what other things you can learn from your teachers and the other kids."

He rolled his eyes. "I just want to storm out."

"Remember the mindfulness activities your therapist taught you?"

When the time came for Josie to go to college, guilt plagued her. Abandoning Nick and her father to pursue her dreams felt selfish. She'd told her dad she didn't want to leave home, but he'd refused to accept that.

"If I thought you wanted a job that didn't require a college education, then I'd listen. But you're interested in things like marketing and graphic design. It's important you learn from the best. To do that, you have to go to college,"

She chewed her lip in indecision.

"And it's only four years," her father had said.

After being away at school for just a couple weeks, she'd realized something amazing about her father: he could do anything. While still pulling long hours at work, he was able to manage helping Nick with his homework and his after-school activities. He also traded his natural skills in electrical service and repair with a behavioral therapist in a nearby town who would visit with Nick once a day during the week to make sure he had a schedule for the rest of his afternoon and evening. Josie settled into her classes and, before long, being away felt normal.

But her years at college had been a colossal waste of time.

That fateful day three years ago, the phone had rung in Josie's apartment bedroom, pulling her from her thoughts about pizza with Julian and bringing her back to the present.

Delighted to see her father's number, she answered quickly.

"Hey, Dad," she said, shutting her laptop and rearranging herself into a cross-legged position on her bed. She scooted a few books to the side, the phone wedged against her shoulder.

An odd, unrecognizable sniffle had come through the line.

"Dad?"

"It's Aunt Zelda."

She barely knew her dad's younger sister, so the fact that the woman was using his phone was jarring. Josie couldn't recall the visual of that exact minute when she'd heard Aunt Zelda's voice, what she was doing with her hands, or the view from her sunny window, probably full of normalcy outside. It was as if she had already plunged into the blur of her next life. She knew right away that something was wrong.

Another sniffle.

"I didn't have your number, so I found it on your dad's phone. I'm at your house."

Of course she didn't have Josie's number. Josie would be surprised if Aunt Zelda had a phone, since the monthly payments would require some semblance of responsibility. She traveled around sleeping on friends' sofas and flitting all over the country, not a care in the world about her family. The last Josie had heard of her was about a year ago when Zelda had told Josie's father that she'd gotten a job and was looking to put down roots in their town of Lox Creek, although nothing in Zelda's past had given Josie reason to trust the information.

"I have some terrible news."

She'd expected Aunt Zelda to tell her she'd lost the job and was now living in Josie's bedroom or something similar. But, no, it wouldn't be that.

"With your exams, your dad called my number instead of yours. He never calls, but he needed family and didn't want to burden you."

"What?" Her aunt wasn't making any sense.

"He only had a few minutes on the line before... He loved you and Nick so much. He wanted me to tell you that."

"Aunt Zelda, what's going on?"

"Your dad had a massive heart attack."

The disorienting swirl of thoughts and worry plummeted Josie into a haze of confusion. She wanted to know how her dad was, she needed to check on Nick, she had to call her professors right away to tell them she might have to make up her exams, she had to go home, to make sure everything was taken care of while her dad was in the hospital. Did Dad have insurance? She wasn't sure—

"Josie." Aunt Zelda's voice cut into the fog. "We lost him." A sob escaped through the phone, ripping past the silence.

All thoughts drained from Josie's mind in an instant, leaving it as dark and empty as a vacant building. The first feelings that registered were the trembling sensation that had taken over her entire body and the absence of breath in her lungs. She'd squeezed her eyes shut as she'd attempted to process what Zelda had said, the visual of her mother's shiny casket going down the aisle of the church swimming into her consciousness as if to say to her muddled brain, *Yes, this is what's happened. Again.*

Tears pricked her eyes and nausea filled her stomach, her vision blurring with the deluge of tears.

"Where's Nick?" she'd managed, ever his protector.

"He's with the Andersons, next door. They picked him up from school."

The confusion and utter despair that had consumed her when her mother died erupted within her. As a newborn, Nick hadn't experienced the pain of her passing. Change was difficult for him, as was handling his emotions. Josie's maternal instincts immediately set in, and she wanted to shield her brother from the feelings. She'd need to be his teacher once more, this time showing him how to manage his grief.

"Is he all right?" She wiped at the tears spilling down her cheeks.

"He's asking for you."

"Tell him I'm on my way. I'll be there as soon as I can."

Josie didn't sit for her exams that year, she didn't go on the Florida trip with her friends, and she never went back to the university. Nick needed her, and nothing else mattered.

CHAPTER FOUR

At breakfast the next morning before work, Josie was scrolling through a news page on her laptop when something caught her attention. She turned the computer toward her brother.

"This is interesting. A Dr. Randolph McDonough is offering a full-ride college scholarship, with a yearly stipend for incidentals, to one math scholar through this Battle of the Mathematical Minds competition," she said while Nick scribbled numbers in his spiral notebook. "The winner would have twelve months to prepare for school and attend the following year."

Nick got up as she continued speaking but then seemed to reconsider and sat back down. He was clearly disinterested in the conversation. He had pursed his lips the way he did anytime he forced himself to pay attention to her, which she always found adorable. Listening when he wasn't interested was his way of showing his affection for her.

"A four-year school, totally paid for. Did you hear that part?"

He nodded before picking up his pencil and jotting down

a few numbers in his notebook. She couldn't tell if he'd grasped the importance of what she was saying.

"It beats community college," she added. "You hate our community college. You said so yourself."

"The instructors are awful."

Frustrated with school and the lack of enrichment he'd received, Nick had long given up on learning, failing subjects he could get straight As in because he was so far above level he'd lost faith in the process. In an attempt to help him move forward, Josie had taken him to the local community college in a nearby town, hoping that if the administrative team met him, they'd let him in despite his terrible transcript. She'd explained that he'd completely given up on high school, so his grades were not indicative of his talents in any way, and she'd had them convinced. The instructors wrote a few problems on the board and Nick solved them in a flash, stunning them all. But when he'd been asked to explain his process, her brother had walked out of the meeting, telling her community college was high school all over again—a waste of time.

She pushed aside her empty breakfast plate and scrolled down the article. "It says even if you're already committed to a university, you can apply the funds to your tuition if you win."

"I'm not committed to a school," Nick said.

"I know, but what I'm saying is that if you win, you can *choose* your school. And you'd have a year to brush up on the tough subjects. The sky's the limit, Nick."

He turned the page and wrote a string of numbers, then erased a few and added more. Solving complicated math problems in a notebook had been his coping strategy to manage his pain during the days after their father's death, and the ritual had continued. When things overwhelmed him, he worked in his notebook.

Wanting so desperately to connect with her brother, Josie

had asked him once what the problems he was working on were, and he'd attempted to explain.

"I'm trying to calculate particle masses that haven't been calculated before."

That hadn't helped her understand any better.

On one of her days off, he'd left his notebook at home when he'd gone to school. She'd taken it to the community college and run the page-long problems by one of the math teachers she'd met named Mr. Haskins. Unsure of what Nick was doing, he consulted one of the physics instructors, who'd also been perplexed. The man had to search his books to figure out what Nick was solving. Then he said it seemed as though Nick could be using a basic theory in particle physics in which parameters could not be calculated hypothetically, given the knowledge that existed today.

"It looks like Nick's trying to find an answer that, as of now, doesn't exist," the instructor had said.

When she told Nick's therapist about it, his guess was that Nick was subconsciously trying to solve a problem that was unsolvable to mimic the confusion of emotions he was experiencing from losing his father—because the discomfort of loss was unsolvable to him.

"He's definitely a brilliant mind," Mr. Haskins had said, but like a doting mother, Josie already knew that. "Get him into anything you can that involves math and science. He might end up cracking codes that no one ever has."

Today, she was trying to do just that.

"It's an advanced mathematics competition," Josie continued, trying to get his attention by reaching over and offering him another piece of toast. "That's your wheelhouse."

"Is it in New York City?"

Josie shook her head. New York was the home of the National Museum of Mathematics. Nick had seen it in one of her math textbooks years ago and wanted to go ever since.

She'd felt guilty about not being able to take him, given her skimpy paycheck.

"The competition's in Florida," she replied.

To her utter disappointment, he declined, scratching number after number in his notebook. "I'm not going to Florida."

"Florida's good too," she offered, trying to stay composed when she wanted to put her hand on his to stop the writing and explain what a great prospect this seemed to be.

He didn't look up. "What's in Florida? There's nothing to do with mathematics there."

"Well, from the look of this competition there will be for a couple weeks. And you've never seen the beach before."

His pencil stilled and he finally made eye contact. "How did you hear about this?"

"An ad for it came up on my homepage," she replied. "I wish we'd found it sooner. The competition starts July seventeenth. That's only two months away." A tiny voice inside told her the timing didn't matter. She needed to get him to enter. It was a good shot at something great for him. And in their town, good shots at anything were hard to find. She leaned into his space to keep his attention, but she'd already lost it again to his notebook.

Rolling her head on her shoulders, she pulled her hair back and tied it with a band, ready for her breakfast shift. Nick only had a couple weeks left in his senior year, and then her morning routine would relax a bit because he always slept in during the summer. If she could just get him to apply for this opportunity...

Trying to keep her disappointment in check, she decided that if Nick wouldn't enter the competition, maybe this summer she could at least spruce up their house and they could have a more pleasant space to live in while they figured out their futures together.

As she was a legal adult when her father died, Josie inherited her family's small mountain house. Right after, Zelda had offered to buy the house and land with money her aunt had received when her own parents had passed before Josie was born. Josie couldn't believe Zelda hadn't already blown through the money. The offer wasn't much, but it was enough. Nick didn't feel connected to his therapist's ideologies, so they weren't helping him move forward in life, and she'd thought about taking the money and selling everything to find her and her brother something better. But as Josie had no concrete career plans, she and Nick had nowhere else to go. Besides, neither the sale of the house nor her waitressing money would be enough to pay for further education for Nick, and that's if they'd resolved the issues with his grades. She'd thanked Zelda, but declined the offer.

Nick wouldn't get an academic scholarship, so this Battle of the Mathematical Minds competition seemed to be the perfect fit. *She'd* missed out on an education and a future, but this chance for Nick had fallen right into their laps. He was too brilliant to waste his intellect, and she knew deep down he wouldn't be happy living the life she did. He had to do something to keep his brilliant mind busy. If she didn't give him every opportunity to do that, she'd have failed both her parents.

"So it's a competition?"

She sprang into focus, realizing Nick had actually asked her something about the contest.

"Yes. I just found it."

She dared not admit to herself that the ad had probably popped up because she'd done so many searches of photos of Rosemary Beach, along the Gulf Coast. The area had always felt like a shooting star she'd almost caught but never quite reached. It was the only thing from her past she went back to. Perhaps because the photos seemed so happy and joyful they made her feel the same. Or maybe she felt she'd let her father down by not going to the one place he'd wanted to see, so she went there in her mind the way he had. Either way, she couldn't deny the pull the area had on her.

"It's a math competition," she repeated, watching her brother for a reaction.

"And the winner can go to any college?"

Josie tried to hide her excitement so he didn't get overwhelmed by her and tune out again. She scrolled on her laptop.

"It looks like it."

She worried about how he'd handle college—the change of living somewhere else, meeting new people, and whether or not his time-management skills would do him in—but she'd cross that bridge when they got to it. Over the last three years, she'd learned to take one day at a time, one step at a time.

"They won't let me in with my grades."

"This says, 'Dr. McDonough came from humble beginnings. He struggled in school and had to work from nothing to attain the wealth he's achieved. Now a multi-billionaire in the tech industry, he wants to give back, so he's offering this enormous opportunity...'" With Nick's focus still on her, she kept reading. "'Prior grades aren't given the same weight as they are for regular university applicants. The goal is to find the next generation of high-level mathematicians.'"

Nick's face gave no indication of his thoughts on the matter. "How many candidates will there be?" he asked.

She scanned the page. "No more than fifty."

He gave her a skeptical squint, his opinion evidently so strong it had made it to the outside of his body. "What do I have to do to win?"

She turned her computer again to show him the entry requirements. "You'd need to fill out the online application, which includes an essay and a comprehensive exam, and if you're chosen you'd have to compete against the other forty-nine applicants in a two-week competition with supervised prep work, studying with leaders in the field, and two hours of competition each day." She looked up at him. "You could totally win."

Nick pinched the last corner of his piece of toast. "Where is it again? Florida?"

"Yes. The doctor retired in Rosemary Beach on the Gulf Coast, so the competition is there."

Just saying "Rosemary Beach" out loud took her back to three years ago. Though she indulged in looking at images of the place she'd been going to visit, and which her father so longed to travel to, she hadn't allowed herself to wonder about the people she'd left behind that fateful day. Once consumed with the business of her father's death and consoling her brother, she wasn't the same person anymore, so relating to her friends' daily goings-on had been difficult.

Brit had sent her condolences with a bouquet of wildflowers in the days after she'd left. Maisy had mailed a card, and Julian had tried to call her quite a few times, but Josie had been too overcome by her heartache and her duties to respond. After a while, the calls and messages had stopped. It had been for the best. Her old housemates had their entire futures ahead of them. The last thing they needed was to be weighed down by her troubles. And if she had allowed herself to miss that life, the what-could-have-beens with Julian would've eaten her alive.

When she surfaced from her thoughts, Nick's gaze had dropped down to the battered kitchen table. Hanging on his every move, she stared at the freckles across the bridge of his nose that had remained from childhood.

"Are you considering entering?" she asked.

"I don't know..."

His response made the grand opportunity feel as if it were a slippery object, tumbling through her fingers.

"Why don't you know?" she pressed. "What is there to decide?"

Nick's silence was agony. She was on eggshells watching as he swallowed a bite of toast and then sipped her orange juice.

"How will we get there? There's no way your old car will make it to Florida. And if we do manage it, where will we live for two weeks? Isn't it expensive?"

"I'll figure it out."

"What about your job?"

"Hang on. One thing at a time."

In an effort to quiet his fears about money first, she did a search for cheap hotels in Rosemary Beach in the month of July, figuring she could give him a price and explain how she could use her next paycheck to pay for it, but when the results loaded, her heart fell. The cheapest room was over three-hundred dollars a night and that hotel was already at capacity.

"Maybe I can find another waitressing job there. We can take Dad's tent and sleep in a campground or even in the woods somewhere, for all I care. If we have to, we can wash up in a public restroom. It's only temporary, and we can do anything if it's temporary, right?"

He shrugged, picking up his pencil and scratching down more numbers.

Her fingers tingled with the fear of him being too over-whelmed by all the change and unknown to apply. She also needed to get going for the day, so she didn't wait for a "yes" from Nick to continue. She clicked on the entry requirements.

"It's free to enter, and I know you can do the exam part with your eyes closed. But to be considered, you have to write an essay on one of these topics: the logic behind and use of number theory in everyday life and how it could relate to soci-etal concerns over disadvantaged youth..."

He stopped writing, appearing to listen.

"Or debate the purpose of homological algebra and explain your opinion regarding how its uses have impacted our society and/or the planet; or explain the random variable in the theory of probability and how it conveys to mathematics as a whole."

Just reading those descriptions overwhelmed *her*, yet Nick brushed it off as if she'd just asked him to count to three.

"It'll be judged by a panel of top mathematicians," she added. "And it says here that if you need any modifications for disabilities or medical concerns, you can apply your high-school accommodations from your IEP to do the essay. You just have to provide the documentation from your school. We have a copy of your educational plan that says you can have more time and someone to read aloud to you."

He continued to write in his notebook—erasing and writing, erasing and writing. When he'd almost put a hole in the paper, he turned the page, put his head down, and began scribbling more numbers at warp speed.

She wished she could impress upon him that an opportunity like this would help him focus on something other than the death of their father and his lack of educational enrichment over the years. Nick had lost faith in life, resigning himself to the routine and not really tapping into the drive she'd seen in his younger days. He'd decided he needed to conform to keep the peace—one of the traits a career in his small-town public school had instilled in him.

He often skipped school to go for walks where it was quiet, went off with his few friends to who knows where until dark, never giving her any answer as to whether he had homework or not. He didn't possess the self-confidence to see the possibilities of life anymore, and she knew that just reading the details of the competition to him wouldn't be enough to convince him. There were too many other voices telling him otherwise. But she did have one final idea for how to reach him.

"Do it for Dad. He always wanted to go to the Gulf Coast."

Nick set down his pencil and looked at her. His large eyes were undeniably like their father's, as if her dad were surveying the world from inside his son.

"And he'd want you to try," she said.

Any time Nick did poorly in school, or when he struggled to handle the demands of his regular friendships with other kids, or stumbled when asked to participate in social gatherings, their dad had always told him, "You'll never know if you don't try." And Nick had always tried. For his dad.

"Just attempt to write the essay," Josie said. "After that, do the exam. Get accepted first. Then we'll figure out the rest."

"All right," he said, but the exhale accompanying his answer told her he wasn't terribly sold on the idea. He picked up his pencil and began working the problem again.

Josie reached across the table and touched his hand. "The essay is open-ended," she said. "This is your chance to really shine. You'll be speaking to other people with top mathematical skills, just like *you*. They'll understand what you know. Just pretend like you're talking to them." She squeezed his fingers as if she could pass him her courage.

A tingle of excitement slipped down her spine when the light of interest flickered in his eyes, and he nodded.

She copied the essay topics from the website, opened a blank document in her word processor, then pasted the options into it. She minimized the browser and slid her laptop toward him.

"Here. You still have about an hour before the bus. You can use my computer for the essay and then do the exam. I can look over your writing and give you pointers on grammar tonight if you need them."

He brushed the toast crumbs off his hands and pulled the laptop toward him. Josie pressed her fingers against her lips to disguise her utter delight when Nick started to type.

Not wanting to put any undue pressure on him, she got up and started wiping the counter to clean up quickly before she left. Out of the corner of her eye, she saw Nick type a few sentences, pause, and then delete them before starting again. He continued typing awkwardly, then deleting while chewing his lip.

"Just let me know if you need me," she said quietly.

He didn't answer, so she let him go.

Nick typed a few more lines then he banged his fist on the table in anger, and for an instant, she worried she'd made the wrong decision suggesting he enter a competition that required an essay. With a heavy sigh, he punched the delete key over and over.

She went back and sat down next to him.

"The thing about essays is they're really like talking." She gently took the laptop and read the few lines left on the page: *I like math because it doesn't matter how you solve it, you get to the same answer. Life isn't like math most of the time…*

"I love this," she said.

His eyes widened, the surprise clear.

"Don't type," she instructed. "Just tell me. How is life different from math?"

He licked his lips and his brows creased. "Like when you talk to people?" he said, seeming unsure.

She gave him an encouraging nod. "Yes. Tell me more."

"Sometimes when I say something I think is funny, it makes people laugh and smile. But other times I say something I think is funny, and it makes people uncomfortable. Math isn't like that. It's always a smile."

"You just wrote your next four sentences. Want me to type them for you?"

"Yes. Thank you," he said, his shoulders dropping, his relief clear.

She texted Helen at work and told her she'd be in as soon as possible. Then she and Nick talked and she typed until Nick left for the bus. The more he explained the differences, the more that sparkle of excitement shone in his eyes.

"Do you think they'll pick me if I know the exam questions?"

"You're so smart, Nick. You've got as good a chance as anyone."

He smiled. "Thank you."

"You're welcome." Josie wrinkled her nose at him.

A buzz of anticipation filled the air, and she couldn't help but wonder if this might just be the thing they needed to shake up their monotonous lives.

CHAPTER FIVE

As she drove to work, Josie felt something she hadn't in a long time: hope. If Nick wasn't selected for the competition, so be it. At least she'd done her job. But she had a great feeling that he would get accepted. This competition seemed tailor-made for his particular abilities.

After she pulled in at the diner and parked, Josie jumped out of the car and ran past the dumpsters, through the back door, and into the break room. She passed the utensils station searching for her boss and found her in the main dining room straightening chairs.

"Helen, may I speak to you?" Josie asked.

The older woman adjusted her denim apron. "Of course."

"I know you're already short-staffed this summer, and I'm so sorry to ask you this now, but I might have a *possible* opportunity in July..." She was distracted by the glimmer of interest, not worry, in Helen's eyes.

"Thank the good Lord. We've all been wondering when you were going to get yourself out of here."

"What?" Josie asked, surprised by her boss's response.

"Ruth and I talk about it quite a bit."

"You do?" She hadn't imagined Ruth would talk about her at all, let alone have full conversations about her with Helen.

"You had to handle a lot when your dad died, but neither of us expected you to stay as long as you have. On more than one occasion, Ruth has told me she wished she had your smarts because she'd be out of here in a second if she were you. She can't believe you're still here."

Was that why Ruth had seemed so distant? Was she upset with Josie for staying?

"We've both said you're destined for great things, and we've been waiting for this moment." Helen clapped her hands together happily. "Now Ruth owes me twenty bucks."

"For what?" Josie's mind was reeling with this new information.

"Ruth didn't think you'd actually go on and do something more. She bet me twenty dollars you'd still be here by next year. But I knew better." Helen smiled, her face alight with pleasure. "So what's this opportunity you have?"

Josie's cheeks burned with the answer. "It... actually isn't for me. It's for my brother, Nick."

Helen's grin fell. "Nick?"

"Yes. I'm not leaving." Josie worked to produce a cheerful expression. Knowing her coworkers had a wager on whether she'd stay or leave drove home the loss of her former life. But how in the world would she be able to take an opportunity for herself when she had Nick to think about?

"I was just coming to tell you I might need to ask for two weeks off. But only if Nick gets chosen for a math competition he entered. If he *is* chosen, we might have to go to Florida. I just wanted to give you a heads-up."

Helen put her arm around Josie, her face contorting with that empathy people gave her that she didn't want to see again.

"Baby girl, you go wherever you have to go. My hope is

that maybe, along the way, you'll find out what *you* want to do, and I won't be upset at all if I come to work and find that apron still hanging on the hook."

"You're hoping I quit?" The idea seemed absurd.

"Yes," Helen replied. "I hope you find what sets your world on fire, because I'm willing to bet it isn't this."

Josie squared her shoulders. "How do you know? And what about you? Doesn't this set your world on fire? You seem to love it. Can't I love it too?"

"I didn't have anyone to tell me to get outta here. And now I'm too old. But you have your whole life ahead of you. Don't waste a single minute."

Feeling lost, Josie reached into her pocket and gripped her brass compass. Walking away from Lox Creek wasn't as easy as that. Her decision to stay wasn't only about her. She had Nick to support right now. Neither Ruth nor Helen seemed to understand that.

She raised her eyebrows as if she were excited by the prospect of leaving, which she knew wouldn't come to fruition, and then went about her day.

———

All day while waitressing, Josie had put on that manufactured smile and greeted people at her tables the way she always had, but she felt more like an outsider. No one wanted her there; they were all hoping for something different for her, and because of that she was faltering inside. Deep down she wanted more, but this was the life she'd been dealt. Her job was raising Nick.

Besides, she didn't know what she wanted to do anyway. Was she supposed to sell everything and go figure out her dreams, dragging Nick along? That wasn't fair to him. But as she worked, an idea began to brew, like a tiny whisper in the back of her mind.

She'd worked the busy breakfast shift with a slew of truckers deciding the diner would be the perfect place to stop for their morning bite to eat. It had been so busy that the breakfast hour waned and lunch had begun with little to no lull in between, except for the ten minutes she'd used to call Aunt Zelda with the idea that had now taken shape. Then the dinner crowd filtered in. She cleared tables, took orders, and by the time she was on her way home, nervous energy swam through her veins.

Josie went over what she was about to do while she drove. After changing into her comfortable clothes, and making and eating dinner, it was time. Nick left to take a walk, then she left the house too.

She drove to the empty lot she often visited when she wanted to feel close to her parents. Josie had always gone to the lot to fly kites with her dad when she was younger, so it was the place where she felt she could reach him. She got out of her car and walked, her flip-flops dangling from her fingers, down the old dirt path to the lot on the edge of the thicket, about a mile from home. She relished the soft dirt under her sore bare feet, channeling the days of her youth. After eight hours of standing and rushing between the diner's kitchen and tables, she was exhausted and needed the reprieve.

Dad? Mom? Can you hear me? She sent the thought into the air, hoping to catch her father's voice on the wind. She'd love nothing more, but in all the times she'd come, she'd only gotten silence. *I feel like Nick and I are stuck, and I think this math thing might be something amazing, but I don't know. Give me the courage and guidance to figure it out.* She walked the perimeter of the lot, straining to hear something—anything. *I just want a strong family... I'm doing my best, but I need you.*

With no answer, she turned her attention to the road, and waited for Zelda. They both knew this spot through her dad. It was also the spot where he used to meet his sister on her way through town whenever she was nearby, which was rare. The few times Aunt Zelda had spent the day with them, they'd met there too. It was the only clearing in the massive expanse of woods, so it was easy to locate and the perfect place to have this discussion. The unspoiled nature and good memories would steady her.

She hadn't told Nick where she was going. She would explain it to him in her own time. But Josie had a good feeling that she was making the right decision for the both of them. She hoped, anyway.

As the sun started setting behind the tree line, Josie squinted and dropped her flip-flops in the tall grass. She sat on a log, the only piece that remained from a neglected tree that had fallen in a storm years ago. This was the place where she'd nibbled sandwiches and drank lemonade from a thermos with her dad, and then later with her brother while he chattered about the aerodynamics of kites and why the cheap plastic ones she and their father had been using could have been better designed.

She tipped her head back and took in the blue sky and billowing white clouds before closing her eyes and letting the late day sun warm her face. Whenever she'd wanted to get away, this had been the location she'd retreated to. The scent of wildflowers and the sweetness of the honeysuckle at the edge of the lot helped to clear her mind.

On a previous visit to the area, Josie had asked her parents what she was supposed to do with her life. She'd felt lost and unconnected to herself and forgotten what it felt like to have wants—such a thing seemed a luxury. Was her purpose in life similar to her father's, to work to give her little family what it needed to put food on the table? After she'd accepted that destiny, she hadn't asked her parents about herself anymore. Most of the time, she just told them how she and Nick were doing and about the life events she was facing. Sometimes when she worried, when helping Nick had gotten too difficult with his therapy, his grieving, and his troubles at school, and she wasn't sure what to do, she'd come to the lot to ask for help. She'd never heard an answer, but things always seemed to work out.

Mom? Dad? she thought again, channeling her inner voice, and attempting again to propel her words through space. She grabbed hold of the compass in her pocket for strength. *If you're watching, you know what I'm about to do, and I just want some sign that it's the right thing.* She peered around at the top of the tree line, the shapes of the clouds, the tall buttercups giving way to the wind. None offered an answer.

Just then, a warm breeze blew over her, yet it gave her a chill. Had that been her sign? She rubbed the goose bumps from her arms, trying to decide. The sound of crunching earth under tires pulled her from her deliberation.

Aunt Zelda's van came to a stop, a plume of dust settling behind it, and she hopped out. Her long, wiry hair—a mixture of gray and the dark chestnut color of her youth—blew behind her shoulders as she walked. Josie stood and moved toward her aunt, leaving her flip-flops behind, the hot ground familiar and comforting. She rubbed the compass in her pocket with her thumb as if she were summoning a genie from a lamp.

"How's it going, kid?" Aunt Zelda asked, a million thoughts Josie couldn't decipher hiding behind the same green eyes they all shared on that side of the family. That look had always been present whenever she'd seen Zelda, but it seemed stronger now—whatever it was. Over the years, Josie had tried to figure it out, but never could. It seemed like an underlying sadness or anxiety.

"It's going." Still hoping for clear confirmation from her parents out in the cosmos, Josie gave the compass one last caress before gesturing to the log. "Let's sit."

They made their way through the rippling grass, matching stride for stride, and lowered themselves to the log as a warm breeze blew across the field.

"What did you want to talk to me about that was so important I had to come out to meet you?" Aunt Zelda asked.

Josie filled her in on the competition in Rosemary Beach. "I'm being proactive because I don't know if his essay will be selected, but *if* it is, we'd leave for Florida in mid-July for a two-week competition."

"Wow." Her aunt's eyebrows lifted, then contemplation slid down her face. "Do you think he's up for that much commotion? That's a lot of people."

Josie tried not to let Aunt Zelda's sudden concern prick a nerve; she hadn't bothered to help with Nick for the last eighteen years.

"I considered that, but they're math students, which are *his* type of people. That has to help, doesn't it?"

Aunt Zelda shook her head. "I don't know."

Zelda was right; she *didn't* know. Josie had always been Nick's "person." She was the one who could calm him during his storms. She was the one who was always there to listen without judgment. She heard his worries about not having other people in his life who enjoyed the same things he did and whether he'd find that special someone one day. She reminded herself not to be on the defensive and to think positively. Everyone was capable of change—even Aunt Zelda. Maybe Josie's father's death had affected her somehow.

"If he's selected," said Josie, "I have to make this competition happen for Nick, no matter how hard it'll be."

"So what do you need from me?" Aunt Zelda asked.

Josie drew in a deep breath, reached into her pocket, and clutched the compass. "The competition is in a pretty affluent area. I can't afford the deposit to reserve a room there."

Zelda tensed, and Josie knew right away her aunt assumed she was asking for money. But after what Helen had said to her at work, she had a totally different, totally terrifying opportunity in mind for her aunt.

"I have a proposition for you," she heard herself say.

Silver strands of hair blew in Aunt Zelda's face with an abrupt gust of wind, and she reached up to hold her hair back.

"What is it?"

Josie couldn't believe what she was about to say, and her cheeks heated with the trepidation that she might regret the proposal. She'd thought about it all day and had nearly convinced herself, but now she was faltering. This one moment could change the course of both her life and Nick's forever.

"If Nick's entry is chosen, I'll sell you the house."

Her aunt's eyes widened.

Josie had weighed this out. Yes, the house was the only thing she had left that had belonged to her parents, and she couldn't afford to buy anything else, but when she'd first left college to raise Nick, she'd decided she and her brother would live there until something better came along. Well, this was their something better. She wasn't sure what would happen after the competition or where they'd go, but she knew anywhere was better than Lox Creek.

There were no jobs in their hometown that required Nick's skills. He'd been contemplating going to a vocational school to learn a trade, but he hadn't moved forward because he wasn't passionate about any of them. And if he went into a trade, he wouldn't be using his incredible mathematics potential, and it seemed like an utter waste. And the only opportunity available to Josie was waitressing at the diner. Neither of them could have any kind of life if they stayed. With money from the sale of the house to Zelda, she could find short-term accommodation until they figured out what to do. It was risky to uproot Nick, but she knew it was for the best.

"Believe me, I've thought this over. If I keep the house, Nick will be so comfortable in his everyday routine he may never leave, and with his incredible abilities he needs to see what else is out there. I owe it to him and my parents to push him out of the nest, so to speak."

"And what about you?"

The concern in Aunt Zelda's question was enough to dig deep into Josie's insecurities. Her conversation with Helen was still fresh in her mind. She wondered if what her aunt really wanted to know was how Josie would manage with no degree and no experience doing anything more than waitressing.

The truth was, Josie didn't know either. While the money from the house would last them a while, she couldn't stretch it across her and Nick's entire lifetimes. Unless Nick could live independently, she'd have to be there to take care of him. Maybe, eventually she could take a class or two here and there until she'd earned a degree, but Nick was her priority.

"I'll be okay," she replied, refocusing on the task at hand. "My guess is the appraisal will come in at around $75,000."

"I got a job. The night-shift clerk at the hotel in town," Aunt Zelda said.

Josie worked to hide her shock. "You have a steady job?"

Her aunt nodded. "I'm trying to get settled. After your dad died, I just didn't see the point in..." She seemed to get lost in her thoughts. "Anyway, I don't see the point in running around anymore. I want to have a life of my own, something to be proud of." Her gaze dropped to the grass and then flitted up toward Josie. "My years on this earth are slipping away from me and I realized, after my brother died, that we aren't given much time to create our lives."

Aunt Zelda's words rang true. Josie was trying to make a life for Nick. She lived for him, and if she could help him live a full life she absolutely would.

"I can probably only get a loan approved for around $60,000," Aunt Zelda said. "But I have $10,000 in cash—most of my savings. So I could pay 70."

That would give Josie enough money to get Nick where he needed to be, and the rest could be added to her savings, giving her some breathing room.

She had no idea where she'd live if she sold their house, but it didn't matter. She'd survive. As her father had said, she'd never know what could come for Nick if she didn't try. And Nick had the biggest chance for success of the two of them.

"Done," Josie said to Zelda. "If Nick's essay is chosen, I'll sell you the house for $70,000. We can work out the closing costs and fees to get it to match your offer."

"Are you sure about this?"

No. If she were being honest, she suddenly wasn't.

"Yes."

"When will you hear if he made it to the competition?"

"They say three weeks after he completes the application process."

The finality of the situation settled upon her. If Nick was selected, but didn't win the competition, she'd have failed both of them. Would Nick forgive her for losing their only birthright to take this chance? But if she didn't take it, what were their other options?

Zelda put her arm around Josie, the gesture startling her.

"How will Nick handle having to move?" her aunt asked, as if reading Josie's mind.

"I don't know," she replied, fear bubbling up. She gripped

the log with her fingertips, still wishing she could channel her parents for their guidance.

"How about if I keep your room and his the same?" Zelda asked. "You two can come stay if he gets overwhelmed by too much change."

Tears pricked Josie's eyes at her aunt's kindness. Zelda hadn't done anything like that for them before. She blinked away her emotion, trying to remain strong.

"Thank you."

Though still unsure, she tried to tap into the hope she'd felt when she'd first read about the competition. Was she making the right decision? There was only one way to find out.

CHAPTER SIX

For the last four weeks, Nick's demeanor regarding the competition had changed considerably. When he wasn't studying in preparation, he'd obsessively paced in front of the mailbox, waiting for the letter, nearly sprinting to the mail truck every day. He hadn't been able to stop thinking about whether he'd been accepted. His therapist had tried to get him to open up about his decision to skip his graduation ceremony last month, but she'd barely gotten him to talk about anything other than Mathematical Minds.

The competition was also the sole topic of conversation whenever he and Josie were together, and his notebook scribblings had increased tenfold. The purple bags under his eyes gave away the fact that he probably wasn't sleeping either, ruminating instead over whether his application had been good enough.

Josie began to wonder if she'd done more harm than good by suggesting he enter. Given how invested he had become, what would happen if he *wasn't* chosen? How long would it take him to recover?

When he burst through the kitchen door that afternoon

and shoved into her hands a manila envelope with a Battle of the Mathematical Minds logo in its left corner, she had to take a moment.

"Open it!" Nick pleaded. "I can't do it. You have to." He leaned forward and put his hands on his knees and heaved anxious breaths.

"One second." Josie closed her eyes and sent a message to the heavens. *Mom? Dad? Help me handle this, no matter what.* Then she opened her eyes and tore off the end of the envelope. She slid out the top sheet of paper. Working to steady her trembling fingers, she scanned the first few lines, trying to decide how best to paraphrase the news if it wasn't good.

The paper fell from Josie's hand and fluttered to the sunspot on the table next to Nick's spiral notebook, the first paragraph still in her line of sight.

Congratulations, Nicholas Wills! You have been selected as one of the fifty arithmeticians and statisticians from across the United States to compete in the Battle of the Mathematical Minds competition the week of July 17th in Rosemary Beach, Florida.

"Oh, my goodness." Josie threw her arms around her brother, making him jump and laugh simultaneously. "You did it!" she squealed.

For the first time that she could remember, a glimmer of optimism filled her brother's eyes.

"Nick, you did this all on your own. I'm so proud of you."

He sobered quickly. "I got past the initial round, but the real work still needs to be done."

"I have full faith in your ability to do it." Unable to contain her excitement, she clapped and jumped around the kitchen, feeling as if they'd just won the lottery. She wondered if their parents could see them right now. She hoped they could.

Pride filled her. She'd done right by Nick, and she was so happy she'd be able to give him the opportunity to do something amazing. That was all she and her dad had wanted for him. Yes, they still had a long way to go to get through the two-week competition, but everything began with one single step forward.

"I don't know why you're so ecstatic," Nick said, dropping onto the kitchen chair. He picked up his pencil and tapped it on the front cover of his notebook. "There are forty-nine other people holding the same letter."

"I have a good feeling about this," she said excitedly, ignoring his warning.

He rolled his eyes. "Based on what criteria?"

"No criteria except that you got in."

"How does that make you happy? I haven't won anything yet."

"You have! Your essay was chosen, and you must have scored incredibly well on the exam—that's the first win. I just have a good feeling," she said.

Nick shook his head and opened his notebook. "That makes absolutely no sense."

His perspective in situations was always entirely factual, so the sheer elation based in hope didn't compute for him, but Josie wouldn't let his perspective change her outlook. She'd have enough hope for them both.

"I have to call Aunt Zelda." She grabbed her phone off the counter.

"Why?"

In her excitement, she'd spoken without thinking about whether it was a good idea to tell him she was selling the house at the same time he received the letter. She'd been organizing as well as making repairs, but Nick hadn't connected her actions to anything yet. Telling him at this very moment might be too much for him, and in retrospect she probably should've given him an hour or two to process the first bit of news before dropping this bomb, but there was no going back now. She had to answer him.

Josie set her phone on the table and took a seat across from him. "Okay, I have something to tell you." She explained what she'd promised their aunt if he was accepted for the competition.

"What?" Nick boomed, pushing away from the table and standing up, his chair flipping backward and his pencil clattering to the floor. "No! You're not selling our house for a contest." He gaped at her, utter shock and unease filling his face.

She stood and righted his chair. "It's not just a contest; you know that. It's a chance for a future you probably won't get otherwise."

Nick paced the small kitchen, crossing it in only a few strides, like a caged animal trying to find its way out.

"What if I *don't* win? Have you thought of that?"

"Yes," she said quickly. "I have." She put her hand gently on his arm, but he pulled away. "Nick."

He stopped and offered her a frustrated pout.

"Look around, Nick. What in the world is keeping you here?" She waved at the dull kitchen, the walls needing paint, the old linoleum floor peeling up in places.

He squinted at her, his confusion over her question evident. He seemed to have an answer that she should absolutely know. "What is keeping me here?" he asked.

"Yes."

"Dad! Dad's keeping me here. It's his home. And *I* live here. This is *my* home. I'm not going." Nick grabbed the acceptance letter, crumpled it in a ball, and slammed it into the trash can.

Josie lunged toward the bin and pulled it out, yanking the paper away from Nick when he pawed the air for it.

"Dad worked extra shifts to send me to college. He wants us to do great things. *He* would sell this house for us to give you this opportunity." She smoothed the paper against the wall next to her. "I've already started the paperwork to sell Aunt Zelda the house."

Nick gritted his teeth, shaking his head and snatching his pencil off the floor. He jammed it into the spiral of his notebook and held it to his chest as if she were taking everything from him and the notebook was the last thing he owned.

Josie softened, knowing how difficult this was for him. It wasn't exactly easy for her either. "Aunt Zelda says she'll keep your room for you. She won't change it."

Nick's tense shoulders fell and surrender showed in his eyes.

Josie held out the wrinkled letter. "We'll take it one step at a time."

"It's not a given that I can win this, Josie. I might not stand a chance."

"You'll never know if you don't try," she said, repeating their father's words.

He reached out and took the letter, peering down at it.

"This could be your shot, Nick."

"There's so much to consider. I have to win. That's a lot of pressure, especially after you've sold our house to do this. Then, if I *do* win, I have to manage going to college—something I'm not sure how to do. What if I get to college and it's just like high school? What if everyone hates me and the professors don't understand where I'm coming from?"

"That won't happen," she assured him. "I've been to college, remember? I can give you a true answer on this one." She stepped toward him. "You won't find the kids at high school there. After your basic courses you'll be in classes with others who know, or at least want to know, the information that you do. They'll be interested in the same things. The professors will either want to teach you or learn from you. It's a different ballgame."

He showed a hint of interest and his tense muscles visibly relaxed. "Okay. I trust you. I'll do it."

Josie held her phone in the air between them. "I'll call Aunt Zelda."

CHAPTER SEVEN

After packing up their personal things and finishing the repairs for the appraisal, when July sixteenth arrived, Josie and Nick were ready. With a cash advance of $10,000 from Aunt Zelda, two suitcases full of new beach clothes Josie had rush-ordered online, and a full tank of gas, they pulled out of their gravel drive, headed south to Florida.

Nick put on his noise-canceling headphones, reclined his seat, and closed his eyes. He would face a lot of change in the coming days, and he'd already had to choose what to take and what to leave behind. He would inevitably be nervous about the unknown of where they were staying and what their new schedule would be. Because of this, Josie had decided to limit the change he was experiencing as much as possible, and asked Aunt Zelda to pack up their dad's things for them. She'd also worked with Nick to go over the competition's detailed itinerary in his information packet so he would know where they'd be and when, and they'd discussed the structure of the competition.

"The first couple days are informational, so you can ease into it and get your bearings," she'd told him at dinner last night. "After that, every day will begin with an orientation and whole group meeting at nine o'clock, followed by break-out study sessions."

Nick eyed her intently. "That's the whole morning?"

"Yep. They provide a lunch stipend so you can get lunch using your badge, but I put some cash in your wallet in case you need it."

"When do I compete?"

"After lunch each afternoon there will be two to three rounds of competition, depending on the day."

Hopefully, knowing what was coming would ease the disruption. The rest, as she always said, they could take one step at a time.

She'd waited until last night to call Helen about her shifts. She was still uncomfortable knowing her boss and Ruth had wanted her to do more with her life, and while she was leaving, the trip wasn't furthering her future. But then she realized that maybe, in a roundabout way, it was. If she could get Nick in college and on the way to a successful job and making a name for himself, she'd be able to follow her dreams.

She had done one thing for herself. With some of the money from Aunt Zelda, she'd rented a fancy condo for the two weeks. After that, she wasn't sure what they'd do, but with everything she and Nick had been through, they deserved to see how the other side lived. It was a splurge, but when she'd talked to her dad as she lay alone in the dark one night, she'd asked him what to do. The memory of the trip she'd been planning with her friends came to mind and wouldn't let go, and she wondered if her dad was urging her to take the vacation she'd missed. Since this already seemed like a once-in-a-lifetime shot, she'd rented the condo.

With his notebook in his lap and a pencil lodged in the spiral, Nick seemed to have fallen asleep. Josie clicked on the radio. The road stretched out in front of her in one long straightaway, as if it had been paved to lead them to their future. She didn't look in the rearview mirror, choosing instead to drift into thoughts of what was ahead of them. The road was filled with new prospects. Nothing could interfere now. Nick would win this thing—she could feel it. He'd go to college and get a degree. With him away at school, she pondered what classes she might enroll in if she could afford it. Maybe she'd finish her marketing degree and find a job that inspired her. There was no limit to the possibilities.

After leaving their modest house behind, she felt the release of also leaving the things that had held them both back for so many years. This was their time to shine. She turned up the radio, rolled down her window, and stuck her hand out, her fingers following the wind as if they were bumping over imaginary mountains.

She'd had to grow up so quickly, especially during the last three years, but the warmth of sunshine on her skin and the drumbeat in the music made her feel like a kid again. The care-free feeling was a foreign sensation, as if she'd slipped into someone else's body. The closest thing it felt like was how she'd once imagined heaven...

Before Nick was born, Mama used to read to her from the Bible and tell her about heaven.

"It's a place of great beauty," Mama had said, brushing the hair off Josie's face. "Everything there is perfect. There's no worry and no sin. Only joy."

Josie's four-year-old brain had struggled to process those big concepts, so she'd closed her eyes and imagined that heaven must be like riding that red bicycle she'd seen at the shop in town. It was more than Mama and Daddy could afford, but in heaven there was no money, so she could climb right on that bright white seat, grip the handlebars, position her dirty bare feet on the pedals, and ride away.

Having not ridden a bike yet at four, she'd imagined it

must feel like running but without the *clop-clop* of her feet hitting the ground. The cool wind blowing her hair, the sun on her face—that *had* to be what heaven was like. If she did what was expected of her, which according to Mama was helping others, being kind, and following the Word, one day she'd get to go to heaven. When Mama had gone before her, Heaven was all Josie could think about for a very long time.

While she drove and Nick slept, she let her mind wander once more. Aunt Zelda was probably already packing up their father's things and living in her new house. As far as Josie knew, it was the first residence her aunt had owned. Leaving hadn't been quite as hard for Josie as she'd feared, since it was still in the hands of family, although that term was used loosely with Zelda. Then again, Josie had left home once before to go to college, so she'd had some practice.

The wind in her ears, her mind free to wander, she allowed herself to consider what had happened to her friends from college. What would they be doing now that they'd graduated? Brit had been in the nursing program. Would she have her first job at a hospital? Maisy was a biology major. What had she done with her degree? And then there was Julian... When she'd left, he still hadn't declared a major and they'd been urging him to select something. With his personality, she was certain he'd be a success in anything he chose to do.

The image of his sandy-brown hair falling across his forehead and the glimmer of affection in his eyes when he looked at her floated into her mind. It struck her how, with so many people at the university, they'd managed to meet. Julian had been easy to fall for. He was all the things she'd heard Mama say a good man was. He was the first to help others, and he was kind and thoughtful without trying.

Her mother believed God put people in the lives of others for a reason. As if she'd known she had a limited time to impart her knowledge, Mama had told Josie this by the time she'd turned five. Josie wondered why Julian had come into her life only to be ripped back out of it. What had been the purpose of that? But she hadn't doubted Mama at the time, and she wasn't going to start today. She forced her shoulders to relax, inhaled the smell of summer, and let the open road lull her into a tranquil state.

After two restroom breaks, nearly five hundred miles, and about eight hours in the car, Josie stopped at a traffic light on a road that was perpendicular to the scenic state road 30A that paralleled the turquoise Gulf Coast. It was a two-lane road hugging the coast, edged with sand, brightly painted shops, and full of vacationers.

A group of people in bathing suits, with gauzy cover-ups flowing behind them, rode in front of her on pastel-colored beach cruisers, their front baskets full of fresh fruits and take-out bags. Josie breathed in the humid summer air with its perfume of honeysuckle, restaurant grills, and salt. It was like nothing she'd experienced before. Just being there made her feel as if they'd already won somehow.

Leaning across the center console, she roused her brother from his sleep. "Nick. We made it."

He sat up, groggy, his hair pointing in wayward directions. With a yawn he righted the seat and put his elbow on the open window, his other hand protectively on his notebook.

When the light changed, Josie made a left-hand turn, heading toward a line of beautiful beach houses along the coast. They ranged from front-porch bungalows sporting brightly colored rocking chairs to imposing three-floor mansions with palm trees peeking out from their rooftop observation decks. Between them all, she caught glimpses of the emerald coast she'd only seen online, and she couldn't deny the lift in her spirits. She passed cafés with cheerful colored umbrellas and lines of sandy-footed vacationers who were grabbing an early dinner, their skin pink from a day in the sun.

They drove past village after village until they reached the spindly tree-lined, cobbled streets of Rosemary Beach. Josie slowed to a stop at a red light, and a group of vacationers—the women in bright sundresses, and the men wearing polo shirts and flip-flops—crossed the road to a grassy park.

The stretch of green sat in the center of a charming string of European colonial-style beach retailers with tucked away coffee spots, bookstores, and souvenir shops that made Josie feel as though she'd gone back in time to the Dutch West Indies she'd read about in her history books. It was as if she were in some totally different dimension—a happier one, where everything was perfect and nothing could go wrong, and she wondered if Mama had somehow sent her and Nick to heaven on earth.

"This is it," she said as she followed the navigation on her phone, turning into a small grouping of condos. She parked the car and pulled up the email on her phone with the details for the condo.

"We can afford this?" Nick asked, wide-eyed.

"Yep. For the past month I've been working on the appraisal for the house and compiling the necessary paperwork to sell it so Aunt Zelda could put in her offer. I've got my computer with me to finish the sale online, and until that money comes through, Aunt Zelda sent a cash advance to my bank account."

She got out of the car, relieved the vehicle had made the journey, and opened the trunk. A family rode by on bicycles as she pulled out their suitcases and set them on the gravel drive. Nick met her at the back of the car.

"Don't worry," she said when he reached her. "We have all the money we need for now."

"I still can't believe we're doing this." Nick gripped his notebook so tightly his knuckles turned white.

A gust of briny air blew around them as the waves sang a shushing lullaby, and Josie couldn't think of anything better to calm her brother. He just needed to get settled and relax.

"Oh, we're doing this all right." She handed him one of the bags. He shifted his notebook into his other hand and slung the bag over his shoulder. "No matter what, it'll be great. I promise."

Once they were loaded with as many suitcases as they could carry, she locked the rest of their incidentals in the car, and they made their way to the condo. A flight of steps and two turns later, they'd arrived. Josie dropped her bags to enter the passcode from the email into the keypad. The latch clicked and she opened the door to reveal a stark white interior, dotted with peaches and teal greens. The serene, coastal vibe was a far cry from the dingy walls they'd left, and the colors immediately soothed her.

She slid her bags onto the shiny tile and followed the hallway to the back of the condo, where two glass doors overlooked the Gulf of Mexico. The light blue sky gave way to the azure and emerald water, the color lightening to teal as it danced toward the shore, eventually crashing in a foamy spray onto the sugary sand. Josie sucked in a deep breath and closed her eyes. They'd made it.

"I'll get the rest of our stuff from the car," Nick said.

She turned around. "I can help."

"It's fine. You keep looking at the view." He left down the hallway.

Josie let him go, wondering if he needed some alone time.

She opened the glass door to the balcony and was greeted by another blast of warm wind, the static rhythm of the ocean drowning out the chatter of vacationers and the squawks of the seagulls. She sat in one of the Adirondack chairs, resting her hands on its arms. The residue of sea air lingered under her fingertips. If nothing worked out from here on, she was pretty sure this serene moment was enough to carry her for the rest of her life.

Sometimes, late at night after Nick had fallen asleep, Josie would notice how alone she was, and it worried her. She was strong enough to manage on her own, but she was terrified she'd wake up one day, years down the road, and Nick would have found his purpose while she was left with nothing and no one to share her life with. While growing up, she'd always imagined what it would be like to have her own family. At the young age of five she'd promised her mother she would use everything she had been taught when she became a mom... She pushed the memory away and focused on the present—one of the coping methods she'd used after her father died.

The atmosphere was different here, lighter. The warmth and the scents of iodine, salt, and magnesium made her feel as if every breath was repairing her battered soul. It was even better than being on the empty lot back home. If she did have to go back to Lox Creek, she couldn't imagine feeling the same as she had before, now that she'd been to this place.

The clunk of the front door opening and then shutting drew her attention back inside.

"I got everything else," Nick said, dropping an armful of bags in the hallway and then passing through the small living room to reach her. He put his hands on his hips and surveyed the coastline. "It's hot out here."

"Yes, it is," she agreed.

Nick sunk into the other chair. "I'm starving. Are you hungry?"

Preoccupied with the view, she hadn't thought about it until that moment, but when she assessed the state of her stomach, she realized she was hungry too.

"Why don't we take a walk and find a nice café with fresh seafood and beachy cocktails?"

Nick put his hands in the pockets of his cargo shorts. "I don't eat fish. But okay."

"We'll get you a burger." She grinned at him.

They made their way back down to the stone walk leading to a wide array of boutique beach shops. Josie walked slowly, taking it all in, as they meandered past the bookstore and the coffee shop she'd seen on the route to town, as well as a few boutiques full of summer dresses and trendy straw hats.

They arrived at what seemed to be the perfect spot: a restaurant called The Salty Shark. Outdoor tables with bright red umbrellas dotted a large wooden deck, providing a clear view of the Gulf. They looked at the menu on the wall and saw the restaurant served both burgers and the catch of the day, along with rum punch. There was a short wait, and Josie gave the hostess her name, then went out to the boardwalk that arched over one of the dark sapphire coastal dune lakes that were nestled in the mounds of sand leading to the shoreline.

"What do you think of this place?" she asked Nick.

"It's pretty good. Did you know the sand is white because it's made of quartz?"

"I didn't," Josie replied. "That would explain why it's so beautiful."

He nodded. "I looked it up on my phone."

"Should we slip off our shoes and take a walk in the sand while we wait for our table?" She gestured toward the end of the boardwalk, which dropped down across the seagrass.

Nick squinted, considering. "I wonder if the sand will bother me."

Josie shrugged. "You'll never know until you try." She smiled at him.

"All right." Nick sat on the boardwalk and untied his

sneakers. He rolled down his socks and pulled them off, shoved them into his shoes, then lined the shoes up neatly on the edge of the walk. His white feet stood out from the bronzed skin of passers-by.

Josie slipped off her sandals and they moseyed down the warm wooden path leading to the water. They stepped off the last stair and onto the soft ground. Grains of sand tickled her feet as the wind blew it over her toes. Nick winced whenever a gust came. He was clearly uncomfortable, but putting up with it for her benefit. When they reached the shoreline, the remaining stress sitting on Josie's shoulders from the drive melted away as her toes sank into the cool water of the Gulf. It glistened as if dancing just for them.

"How are you feeling?" she asked, glancing at Nick.

"Okay," he said. "It's not so bad." He leaned down and scooped up a handful of sand, then let it slowly pour through his fingers to the beach below. "It feels amazing, actually. Now we're off the wooden boardwalk."

"I agree." She stepped further into the water and put her hands on her hips. The tide pulled away and then bubbled over her toes once more.

Nick hung back a few paces, choosing to remain in the sand. "I wish Dad could see this."

She turned to face her brother. "Me too."

With only a second to ponder Nick's comment before her phone pinged, she let the thought go. "The table's ready."

They walked back, rinsed their feet at the public spigot, put on their shoes, and then climbed the steps up to the deck. When they reached the hostess stand, the woman led them to their table. A waitress came by right after and took their drink orders. Josie got the signature rum cocktail and Nick decided on a Coca-Cola.

"When we get back to the condo, we'll look at the itinerary to see where you're supposed to go tomorrow." She rearranged her silverware on the paper napkin in front of her and pulled her dark hair to one shoulder to keep the wind from blowing it. "How do you feel about the competition?"

"Good," he replied, as if a mathematics competition between some of the greatest young minds in the country wasn't a big deal. "I'm just going to approach it with what comes naturally to me. That's the best way to handle it."

"I think you'll do great, Nick. I really do."

The waitress brought their drinks and disappeared once more.

"We have no idea who I'm up against," Nick said. "It's probably beyond my knowledge."

Josie shook her head tightly. "No. No, it won't be. Your essay and exam scores earned you a spot. You have just as much of a chance as everyone else."

He looked around, his shoulders rising the way they did when he got tense. "I wish I'd brought my notebook. I should probably go get it."

"I think you'll be okay without it. We won't be here very long."

He chewed the side of his lip. "I should probably get it."

"How are y'all doing tonight?" a deep voice cut through the conversation.

Nick stayed put.

This voice was not the waitress who had taken their drinks order. Josie looked up to find a familiar pair of blue eyes on her.

She drank in the sight of him. The golden strands in his hair lifted on the breeze and his faded T-shirt sleeves fell right in the center of his biceps, drawing her attention to the round-ness of his muscles as he set their drinks in front of them. Seeing him pulled her back in time. His expression, curious and awestruck, was the kind someone would offer a best friend after years apart. It was clear he was just as surprised as she was.

It was him. Plain as day. *Julian.*

On the outside he'd barely changed at all. She couldn't say the same for herself. She wondered how haggard she looked after the three years she'd just endured, not to mention the car ride to get there.

"We're doing fine, thank you," Josie finally said with an uneasy smile, her heart about to pound out of her chest.

"Josie?"

Before she could respond, one of the waitresses called him over.

"Sorry," he said, outwardly frustrated that he was being summoned. "Be right back."

He didn't need to worry; she was perfectly happy for him to leave them. What would she say to him if she *was* given time to talk? The remnants of the girl she'd been that lurked in the shadows of her soul was clouded by who she was now. The only things she had to talk about these days were her shifts at the diner.

Josie stirred her orange-and-yellow cocktail with the striped straw, taking in a slow draw of warm air, trying to calm her pulse.

"So where were we?" she asked Nick. She took an enormous swig of her fruity drink, giving herself an immediate brain freeze.

Nick slid his finger up his glass of Coke to catch a runaway drop of condensation. "I was about to ask what in the world we think we're doing." He lifted the glass, the ice clinking. "I have no business being here." He paused. "I need my notebook."

Julian was busy by the bar, but she caught his glances at her in her peripheral vision. She turned away from him so she could focus on Nick. With a steadying breath, she opened her mouth to respond, but her brother cut her off.

"I'm competing against forty-nine people. You really think I'm the smartest of all of them?"

Nearly his whole teenage life, Nick had looked to her to help him find his way. She'd gotten him therapists covered by their insurance, tutors who worked for free after school, and a psychologist who specialized in grief, and still he'd struggled. She'd lost track of her friends, worked long hours on her feet all day, only to go home and fall into bed exhausted. And why had she done it? Because even though he struggled, she believed in him.

"I'm willing to bet my entire future on it."

Nick stood. "I'm going to get my notebook. I'll be right back. Order me a plain hamburger."

Julian passed Nick as he returned to the table.

"I'm so sorry for that," Julian said. "We're a bit short-handed. Your waitress quit after taking your drink orders."

Josie tried not to return the playfulness that still lingered in his eyes.

"She quit?"

A job may have just opened up right in front of Josie, but she didn't want to think about it. There was no way she could work with Julian. Too much had happened in the last three years, and he probably wouldn't understand that. His smile right now illustrated his lack of understanding. He very likely thought she was the same person who'd left college three years ago, but she wasn't. And she didn't want to spend the next two weeks explaining herself.

"Yep. Just walked out. I'm filling in, so it's fate." He squatted to her eye level, a kind of knowing in his gaze that made her self-conscious. "Long time no see. How are you, Josie-Boo?"

The hair on her arms stood up at the ease with which his old pet name for her rolled off his tongue. But this was neither the time nor the place to tell Julian Russel how she really was.

"I'm fine."

She looked down at her menu to avoid the flash of skepticism on his face. He had always been quick to catch her mood, and she knew what he must see. To him, she was the girl who didn't get to finish school and reach her potential because of a tragedy, the girl who was forced to grow up and raise her brother. And she couldn't deny that it was all true. But she didn't need pity. She did still have dreams; they'd just been buried under... life.

"I tried to call you..." he said gently.

She really didn't want to get into the specifics of the days after her father's death. Nick would be back in a matter of minutes, and she needed to keep him in good spirits so he'd make it to the battle's opening day tomorrow without any apprehension.

She offered Julian a weak smile. "Yes, I know you tried." With a bob of her eyebrows and a deep breath to clear the moment, she picked up her menu, but the hint didn't have the effect she'd wanted.

"I just graduated. It took me five years." He offered a sheepish grin, and she wondered if he'd wrestled with finding a major longer than she'd thought he would. "I'm living here and bartending for the summer while I get serious about the direction of my career."

"So you finally chose a major?" she asked. Allowing herself that tiny bit of connection to her old life felt indulgent.

"Business Administration."

The playful wrinkle of his nose made her aware of the burn of alcohol mixing with the anxiety churning in her empty stomach.

"Why don't we get a drink later or something and catch up?" he asked.

She shook her head. "I... can't. I'm busy." Hanging out with Julian would only make everything harder. She couldn't just run off into the sunset like he could. Her time was not her own. She had Nick to take care of. And Nick had a very big day tomorrow.

"Oh, perfect timing," Nick said, arriving back at the table, slightly out of breath. He put down his notebook and opened it to a page full of numbers. "I'll have a plain hamburger. No cheese or anything. And fries, please." He began writing more numbers in his journal.

When Julian and Josie both hesitated, Nick stopped writing.

"You're our waiter, right?"

"I'm Julian, a... friend of Josie's. *And* I'm your waiter."

"Oh, good," Nick said, returning to the math in front of him.

Julian blinked a few times, evidently trying to get a footing between the prior conversation and this one. "And you?" he consulted Josie, more in his gaze than his words. "What would you like?"

Her two lives were intersecting for the first time. Julian hadn't met Nick before, and Nick's abilities weren't something that came up in Saturday night conversation back in college. She didn't really have the kind of time needed to delve into her family life with people.

Refocusing, she scanned her menu. The words blurred in front of her.

Nick erased one of his numbers and brushed the eraser dust off the paper.

"Um... I'll have whatever your catch of the day is. Or..." She was so caught up in her thoughts she was unable to give him a clear response.

Julian's empathetic pout didn't make the situation any easier.

"I'll surprise you," he said.

He'd already done that.

Chapter Eight

The next morning Josie was the first one up. She made coffee and poured some into a shiny white mug, then padded out to the balcony to catch the final moments of the sunrise above the water. The busy beach she'd seen yesterday was serene and quiet in the early morning. She lowered herself into one of the chairs and watched the sun slowly rise to cast a golden glow along the powder-white sand. A couple walked down by the low breaking waves holding hands, and a vehicle drove along the beach, stopping every few paces to allow the passenger to jump out to set up chairs and umbrellas for the vacationers.

Josie sipped her nutty coffee, trying to channel the calm the view offered, but her mind was busy. She closed her stinging eyes and let the morning heat warm her face. Sleeping in a new space last night had been difficult for Nick—she'd heard him tossing and turning throughout the night. She'd stayed up late, going back and forth between worrying about what was keeping Nick awake and thinking about Julian.

With the waitstaff shortage at the restaurant last night, Julian was pulled away after delivering their food, and another server had taken over, much to Josie's relief. After paying the bill, she'd looked for him to tell him she'd liked the mahi-mahi dish he'd chosen for her, but she didn't see him in the dining area, so she'd slipped out.

All night the two sides of her life battled for her consciousness. A part of her was wistful that Julian had finished his studies and could now kick back for an entire summer of rest, but before the thought took hold, guilt settled in. She had a duty to be her brother's guardian and mentor, and she believed that, in time, he had a chance at holding a fulfilling job and living a happy life. But until then, he had no one else but her, so she shouldn't be thinking about Julian's restful summer and why, with no secure plans beyond the two-week competition, she might not have one.

She turned to view Nick's door through the glass. It was still closed. His notebook sat open on the table in the kitchen, the pages curling from use. While she hadn't let it show last night, she had also hoped Nick wasn't right about being in over his head. His abilities were well above anything she could understand, and she had no idea if he was out of his depth. What if she was setting him up for failure? What if she'd sold his only home and given him this hope and things didn't work out? Could that question have been what had made him restless last night as well?

Take one thing at a time.

Josie held her mug in both hands, consciously releasing her fears and relishing the moment. During the last three years she'd learned to steal these little snippets of time for herself and pile them up to keep her going when things got hard. She closed her eyes again, the sea breeze blowing against her skin. She imagined what memories she could've made with Brit, Maisy, and Julian had she taken that trip with them. A lump formed in her throat, and she swallowed it back down. Why did some people have it easier than others?

She reminded herself that things could always be worse, and she was genuinely thankful for what she'd been given. She adored taking care of Nick. His quirky sense of humor, the way he showed her love by leaving notes around the house for her that said things like "*I will lock the door tonight to keep you safe*," and the endearing way he tried to listen when he wasn't interested at all, sometimes walking off and then evidently reminding himself to come back to show he cared about what she was saying. He was a wonderful brother in so many ways, and they had a bond she couldn't replicate with anyone else. She had to hold on to that when she felt low about not getting the breaks her friends had. The only thing she could do was focus on the moment and try not to worry about anything else.

Anyway, she'd finally made it to paradise. She'd been given that gift. If only her father could've seen the Gulf with her. Perhaps he still could through her eyes.

"Morning," Nick said, coming out with a yawn. He was squeezing his notebook and pencil, revealing his apprehension. He dropped into the chair beside her and squinted at the sun that had climbed higher since she'd first come out. "Do we have breakfast?"

"We should probably go to the store. Want to grab a cinnamon roll or something at the coffee shop and then go shopping? Your check-in isn't for another two hours."

He made a face. "I'll take the cinnamon roll, but pass on shopping. It's so cold in the grocery store."

"Fair enough. How about I shop this afternoon after registration and orientation, and then you put things away when you get home?"

"Yes. That works."

Josie hoisted herself out of her chair and stretched her back, taking in another view of the shoreline.

"Okay. Let me get ready. Then after breakfast, you can relax until registration."

When Nick didn't respond, she peered over at him, but he was already madly scratching numbers in his notebook.

———

"I knew this was a bad idea," Nick said as they approached the convention center. He hung back and gawked at the line of other applicants and their families that wound past the outdoor beach pavilion and down the sidewalk. While the other candidates stood with their arms full of books, Nick had nothing, not even his notebook. He began to pace the sidewalk.

Those who weren't in line were drilling each other on their laptops or sitting on the ground in groups with their noses in the latest research articles with headers like "Mathematical Physics" and busily jotting down formulas and scratching their heads.

"I'm definitely out of my league," Nick said.

"Don't let them intimidate you," Josie said gently, following him back and forth. "Maybe you don't need to study like they do. Maybe they've never met anyone as smart as you and they need to brush up on things you already know."

Even though she'd advised Nick against feeling threatened, she felt the pull of fear herself. He was faced with crowds of people, blinding sunlight, and the worry that he wasn't enough.

Nick began to back down the sidewalk in slow, methodical steps, and she tenderly grasped his arm. He pulled away from her, his lips pressed firmly together as the entrance line grew, inching toward them.

"I'm not doing this. The whole trip was a waste of time."

"Nick, you owe it to yourself to find out if it truly is a

waste of time or not. It could be everything you're looking for."

"Excuse me. Are you in line?" a light but matter-of-fact voice said from behind them.

Nick stilled in response.

Josie shielded her eyes from the sun and saw a girl of around eighteen with her blonde hair pulled back in a messy ponytail. She wore a gauzy cotton dress, loafers, and an oversized brown cardigan despite the heat. Her pale face was nearly hidden by a large pair of glasses. She wrinkled her nose and clutched her armful of books tighter.

"I'm not in line," Nick said.

"Okay." The girl stepped around them and stood at the end of the growing group of people that had now reached them.

Nick stood frozen, peering over the girl's shoulder. "Is that a book about quantum electrodynamics?" he asked her.

She turned around. "Yes." She wrinkled her nose again, making Josie wonder if it was a nervous tic or a way to keep her glasses in place. The girl beamed at Nick. "Do you have a study partner?"

Nick blinked repeatedly as if the question had come out of left field. Josie gave him a discreet nudge from behind.

"No, I don't." His fingers wriggled by his sides. "I'm... not registering for the competition."

"Oh. You look like you belong."

In that moment, it was as if the sky had opened up and illuminated the whole place with the most magnificent sunlight. The girl couldn't have used a better word than "belong," and Josie's heart sang for her brother.

"What is your name?" Nick asked.

"Rainy."

His face contorted into a look of confusion. "Like the weather?"

Rainy seemed unfazed. "Yes. Rainy Morten."

Nick searched the sky as if the reason for the girl's unique name was somewhere in the clouds.

Josie gently nudged him again. "Tell her *your* name," she whispered.

"I'm Nick Wills."

Rainy squinched up her nose once more. The two stood in silence until the line moved. Rainy stepped forward, and Nick looked at Josie as if asking what he should do.

"Go," she urged him. "Get your name badge and the event packet."

Nick stepped up next to Rainy. "I'll be your study partner. I am going to register after all." Then he turned to Josie. "That's my sister, Josie."

Josie gave Rainy a wave. "Hello."

Rainy grinned at her. "Hi."

"Where's your family?" Nick asked her.

"Oh, my parents let me come by myself. They had to work."

Nick nodded; his interest evident by the directness in his gaze. He turned and addressed Josie, "You can go if you want to. I'll meet you back at the condo."

Josie wondered if he was curious about Rainy's independence and suddenly wanted to try out this freedom for himself. "You sure?" she asked.

"Yes." The word was short and choppy, his attention on Rainy.

Josie suppressed her grin. Had Nick just found himself a friend?

"All right. I'll see you at the condo," she said. "I can't wait to hear about everything."

Rainy and Nick shuffled forward in the line, and Josie turned toward the sidewalk leading to the beach, leaving Nick with his new acquaintance.

For the first time in a very long time, she didn't have to be anywhere, so she decided to take a stroll. It felt unusual and liberating at the same time. When she made it to the board-walk that crossed the sand dunes, she slipped off her flip-flops and carried them until she got to the other side where she dropped them in the sand next to a few other pairs abandoned by beachgoers. She stepped onto the powdery soft beach, her toes sinking into the warm grains.

The water fizzed onto the sand in front of her. A sand-piper tiptoed through the bubbles, running up to the edge of the breaking waves and then back again, leaving hairlike foot-prints. She wished again that her father could see it. For so long he'd wanted to visit this place and hadn't. Nowhere else had seemed to capture his attention the way the Gulf Coast did. She wondered how, with so many beautiful beaches in the world, he'd stumbled upon this particular area in his research.

The tide rushed toward her, erasing the bird's footprints. She couldn't remember when she'd last been able to slow down and take in her surroundings. She was thankful to have the chance now, although it felt odd not to be needed. She was constantly running to the diner and school meetings and doctors' appointments for Nick. Her late nights were spent organizing bills and reconciling her bank account to be sure they had enough to cover them, cleaning and straightening the house to keep it livable, or planning for the next day. When she finally fell into bed, she'd slip into unconsciousness almost immediately.

The constant bustle of her regular life made the more leisurely pace difficult. She tried to relax, consciously lowering her shoulders, taking in deep breaths of briny air, tipping her face toward the sunshine, but her mind wouldn't settle. She was concerned about whether Nick had everything he needed for entry—would he be okay registering alone? Did he know that orientation followed registration? Would he know where to go?

His good mood was often delicate. It occurred to her that he'd shooed her away before she could really tell what Rainy was like. Would the girl do or say anything Nick would struggle to understand? Would she rush off and send Nick into a tailspin of anxiety? He didn't need that right before the competition—one slip in the wrong direction could change the course of his day.

Josie stopped herself. She was used to worrying about Nick. She'd been doing it for eighteen years. And, if she were being honest with herself, she wasn't sure she knew how to live without the apprehension. Looking out for Nick had become a part of her.

She could vividly remember her mother sitting on the edge of her bed, brushing her hair off her forehead, and singing a made-up lullaby.

"Sleep well, my angel girl. Your dreams are here to guide you through the night. They keep you company and hold your hand until I do…"

When her mother died, Josie took over for Nick, singing him the same thing—"*Sleep well, my angel boy…*" By taking on the duties of her mother, Josie had felt closer to her. Caring for others was a connection to her mom, and without that tether of caring for Nick, Josie would be completely alone, left behind by literally everyone. Just considering it caused a tear to form. It spilled down her cheek, surprising her, before she brushed it away with the back of her hand. This was supposed to be a happy trip, she reminded herself. There was no need to fret about things that hadn't happened. Even if Nick didn't win the competition, it was about the journey. She'd been able to show him the coast—a place their wonderful parents hadn't had the chance to take them. And while Nick might not feel the same excitement about it, the memories of their time together would be with him forever.

Josie walked along the edge of the surf, letting the cool water bubble over her toes and savoring the crisp sensation. The sun hugged her skin, making her feel alive. She put her hands on her hips and peered out at the perfect line of the horizon, dividing the blues of the water and sky into two perfect sections.

"Josie?" A voice floated on the coastal wind.

She held her hair back, turned toward the voice, and found Julian jogging toward her.

"I'm so glad to run into you. I didn't see you leave last night," he said when he reached her.

"I know. You were busy."

The corner of his mouth raised in that adorable half grin she hadn't forgotten. "I'm never too busy to say bye."

She shifted her weight uncomfortably in the sand.

"But it doesn't have to be goodbye anyway. Want to get a drink or something tonight?" Julian asked.

"I can't," she replied in a knee-jerk reaction. She may have been interesting to him in college, but she was nearly certain she wouldn't be now. When it came to general conversation, she came up empty. And she knew better than to indicate that she could hang out with him for any length of time. Nick would be coming home after orientation today and she'd want to know how it went. *And* she needed to make sure her brother got dinner.

"Okay. How long are you here for?"

"Two weeks." And although she had nowhere to be just then, she looked at her watch. "I need to go."

"All right." Julian pulled out his phone, tapped the screen, and held it out to her. "Is this still your number?"

Her shoulders tightened at the sight of the contact name:

Josie-Boo. "I always hated that name," she said to hide the flutter that surfaced in her chest.

He laughed. "Not true."

She attempted to avoid the playful challenge in his eyes.

Julian pushed the phone farther into her personal space. "Is this still your number?" he repeated.

"Yes."

"Great. I'll call you." He slipped the phone back into his pocket.

"Okay," she said, even though it wasn't really okay. It was a lost cause to get herself worked up over him when they had very different paths in life. The last thing she wanted to do was waste his time. Or hers.

CHAPTER NINE

Josie sat on their balcony, a retreat she'd become fond of. At that time of the afternoon, the space was shaded, the cooler air a relief after being in the heat while crossing the parking lot.

She'd pretended to need to go when she saw Julian to give herself time to regroup. And, really, she'd needed to get groceries anyway. She'd gone to the local market and filled a basket with things she and Nick could munch on between Nick's group sessions. Then she'd closed herself inside where she couldn't run into Julian again.

She leaned back in the chair, the buzz of beachgoers rising from the shore below. She barely noticed, her mind on how she'd handled Julian's invitation.

After three years apart, they'd hit that divide where they could rest on their shared experiences or go their separate ways. While he seemed like the same kind Julian, and she'd like to ask him about his plans for the future, she felt forced to choose the other path and make excuses for why she couldn't see him. Then he could go along on his way. She didn't have a lot to offer him.

As Josie contemplated what she would tell Julian about her last three years if they did get a drink, a sinking feeling enveloped her. She'd sold her only house—she and Nick were essentially homeless. She had no plan after these two weeks. She also had no idea what her future held. How would she go back to work when she had nowhere to live? Would Aunt Zelda let her rent her old room if she needed to? She'd been so fixated on this competition that she hadn't thought to ask. None of this was like her. Had her hope in something better caused her to make a horrible mistake?

Josie pulled her compass from her pocket and peered down at the brass needle pointing southwest. It had always interested her how both a compass and a clock were circular—the directions and minutes coming back around if she waited long enough. In life it seemed that both direction and time were linear, always slipping away, never to return. She flipped the compass over and shined up the glass on the leg of her shorts before returning it to her pocket. Then she leaned back and tried to relax, closing her eyes.

The sun peeked around the corner, and its heat began to melt away her thoughts, wrapping her in its cocoon until she drifted off. Every so often a muscle would jump, making her aware of the sound of vacationers, but then she'd fall back into unconsciousness, her body finally letting go of her burdens.

———

What ultimately brought her out of her nap was the sound of Nick's voice as he called out from the hallway.

"Were you asleep?" he asked through the open door, dropping a pile of folders on the table. He picked up his notebook from the placemat where he'd left it and set it on top of his things.

"Yeah." Josie stretched and stood up, noticing the beach

had cleared out. Was it nearing dinnertime? Moving into the cool air-conditioning, she shut the sliding door behind her. "How was orientation?"

Nick shrugged and then sank his hand into one of the grocery bags. "Long. You get chips? I'm starving." He grabbed the Lays and pulled the sides until the bag popped open.

"Did you size up your competition?" Josie asked with a wink before she pulled one of the folders from the stack and peered inside, thumbing through pages of math that was so high level she didn't recognize it.

"There's no way to know the full potential of my competitors," Nick replied, evidently not realizing she had only been kidding. He popped a chip into his mouth.

She closed the folder. "Rainy seemed nice."

"She has an odd name, doesn't she?" he asked, grabbing a handful of chips.

"It's definitely different. I wouldn't tell her it's odd, though."

He stopped and looked at her as if he were filing the advice for later, then clapped his hands together to rid them of crumbs, rolled the bag over, and placed it neatly next to the sink before putting a few of the remaining groceries in the small pantry.

Josie leaned on the counter across from him, her curiosity about Rainy winning out. The girl had seemed to have quite an effect on him when they'd met, and she was dying to know if he'd made a friend. "What did you think of her?"

He shrugged again, but the slight redness in his cheeks gave away the answer. Nick had never brought a girl to the house, and he didn't talk about anyone in particular. But Rainy seemed friendly. Maybe this trip would be even better than Josie had thought.

Nick went around the counter, sat at the table, and opened his notebook—his cue that he wasn't up for any further chitchat. Josie grinned at him, fondness for her brother filling her. It had been a big day for Nick, and she was glad he was back. With him at the table, things felt... normal again.

The silence between them was typical. She'd learned through his counselors that his reluctance to divulge his feelings was based more in his difficulty sharing them than an unwillingness. He didn't always have the words to express what he was feeling. Instead, he would often show his affection for Josie by doing things for her like cooking dinner or cleaning up the kitchen. It was easier for him to do rather than tell. So when it came to communicating how orientation went or his thoughts about Rainy, he had trouble doing so.

"I'm going to take a shower and put on my pajamas," Josie said to give him a mental break. "Then we can bake a pizza and watch a movie on the big TV screen over there." She nodded toward the living room, but Nick was busy working in his notebook.

With her brother clearly shut down for the night, Josie padded into the back bedroom and got her pajamas. Then she gathered a few toiletries and headed into the bathroom. She clicked on the light above the sink and peered at the large oval tub, wishing she had supplies for a bubble bath. For now, she'd have to settle for a shower.

She turned the brushed-nickel knobs, and the water started running into the sparkling clean tub in a warm stream. She pulled up the valve on the spout and the shower hissed into action. Then she undressed, set her compass on the counter, and climbed in, letting the soft spray massage her skin. She closed her eyes as the steam rose around her.

She reached for the complimentary shampoo and squeezed the coconut-scented cream into the palm of her hand, its richness a luxury. She'd never had enough cash to splurge on a product as nice as this one, so she relished the soft foam as she worked up a lather. After longer than she'd ever spent washing her hair, she rinsed it and applied conditioner. Once she'd gotten herself clean, she climbed out and wrapped both her body and her head in fluffy towels, feeling peaceful.

Even if she had no idea what the future held, for the first time in her life she understood what it was like to be on vacation. Her skin was still warm from sitting in the sun, her muscles relaxed after the long shower, and with nothing but pizza and a movie planned for the evening, she was in complete bliss. She hung the towels on their silver hooks, put on her pajamas, and combed out her wet hair. Then she set her compass on the dresser in her room and went back out to the kitchen so she could get the pizza started. Her tummy rumbled.

Nick was still at the table, writing in his notebook. "Some guy named Julian is coming over," he said without looking up.

Josie stopped in her tracks. "What?"

"He'll be here in ten minutes."

She threw her hands out as if she could hold off the movement of time. "Ten minutes?"

Nick picked up her phone and opened a text. "Actually, two minutes now."

Josie's mind spun. She didn't know what to do. "How? Why?" she asked helplessly.

"He texted, 'Are you're home, by chance?' and since you were in the shower, I answered for you and said 'yes.' Then he said, 'May I come see you?' I didn't mind, and since we were both here, I gave him the address."

"You can't just go around giving out our address," she huffed, exasperated. "He could be an ax murderer."

Nick's face crumpled. "But you don't have ax murderers in your phone. The screen said 'Julian,' so you know him, and even if you didn't, I remembered him from last night."

A knock sounded at the door and sent her heart hammering. She straightened her pajamas as best she could before peering into the peephole at Julian's distorted face. After a deep breath, she opened the door.

The corners of his mouth twitched up, and his gaze trailed from her wet hair down to her bare feet. She knew that slightly flirty look.

"I was in the shower. My brother, Nick, responded to your texts on my phone," she explained as she let him in.

Nick waved hello from the table and went back to his notebook.

"So I didn't know you were coming." Josie tried to sound as casual as possible, willing her heart to stop pounding. There was something intimate about having Julian in the space she was sharing with Nick. It had been so long and too much had passed in that time to make it feel normal in any way.

"She seemed very distraught by you coming over," Nick added, his comment causing her to plunge further into her mortification and Julian's smile to widen.

Did Nick have to be so transparent at this moment?

"Oh, I'm sorry," Julian said. "I'm off work tonight and just wanted to stop by when you had some time to catch up."

Nick stood and closed his notebook, sliding the pencil into the spiral. "She has tons of time. She was going to make pizza and watch a movie, and I'm exhausted. I'm going to bed."

"What about dinner?" Josie asked, scrambling for any reason to keep Nick there as a buffer. She could have told Julian she'd been planning a quiet meal with her brother and she'd call him tomorrow, except Nick had just announced he was going to bed. Plus she hadn't heard about orientation yet, and they should probably go through the paperwork he'd brought home. She turned to Nick. "Aren't you hungry?"

"I ate with Rainy."

"What?" she asked, befuddled. Nick didn't eat out unless he was being nice. Had he done it for Rainy's benefit?

He tucked his notebook under his arm and made it to the short hallway in a couple strides. "Yeah. We got sandwiches at the shop next to the venue, and they had plain ham. But if you want someone to eat pizza with, Julian probably would."

Julian piped up. "Yes, I'd love to. I'm starving."

"Goodnight." Nick went into his room and shut the door, leaving Josie and Julian in the open space between the kitchen and living area.

A tick of awkward silence buzzed in her ears.

"I'll help you make the pizza," Julian said, looking at her as if he could see the blanket of anxiety shrouding her. His smile had faded once they were alone, and his interest was less playful and more cautious.

She pulled out the box from the freezer while he washed his hands at the sink.

"What's the temperature?" he asked, leaning toward her to view the directions while he dried his hands with a paper towel. His scent of pine and cotton carried her back to a different life.

Josie swallowed. "Um, four twenty-five."

He fiddled with the oven buttons while Josie busied herself with getting the pizza out of the box. Her fingers trembled. Was she really going to sit at the kitchen table and share a meal with Julian? What could they possibly talk about? The last thing she wanted to do was drag him through her life. He was probably on a high now he was ready to jump into the real world with both feet, a degree under his arm, and a summer of fun leading him toward his chosen path, whatever it was.

Julian's hand on her arm made her jump. "I'll set the table." He rooted around in the cabinets, pulling down glasses and plates.

Josie went into the living room and clicked on the TV.

"What do you want to watch?" she asked. She scrolled through the guide to find a movie, but her mind was too full to process the list.

Julian picked up the pizza box and chuckled.

"What?" she asked, whirling around, feeling a bit manic.

"Thick crust."

"What?" she asked again.

"You always get thick crust. I still remember your favorite: Bruno's woodfired, mixed veggie, thick crust with olive oil drizzle."

For an instant, his voice and the mention of a food she hadn't had in years made time feel circular, and she had to force herself not to grab him, bury herself in his chest, and never let go. But she knew time wasn't actually coming back to her; it was an illusion. Those days were long gone.

"I don't really have a favorite anymore," she said.

He cocked his head to the side. "You don't?"

"No." She turned back to the TV, clicked on a sci-fi movie, and walked back to the kitchen, where she grabbed the two glasses and lined them up on the counter. "Milk or Coke?"

"Coke."

She opened the fridge and took out the bottle, glad to have something to do to avoid having to think about anything other than the fizz popping in the glasses as she poured their beverages.

"The oven's preheated," he said, his forehead creasing, his attention on her. An earnestness filled his gaze that made her uncomfortable.

She turned away from him and put the pizza in the oven.

"You seem different," he said.

She closed the oven door and turned to face him. "I am different." She squared her shoulders to avoid crumpling.

Ever the reader of her, Julian seemed to notice, his gaze softening. "Why didn't you let me support you while you went through your dad's passing and leaving school? I wanted to be there for you."

"There was nothing you could've done that would've changed anything." She moved to the sofa, a swell of emotion rising out of nowhere. She swallowed it down.

The people she'd cared for most had been taken from her, and she'd had to learn how to function with the pain of that loss. The ache didn't go away, but she'd become better at moving through her day with it. But this was different because she'd learned to cope without Julian's smile and gentle nature, yet he was right there with her, yanking her back into the past where she knew she could never be again. She wondered if his kindness was pity. Because of that, she wanted him to leave, but she didn't know how to tell him why. He wouldn't understand.

Julian took a seat beside her, not saying anything. He seemed pensive, but he didn't divulge what was on his mind, which was unnerving, given the fact that the Julian she'd known had never been at a loss for words.

"I didn't think you liked sci-fi," he finally said, his gaze on the screen. "Or is that a change too?"

Only then did Josie actually give the movie any attention. "No, I still hate it." She allowed a small smile and grabbed the remote from the coffee table, flipping through the stations.

Julian put his hand on hers, his touch like an electric shock, causing her to drop the remote. The clatter on the tile floor made her fear she'd disturb Nick, but a quick glance down the hallway told her otherwise.

Julian picked up the remote and set it on the table. "You didn't used to be jumpy," he noted. "I can tell you're carrying quite a load."

His assessment might have been worse than the looks of empathy she'd gotten from others. This was direct; she had to respond to it. But what good was it to point out the burden she'd been handed when no one could do anything to lift it? She just had to get on with handling things, because if she didn't, she might fall apart, and that wouldn't be good for anyone.

"Is there anything I can do to help?" he asked.

"There's nothing you can do." She picked up the remote and began flipping through the channels once more. "What do you want to watch?" She quickly set down the remote when she realized her hands were trembling with her rising emotion.

"I can go," he said, then stood. His lips turned downward.

She didn't need the added stress of letting someone down. She had enough on her plate. She didn't want to hurt him, but it *would* be better if he left. She wasn't practiced in answering questions about her life or how she was feeling.

"That's probably a good idea," she said gently. She needed some time to wrap her head around his proximity. She crossed her arms, her hands still shaking.

Julian walked to the door and opened it, then turned around. "I want to see you again."

"Okay," she said, not really sure if she meant it.

"You know where to find me."

He left, closing the door, leaving her in the silence of night she'd become accustomed to over the last three years.

She decided right then and there to protect her aching heart and stay clear of Julian Russel.

CHAPTER TEN

The next morning, the competition's events began under a large tent that had been set up in a wide grassy area in front of the white stucco town hall, its parapet roof making Josie feel as if she were in another country instead of a new town. With the folders Nick had received yesterday under her arm, she dodged a couple of tourists on pastel bicycles and stepped beneath the tent. She and Nick sat down in folding white chairs on the aisle of the third row. Josie opened the folder and scanned the schedule.

"Dr. McDonough is starting today with opening remarks and then you'll have break-out sessions for practice."

Nick was busy looking over her head, clearly not hearing a word she'd just told him. "What's wrong?" she asked.

"I see Rainy." Tentatively, he raised his hand to get her attention.

Her thin blonde hair was loose today, fluttering behind her shoulders like feathers in the wind. She wrinkled her nose under her glasses and smiled at Nick before bouncing to them with a stack of books under her arm. After hellos, she squeezed into their row and sat next to Nick.

"May I have that?" Nick gestured to the folder in Josie's lap.

She handed it to him.

He opened it and turned toward Rainy, and they spoke in a hushed conversation. The hum of the other contestants and their family members filing in made it impossible to join Nick and Rainy's conversation, but they looked like they didn't need Josie's input anyway.

The small crowd was filling the space under the tent, the fans on the edges no match for the close quarters and scorching heat. As the hour got closer, chairs were becoming scarce.

Nick turned to Josie. "It's busy in here."

"Yes. You okay?" she asked.

"Yeah. I've been focusing on Rainy. That helps."

A few contestants wandered around, looking for seats. "I might stand at the back to give my chair to someone who needs it," said Josie.

"You don't have to stay. I'm fine," he said quietly into her ear.

That was the second time he'd told her that in two days. "Shouldn't I stay so I can hear what you'll need to do?"

He shook his head. "I can handle it." He nodded toward his new friend. "Rainy doesn't have anyone here babysitting her and she's okay."

There were a lot of ways Josie could've responded to that. Rainy might not have ever dealt with what they'd had to cope with over the last three years. Rainy might not have had to visit counselors to manage her stress. This all might be much easier for her.

On the other hand, here Nick had structure, time limits, and written explanations of where to be and when, so this might be the perfect place to allow him a bit of freedom.

"You sure you're going to be okay?" she asked.

"Yes."

Josie stood and wiped the sweat off her forehead. "All right. Text me if you need anything at all."

"I will," he said, his tone hurried as if he wanted her to leave.

Josie tried not to take Nick's new demand for independence personally as she walked back to the condo. She decided she'd use the time to get an early start on the rest of the paperwork for the sale of the house. She also planned to figure out what to do after these two weeks were finished. The extra few hours would be helpful.

When she arrived at the condo, she changed into a sundress she'd found online the week before and grabbed her laptop, a pad of paper, and a pen. Then she headed out to the local coffee shop to dig into her tasks and treat herself to a cup of something delicious.

Her boss Helen would've gasped at Josie spending so much on an indulgence. People in Lox Creek didn't buy fancy coffees. And during her two years of college, Josie hadn't been able to study at coffee shops, so she couldn't remember ever paying six dollars for coffee, but when she ordered just now, that was how much she'd given the barista for her latte. It included honey and milk made from macadamia nuts. She'd never had such a thing, but the barista swore it was the best cup of coffee on the Gulf Coast. *For six dollars, it better be.*

Feeling guilty for paying so much, Josie carried her mug with a heart drawn in the foam to an empty table across from a mother and her small girl who looked to be around six. Josie opened her laptop, but her attention remained on the pair. The little one wore a smocked sundress with green and navy sea turtles, matching sandals, and a navy hair bow in her neatly combed ringlets. Her mother was showing her how to place a paper napkin in her lap so she could eat her blueberry muffin. The girl's feet dangled above the floor while she pressed her baby-pink fingers against the napkin to keep it on her tiny legs. They were chatting, and the girl said something that made her mother laugh. Josie watched them, unnoticed, for a good while as they conversed.

She didn't think she'd ever chatted that long with any of her family members, instead spending loads of time by herself. Sometimes she'd put her toes in the soft mud of a babbling brook or run her tongue along the drop of nectar from wild honeysuckle. She'd laid in the tall grass and looked up at the stars, making pictures with them like dot-to-dots. She'd used a nail and a hammer to pound holes in the lid of mason jars for lightning bugs when she caught them on hot summer nights. Had the girl in her dress and sandals done those things too? Maybe that was just the girls who'd grown up without their mothers.

She wondered what it would be like to have a daughter. What activities would they do together? Would her daughter like the same things she had as a girl? Would her daughter be athletic and play softball? Or would she be into fashion and want her nails painted and her hair curled? Would Josie really be a good parent the way Mama had assured her she would?

The child and her mother stood up and scooted their chairs in, drawing Josie away from her questions. She pulled her gaze off them and returned to her laptop. After connecting to the Wi-Fi, she opened her email to sign the certificate of sale and the bill of sale for personal property for the closing of the house. She brought up the first form and scanned the document, then scrolled down to the signature line. Her fingers hovered frozen over the keys.

She didn't know why she was hesitating. She'd already used some of the money from the house to pay for their two weeks at the condo. It had taken almost the entire advance from Aunt Zelda, and she couldn't pay it back. There was no way she could pull out now. Holding her breath, she signed her name and hit Enter. Before she could think too much about it, she signed the next page.

Josie sat back and sipped her coffee. It was worth more than six dollars. Wrapping both hands around the mug, she savored the creamy sweetness. She hadn't tasted a cup of coffee quite so decadent. With the next sip, she closed her eyes, trying to imagine what it would be like to have the kind of life where having a six-dollar beverage in the middle of paradise felt normal. But she snapped out of it quickly to avoid feeling anything but grateful for the life she'd been given.

This trip was a turning point. She had to decide the best way to handle Nick's need for independence until he was ready to move forward and be out on his own. She wasn't sure when that would be, and she could always petition to maintain control of his medical care and finances if he needed that. He hadn't connected to his therapists back in Lox Creek the way she'd hoped, so it might be good to find a new location to call home. While it would be a dream to live and work where she was right then, she knew it wasn't feasible. Rent would eat up her lean savings.

"You'll never know if you don't try," her father's voice came to mind.

Contemplative, she minimized the loan forms and brought up the search engine on her computer and combed through the results for rentals in Rosemary Beach and the surrounding area. As she'd thought, every one of them was way out of her price range.

Right then, an older woman swept through the door carrying all the energy in the place with her. Once at the counter, she leaned on it with her manicured fingers, squinting to see the menu.

"Just a coffee. Black," she said in a confident voice before striding to the table where the mother and daughter had been. The woman sat down and crossed her legs. Her cream pressed-linen trousers and strappy heels with starfish-shaped stones along the buckle were no match for her elegance. With her thin frame, red lipstick, and black hair, she rivaled Audrey Hepburn. She caught Josie staring and produced a bright white smile in her direction.

Josie smiled back uncomfortably and tipped her head down to her computer, although she wasn't sure what she was looking at. She'd already determined she couldn't afford anything in the area. Unable to attend to any more of the sale documents, she shut her laptop and dropped her gaze to her coffee, wishing she didn't have to sit alone. Everyone else was with their families—everyone except her and the elegant woman across from her.

The woman caught her eye once more and Josie scolded herself for looking.

Suddenly she appeared at Josie's table.

"Do you mind?" she tucked a long, shiny lock of hair behind her ear and gestured with her red nails toward the empty chair across from Josie.

"Not at all," Josie replied. What was she supposed to say? From the command in the woman's presence, it seemed as if she wasn't used to hearing "no."

"I come into town every single day, and spend all day here." The sparkle in the woman's eye when she spoke of Rosemary Beach was noticeable. "I'd rather walk among the tourists and talk to people than sit alone at home while my husband works. And I adore this little shop," she said, waving a hand around as she pulled out the chair. "It's such a wonderful place to meet people."

The barista called the next order.

"I'll be right back." She swished up to the counter and retrieved her coffee. "I'm Hazel," the woman said when she returned, setting the cup down next to Josie's mug. "And you are?"

"Josie."

"I hope I'm not interrupting, Josie." She waggled a finger toward Josie's laptop. "Are you here doing work?"

"Uh... Not really. I'm sort of on vacation. It's my first time in Rosemary Beach."

"Ah." Hazel removed the lid from her cup and blew on the steam rising from the dark liquid before taking a dainty sip. "I was 'sort of on vacation' the first time I came to Rosemary Beach as well. You could say I'm a former tourist." She flashed her high-dollar smile. "My husband and I fell in love with the place and couldn't leave." She peered past their table to the street as if a sweet thought had crashed over her. She quickly turned back to Josie with renewed interest.

Josie picked up her mug and sipped her latte. "I can definitely understand how you'd want to stay."

"So where do you live when you're not on vacation?" Hazel asked, only half paying attention when a couple came in and waved hello to her. She greeted them with a smile.

"It's a small town called Lox Creek. In Tennessee."

Hazel's expertly plucked and penciled brows pulled together. "It must be small indeed. I've never heard of it. What's it like?"

The truth was that nothing about Lox Creek stuck out as interesting, and Josie was willing to bet any outsider who visited was only doing so as a stop off the highway for a restroom break while passing through on their way to Johnson City. But she didn't want to speak poorly about the place. The home she'd grown up in had kept them cool in the summers and warm in the winters, the empty lot had given her solace, and Helen's diner had provided the work she'd needed to keep them going. While there was nothing to enrich their lives, and she didn't feel she could go back to it, the town had held her hand through everything.

"Quiet," Josie finally replied once she had a word to describe it.

"Kind of like you," Hazel said. "You seem full of thoughts, but something is holding you back."

"Why do you think that?" Josie's pulse rose at how quickly her preoccupation had shown.

"I'm great at reading people."

"Oh?"

"It's one of my few talents."

"I'm sure you have more than a few," Josie ventured. By the look of Hazel's designer outfit, she must be doing something right. She seemed very successful.

Hazel squinted at her. "How many talents do *you* have?"

Josie had never considered this before. She used to draw, but it had been a long time. She was good at taking care of Nick and she was dependable at work—were those actual talents?

"That's what I thought," Hazel said before Josie had been able to answer. "You're trying to sift through your list of skills to come up with your talents, probably probing yourself with whether you have any at all." She grasped her coffee cup and leaned forward. "And you questioned that I have only a few? It's taken me years to come up with mine."

Her ability to read people was certainly a talent. An intimidating one.

Hazel took a sip. Then she waved a hand between them. "We're not that different, you and me. We're all trying to figure ourselves out."

"How did you do it?" Josie asked.

Hazel set her coffee cup down once more and lifted her eyes toward Josie. "Do what?"

"Find your strengths?"

She shook her head wistfully. "I had to lose many times."

Josie wasn't sure what Hazel meant by that answer, but

she knew what it was like to lose. The idea that the things she'd lost might help her find out if she had any strengths was mildly exciting.

"I can tell you one of your talents, if you'd like to know," Hazel said.

Josie sat up straighter. "Yes. I'd love to know."

"You're able to tuck away every feeling you've ever had well enough that only someone like me can tell."

Josie reflected on her observation. "How do you know?"

"Because I'd only guessed that you were struggling to find your strengths. I got a gut feeling, but most people would see your light grin and your youthful eyes and think everything under that milky skin of yours was just fine." She flashed her million-dollar smile. "So I can see thoughts and you can hide them. Aren't we a pair?"

Josie wasn't sure what came over her or why she wanted to show Hazel something so personal, but she pulled out the compass her father had given her and slid it across the table.

"This was my father's," she said.

Hazel picked it up. The glint in the woman's eyes told Josie that the gesture had warmed her.

"Was?"

"He passed away. He gave it to me when I was ten." She peered down at it. "I've always told myself I carry it around to remember him, but now I wonder if, deep down, I was hoping it could somehow help me find my true north." Admitting this new idea out loud felt like therapy.

Hazel pinched the compass between two dainty fingers and held it up in front of her, running her nail along the broken hinges.

"It's lovely. Do you know where your father got it?"

"I don't know. He had it as long as I can remember, and then he gave it to me."

Hazel nodded, passing it back to Josie. "The beginnings of a family heirloom."

"Yes." Josie took a drink of her latte, the whole moment decidedly more comforting than anything she'd experienced in a long time. Perhaps she'd just needed someone to hear her.

"And will you give it to your children?"

Josie forced down her mouthful of coffee, fearing it would turn acidic when it hit her uneasy stomach. "I'm not sure if I'll have children."

"That's fine," Hazel said. "If it's what you want."

She wanted to tell Hazel about the loss of her parents and caring for Nick, but it just didn't seem to be the right time, and she couldn't change her situation, even if talking would get the stress of not having a big family off her chest. She slipped the compass back into her pocket.

Without warning, Hazel stood and paced to the counter, grabbed a paper napkin, and spoke to the barista, who handed her a pen. She jotted down something on the napkin, came back, and handed it to Josie.

"This is my number. Don't leave before coming to my house for some key lime pie."

Josie set the napkin next to her. "You make key lime pie?"

Hazel tipped her head back and let out a laugh that sounded like wind chimes. "Absolutely not. But my chef does, and it's incredible." She moved her well-made face close to Josie. "I'm not kidding. I want you to come. And the pie *is* incredible. I wasn't kidding about that either."

Josie folded the napkin and slipped it into her pocket, unsure of whether she'd take the woman up on her offer. Visiting her would be far less casual, and Josie wasn't entirely sure she'd know what to do in a home that had its own chef.

"Tell me you'll at least think about it," Hazel said, guessing her feelings once again.

"All right," Josie said. There was something mesmerizing about Hazel, and she couldn't say no.

"Excellent." Hazel blew her a kiss and nearly floated out the door like an angel.

Josie didn't know Hazel from Adam, yet she decided to keep the phone number. The thing she hadn't known she needed until then was connection, and Hazel had provided that, no strings attached.

CHAPTER ELEVEN

Hazel's number in Josie's pocket felt as if it were a grounding force, a tether just like her compass. However, the napkin was different because it connected her to a real, live person, and even if Josie never called, she was comforted just having it.

Sure, she knew Aunt Zelda's number too, but Aunt Zelda hadn't ever *asked* her to call. Aunt Zelda hadn't singled Josie out in a crowd and decided to talk to her, or invited Josie to her home for that matter. Hazel had. And Hazel's attentiveness made Josie nearly skip with joy as she walked back to the condo. Ever since her father died, she'd felt as if others were judging her. Her good friends only offered their condolences. Julian had shown interest in her years ago, but now she feared he only had concern for her. No one had simply shown interest in *her*.

As Josie walked along, the bustle of the town square growing nearer, she considered how Hazel's curiosity was both thrilling and terrifying. And the woman's assumptions about her had been right on the money. The freeing sentiment that Hazel knew only Josie, and not what Josie and Nick had been through, was a feeling she couldn't have gotten back home. It made her think that, maybe, if Nick said he didn't need her tomorrow, she might actually give Hazel a call.

Deciding that her morning had been too exhilarating to simply go back and sit at the condo doing more paperwork for the sale of the house, she continued into the center of town, past the bright umbrellas at café tables lining the cobbles. To find relief from the fierce heat and humidity, she ducked into the souvenir shops and then perused the flower shop, its blooms spilling onto the sidewalk outside. As she wound her way through town, the shush of the Gulf whispered in her ear while the crowds gave way to shady streets.

Josie stopped on the corner, lifting her hair off her neck to stay cool, when she noticed a man ahead on a small wooden seat, paintbrush in hand, stripes of deep blue, turquoise, and pearl white splashed across his canvas. As she moved closer, she understood the pull of the landscape and the reason he'd settled right there to paint. Just past him, between two rows of houses, the water peeked through, showing off its vibrancy.

The starting and stopping of the painter's strokes were in time with the rhythm of the waves. Josie was transfixed with the movement of the paintbrush on the canvas. Her fingertips tingled by her sides, as if his hands were moving for hers, creating the magic that she'd long abandoned with her drawing. The days of exploring art felt as though they'd occurred in a completely different life. She missed how art had made her come alive. The feeling returned like an old friend, wrapping her in its alluring embrace, reminding her how long it had been since she'd held a pencil to paper and let her mind and heart lead.

When the artist finished, he sat back on his stool, crossed his arms, and assessed his work. She wanted to tell him it was magnificent, but she didn't want to disturb him.

Disrupting the moment, a man stepped up to the painter

and whispered something in his ear. Josie shielded her eyes from the blinding sun, trying to make out what was going on. Was he not supposed to paint there? What was the problem? As she took in the roundness of the man's shoulders and the prominence in his stance, she decided the bystander looked a whole lot like Julian. He reached into his back pocket and retrieved his wallet, opening it and handing the artist a wad of bills. After the exchange, the artist stood and removed the painting from its easel. Carefully, he passed it to the man.

The man thanked the artist, then turned, and began walking toward Josie. The minute that grin spread across his face, her speculation was confirmed.

"What are you doing?" she called to him.

"Buying you a gift." Holding the wet canvas by its edges, he hoisted the painting above his head and reached her in a few paces. "I saw you admiring it, and I remember how you used to spend your free afternoons drawing. I loved to watch you draw." He lowered the painting, leaned it against the building next to them, and surveyed the scene. "My tip money was burning a hole in my pocket," he added with a smirk.

"You could've bought groceries with your money instead," she suggested.

"And miss the chance to give you something you so clearly appreciate?"

"Thank you," she said, unsure how to handle the situation. She didn't know how she felt accepting a gift of this size from him, and she wasn't sure if she wanted the monumental reminder of her old life.

"Where were you headed?" Julian asked.

"I was just taking a walk." She waggled a finger at the painting. "But I suppose, now, I should get that out of the heat."

"I'll carry it to your place." He picked up the large canvas and lifted it above his head once more, his T-shirt riding up on his waist.

She turned her head to keep her eyes on the street.

As they walked, Josie considered how different his attention felt from Hazel's. With Julian, she had history, and even after three years it would be difficult to be just friends, given how easily her feelings for him slipped back in when she was with him. He was a constant reminder of simpler times in her life and a future she'd never have.

She needed to give Nick her entire focus. That thought was beginning to feel like her mantra these days, but it had to be. Her brother didn't know how to save money, manage the tasks of adulthood, or organize his schedule yet, and his newfound need for independence had put a timeframe on teaching him those skills. These moments he'd freed her during the math competition were the first time he'd taken the initiative to do something without her, with the exception of hanging out with his friends back home.

Regardless of being on vacation, with all Josie had ahead of her to get Nick ready for adult life, she barely had time for friends, let alone a suitor. Considering the painting Julian had just bought for her, it seemed as if becoming her friend again was exactly what he was working toward.

"Were you following me?" she teased.

"I'm off work, and I was on my way home," he replied, shifting the painting. "Want to go do something after we take this back?"

"I don't know." She looked at her watch. "I was just walking around while my brother completed his practice sessions. I wanted to check on him."

"What's he practicing?"

They returned to the main road in town while she gave Julian the short version of Nick's math abilities and told him about the competition.

"Wow," he said. "That's incredible."

"Yeah. I just hope something comes of it." She dared not go into what she'd given up to get Nick there.

When they rounded the corner and climbed the steps to her condo, Nick was outside pacing, his hands trembling by his sides.

"Hey," she said, worried by his stance and trying to stay calm as she walked up to him.

He didn't answer or acknowledge either of them.

"Nick. Are you okay?"

He swallowed, his Adam's apple visibly moving down his throat, his nostrils flaring, eyes wide.

Julian had hung back a step, but she'd barely noticed, her attention on her brother.

"Were you locked out?" She slipped the key in the lock and opened the door, feeling terrible for not being there when he arrived.

Without acknowledging the fact that they'd shown up with a canvas the size of a dinner table, Nick flew inside and nearly dove onto the sofa, burying his head in the decorative throw pillows.

Julian carried the painting into the condo and eyed her helplessly. Of course he wouldn't know what to do. She went over to her brother.

"What's the matter?" she asked, rubbing Nick's back. All she could think about was that, if this had anything to do with the competition, whatever had gone wrong would be all her fault because she'd convinced him to apply. What if the topics had gotten too difficult for him? Were the required skills stronger than his? Had he struggled to do the group work today? Her mind raced.

Compounding her apprehension, Julian was still standing at the door.

Josie crouched next to the sofa and leaned in toward Nick.

"Hey," she said gently. "Tell me what's going on."

"Rainy." His muffled voice came from the pillow.

"What about her? Is she all right?"

He lifted his head and sat up, the pillow falling to the floor. "She knows more math than I do."

"Okay," Josie said, glad everyone was fine. "She seems so sweet. She could be healthy competition for you. Maybe you can learn from her."

"Or lose to her."

"If you have to lose to someone, I think it would be the best scenario to lose to someone kind like Rainy. Wouldn't you be happy for her?"

"No!" His square jaw ground, heavy breaths huffing through his nose.

"Why not?"

"Because I want to impress her."

A tickle of affectionate amusement swam through Josie. Her brother was smitten.

To her surprise, Julian had walked over and sat down next to Nick. She tensed. What was he doing? He didn't know how to approach her brother.

"I was friends with a girl who knew more than I did," Julian said. "Probably plenty of girls, actually, but this one was different."

Nick's gaze moved to him. "Was she nice?"

Julian nodded. "Very. I adored her." His eyes fluttered to Josie before returning to her brother. "She studied all the time, but I don't think she needed to. She was already so smart."

Nick frowned, visibly withdrawing, evidently not realizing that Julian was talking about her. "Yeah, but it's not the same for me."

Julian didn't flinch. "How do you know?"

"My intelligence is the *only* thing I have to impress people."

A twinge of regret overtook Josie. Nick hadn't said anything like that before. She had no idea he didn't see his other strengths. He was caring in his own distinctive way, and he did thoughtful things for her all the time. Anyone who understood him could see it. Had she not done enough to show him?

"Can I let you in on a secret?" Julian asked. "When it comes to the right girl, no man feels like he has enough of what it takes to impress her."

Nick stood and loped to the table, snatching his notebook. "Well, I wish someone would've told me that earlier. I really like her. Now I've ruined everything!" He threw the chair back, sat down, and opened the notebook to a clean page, then started writing numbers.

Josie didn't know who to respond to first—Julian and his admission about his feelings for her, or her brother and his erratic behavior. She chose Nick. "I don't think you've ruined everything."

"Yes, I have," he said through clenched teeth before scratching out letters and numbers, this time including symbols she didn't recognize.

"How so?" she pressed.

"I snapped at her when I shouldn't have and then stormed away. It was my own frustration that I couldn't affect her the way she affects me." His hands stilled, his face dropping with remorse. Then he slammed his fist on the table. "I don't know how to handle this stuff."

"You can just apologize—"

"No, I can't! What do you know about how to fix this? I've never seen you with a boyfriend!"

In Nick's defeat, his blatant honesty was like a punch in the gut, silencing Josie immediately. Her cheeks burned with Julian having heard it, and she quickly went into the kitchen. She opened a cabinet door slowly and looked through the glasses as if she were searching for a specific one while frantically blinking away her tears.

"Can we talk man to man?" Julian said to Nick from behind her. The kitchen chair made a scooting sound. "It doesn't matter if Josie's never had an official boyfriend. I'm sure she's felt something for someone before."

Josie cringed, grabbed a glass, and walked to the sink while Julian continued.

"Every time you fall for a girl, it's like the first time. You get nervous. You say the wrong things. Your emotions get the better of you and, God knows, you don't always act on your feelings when you should."

Julian glanced at her. The moment was too difficult. She filled her glass with water and looked away.

"We all do stupid things when we like someone," he continued.

Nick set his pencil down. "Like what?"

Julian leaned back in the chair and folded his arms. "Well, you might sign up for a botany class when you don't need it just so you can have a class with her."

Nick eyed him, clearly perplexed. "You did that?"

"Yep. And I got to spend lots of time with her on the class projects."

Nick's eyebrows pulled together. "It seems like an awful waste of money for a college class you don't need."

"Love is bigger than money."

Josie took a long, slow drink from her glass. The regret over the lost opportunity that she'd tried to push down and ignore flooded her like a tidal wave.

"What happened to that girl from your botany class?" Nick asked.

Julian frowned. "I didn't chase her when I should've. I let her go."

"So I should chase Rainy?"

"If you think you might still love her someday."

Nick closed his notebook and swung his long legs around to face Julian. "And what if I find out that I don't love her?"

"Well, then you'll always know that you gave it your best shot, and she wasn't the one. It's the not knowing that'll kill ya."

Josie inhaled deeply to steady her frayed nerves, then walked to the table. "What should he do now? What's your advice for him?"

"Get her something that shows you care."

Nick cocked his head to the side. "Buy her love?"

Julian erupted in laughter. "Not exactly. Get her something beautiful and say sorry. Explain what's on your heart. Then tell her you hope the gift will remind her of how much you care for her every time she looks at it."

Nick nodded, clearly thinking through Julian's suggestion.

Josie's gaze moved to the painting leaning against the wall next to the front door, her heart thumping. Had that painting been Julian's apology for not chasing her three years ago? After this conversation, she couldn't help but think how it would forever remind her of him.

CHAPTER TWELVE

After Julian left to run a few errands, Nick had retired to his room for a nap, exhausted from the day's events. Josie flipped through the folder from the competition, pulling out the visitor's badge and the day's information to avoid thinking about what had just transpired.

Julian had calmed Nick when Josie hadn't been able to. She convinced herself she hadn't had enough time to soothe her brother because Julian had jumped in. She'd really wanted to be the one to offer the life-changing advice he'd needed. Deep down, she doubted, even with time, she'd had what he'd needed.

For a while she wasn't sure why she was in such a tizzy over it, but the more Josie ruminated, she realized exactly why. If she couldn't help Nick, she'd lost her only purpose in life. She'd given up everything for him, been his teacher, his guardian, and without the task of looking after him, she had nothing. Her only promise to her mother would be broken. She hadn't considered until this minute how much it had bothered her the last two days when Nick told her not to stick around at the competition. And here she was now, thumbing through his folder to see what he'd been working on today, still not reaching him.

She'd imagined this competition would be a bonding time between them, where they could connect on the mutual ground of new experiences and a happy vacation. She'd thought they would have breakfast at the table just like they did at home and Nick would chat about what he'd be working on that day. Instead, she'd been on her own most of the time.

Josie reached into her pocket and pulled out the napkin with Hazel's number on it and laid it out on the kitchen counter. Was she so desperate for interaction that she'd call a complete stranger she'd met for a few minutes at a coffee shop? The truth was, she didn't know what to do. She was lost, and she couldn't be good to anybody feeling that way. Though still not sure why Hazel interested her so much, she knew the older woman was the one person in her life right then who felt like a friend.

She picked up her phone and dialed Hazel's number. When there was no answer, she left a message. "Hi, this is Josie Wills. You met me in the coffee shop and gave me your number. I just wanted to call to say hello..." She felt foolish suddenly. She left her number and ended the call. With a huff Josie dropped her phone back on the counter, went to the sofa, and sank onto it.

A sharp object dug into the crease at her hip as if vying for her attention. She wriggled around and pulled out the compass, then stared down at it.

Mom? Dad? Who am I? She sent the thought into the air, hoping for the answer to fall from the ceiling, but of course it didn't. She peered at the painting of the ocean, still leaning against the wall. It reminded her again how long it had been since she'd sketched anything. She couldn't even remember what had happened to her sketchbook.

Then there was the other thing that entered her mind

when she looked at the painting... Julian's words floated on the air like stardust: "Tell her you hope the gift will remind her of how much you care for her every time she looks at it."

Josie rolled over on the sofa and closed her eyes.

She wasn't sure how long her eyes had been shut when her phone went off. Not wanting to wake Nick, she sprang from the sofa and snatched it off the counter, answering without looking to see who was calling.

The smooth Southern accent came through the line. "Hi, it's Hazel. I'm calling you back."

Josie blinked and cleared her throat, trying to get her bearings. "Oh, hi."

"You sound like you've been through the wringer."

"I was just napping," Josie replied, but she was amazed once more at how easily Hazel could tell what was really going on.

"If you're sleeping at four o'clock in the afternoon, you must have had quite a day after leaving me."

Josie didn't answer, the truth of it settling upon her like a heavy weight.

"What do you say we get in our swimsuits, order a cocktail from one of the walk-up beach bars, and sit in the late afternoon sun until we melt?"

Josie smiled despite herself. "That actually sounds amazing."

"I'll text you the address and meet you on the beach in twenty minutes."

"All right. See you soon." Josie ended the call already feeling better. There was something soothing about Hazel that she couldn't deny and after making her afternoon plans, Josie was glad she'd called.

She ripped a page out of Nick's notebook and wrote him a note, telling him where she'd gone in case he woke up before she got back. Then she changed into her bikini, slipped her cover-up on, and slid on her flip-flops. Less than fifteen minutes later, she was combing through the groups of people on the beach, carrying a towel and a folded chair—one of the amenities of the condo—looking for Hazel.

Josie spotted her waving from the beach bar next to The Salty Shark. She was wearing a large straw hat, dark sunglasses, and a beaded white mesh cover-up to shield a black bikini that showed off an incredibly youthful figure for her age. Josie trudged through the sand toward her with her beach chair slung over her shoulder by its strap, and a brightly colored towel with flamingos under her arm.

"The bartender's name is Kyle," Hazel said when Josie arrived. "He looks to be about twelve but says he graduated college and moved to the beach for a slower pace after a tough run of hard classes. He said he didn't know life could be so hard." Hazel chuckled, her gold bangles jingling when she put her hand to her chest, but then she became serious. "You can't blame him."

Josie dropped her chair in the sand. "Blame him?"

"For thinking his classes were so difficult that he needed to completely change his life. That's the hardest thing he's had to experience at this point, but when he's my age and looks back on his life, he'll wish he could have it that easy."

"You think so?" Josie asked, but she already knew the answer.

"I know so." Hazel lifted her black designer sunglasses that matched her bikini and squinted at Josie. "That's why I gravitated to you at the coffee shop. You have a different look in your eyes—a look that tells me you've already lived more life than you should have."

Josie became self-conscious, feeling as if Hazel could see down to the depths of her soul.

"But"—Hazel raised a red nail in the air—"we're here for rum!" She turned toward the bar and snapped her fingers. The young bartender whirled around and greeted her. "I'd like two rum runners, please."

"Coming right up," he said.

"Rum runner? What's that?"

Hazel offered a devious grin. "Heaven in a glass." She removed her sunglasses, the frames dangling from her long fingers. "Two types of rum, blackberry liqueur, banana, pineapple juice, and grenadine."

"It sounds deliciously alcoholic."

"Yes. One of those plus the sun, and you'll forget your problems entirely."

Josie was definitely ready to forget her problems. She just needed to make sure she'd be clear-headed enough to be there for Nick tonight, if he decided to come out of his room. She wanted to chat with him about how his day had gone, and she hadn't thought about what they would do for dinner if he was hungry.

The bartender slid two hurricane glasses their way, and before Josie could offer, Hazel told him to put the drinks on her tab.

"I'll get the next one, whenever that will be," Josie offered as she took one of the glasses and squirmed to remove her cover-up and drape it on her chair. In a way, she was glad to have the burden of repayment because it gave her a reason to see Hazel again. Having grown up without a mother, Josie enjoyed Hazel's mature perspective, and until then, she hadn't realized how much she'd been missing it.

The glass was sweating in her hand as she picked up her folded chair, rearranged her towel under her arm, and followed Hazel down to the beach where she had already set up a spot for herself under a navy-blue umbrella. Josie plonked her seat beside Hazel and sank into the chair, her feet resting in the sand. She swigged the delectably sweet nectar, the rum tickling her lips, and swallowed. The turquoise water lapped in front of them, bringing an offshore breeze with it.

The two of them sat, quietly sipping their drinks as time ticked by under the shushing of the waves and the squawk of seagulls. The quiet sounds lulled Josie into a state of absolute calm—Hazel was right; the buzz of the alcohol mixed with the heat and the hum of nature was the most relaxing experience she'd ever felt. It had slowed time and allowed her to simply be in the moment, unaware of how many minutes had passed. By the time she'd gotten to the bottom third of her drink, she guessed by the position of the sun that they'd been there an hour or so.

"This is really nice," Josie said. "Thank you for suggesting it."

Hazel leaned back and took off her glasses again, closing her eyes. "The beach always makes things better. It was the one constant that held me together in my darkest days."

"Is that why you moved here? Because it helped you heal from something?" Asking the question out loud made her wonder if a cosmic force had put them together—one healed and one still seeking healing. The hole in Josie's heart told her the answer.

"Yes," Hazel replied. "I'm from Dallas, Texas, and as far as I was concerned, there was no better place to grow up. At twenty-seven I married a wonderful man—a pilot in the air force."

The idea that Hazel seemed to have lived an entire life while Josie's had been stopped cold made her curious. She had no idea what it would feel like to spend all her hours with a man she loved, let alone be married. Given the amount of life she'd endured so far, the absence of that experience made her feel naïve somehow.

"How did you meet him?"

"I met him in New York when I was Maid of Cotton."

"Maid of Cotton?"

Hazel sat up and took a drink from her cocktail. "It began at Christmas in 1986. We had a dusting of snow—only about half an inch, but it was enough to make everything feel like a dream. I'd won the Maid of Cotton pageant. It used to be in Memphis, but it had moved to Dallas, so I thought it was fate when Mama let me enter."

"You won?" Josie asked. The glamour of a pageant was so different from the way Josie had grown up. The knowledge caused her to view Hazel through a new lens, as if she were some rare flower.

"Yes, I couldn't believe it. I felt so grown up." She swirled her drink with the straw, her red toenails drawing circles in the sand. "It wasn't just a beauty pageant. We were judged on our ability to communicate, how our personality came through, our manners, and family background. For someone who'd grown up the way I had, it was validation that I was marrying material."

"I haven't really thought about someone being 'marrying material' or not. Aren't we all marrying material?"

"Yes, we certainly are. But in my upbringing no one ever told me that, so I worked really hard to become a polished young woman in the hopes that I'd find the perfect man to take care of me."

"And you did?"

Hazel broke out into a wide smile. "I did. His name was Charles, but I called him Charlie. I was the only one he allowed to call him that." Her cheeks glowed as she spoke.

"You met him in New York?"

"Winning Maid of Cotton made me the Goodwill and Style Representative of the cotton industry for five months, and they flew me to every major United States city on an all-expenses-paid tour. New York was one of the stops."

Josie held her glass, wondering how in the world she'd ended up on this beach, drinking an expensive cocktail with such a fabulous woman.

"How glamorous."

"At only twenty-three I didn't understand that it was glamorous at the time. It was all I knew." Hazel's chest filled with a breath of air, her eyes dreamy. "It was May, the end of my five-month tour. I was at a luncheon, dressed in a bright blue ball gown the color of the ocean." She pointed a finger at the horizon.

"He walked in wearing his crisp white air-force uniform, his dark hair cut short, his skin soft and freshly shaven. I couldn't take my eyes off him. That was the day I knew I'd marry him," Hazel said, sliding on her sunglasses. "I could feel the electricity between us. Have you ever felt that with someone?"

Josie remembered Julian's arms around her at the waterfall, the fondness in his eyes, and the way it made her heart pound.

"No," she lied, knowing if she said yes Hazel would want to hear *her* story, and she wasn't ready to tell it. She sucked down the last of her drink, the sweetness helping her through the memory.

Her phone buzzed. Josie shifted her glass and pulled her phone from the pocket on her chair. Shielding the screen from the sun, she saw a text from Nick:

I'm hungry.

There was nothing at the condo he would be able to throw together on his own. She texted back that she was on her way.

"Sorry, Hazel. My brother's here with me and he's expecting dinner. I should probably go."

117

"Oh, all right," Hazel said. "Maybe we can meet for coffee tomorrow? You know I'll be in town."

Josie slipped on her cover-up, and folded her chair. "That would be nice. I'll treat."

As she said goodbye to Hazel, Josie was excited to know she'd see her again. They were two very different people, but it was as if Hazel could reach a part of her that no one else had been able to. She definitely wanted to know more about her.

————

On the way back to the condo, Josie was feeling beachy and warm from the sun and the rum. She grabbed a burger for Nick from a walk-up stand and then stopped by the local seafood market where she picked up a pound of shrimp and a container of crab meat, something she'd not been able to do before. Bags in hand, she made her way back to the condo, walked in, and kicked off her flip-flops a few steps away from the painting Julian had bought for her.

"I didn't know what to do for dinner," Nick said from the empty kitchen table where he was writing numbers in his notebook. His hair was flattened on one side where he'd been sleeping, and he scratched a pillow line on his face. "We don't have the same stuff we usually have at home."

"I got you a burger and I picked up some seafood for myself," she said, raising the bags. "I've never had seafood before, so I thought we could give it a try."

"Do we still have chips to go with the burger?"

Josie set the bags on the counter and retrieved the Lays from the pantry. "Would you like to try the seafood?" she asked, unpacking and setting it on the counter. She opened the lid of the steaming shrimp, the aroma of paprika, ginger, and lemon making a mundane dinner hour feel like something special.

"No, thanks."

"All right." She passed Nick his take-out bag. "So how's the competition going? You haven't said much about it."

"It starts easy and gets harder."

She attempted to hide her uneasiness by keeping her eyes on the various dinner containers, wondering if Nick would struggle or soar as the competition became more challenging.

"Do you find it easy so far?"

"Yeah. It's just practice right now. We don't start the actual competition until tomorrow." He closed his notebook and turned in her direction.

She was glad he hadn't felt any pressure yet.

"What kinds of things did you work on today?" she asked.

He squinted at her. "I don't think you'd understand even if I explained it. And it would be a lot to explain." He chewed his lip. "We've been working in groups and practicing."

She retrieved two plates from the cabinet and began to fill them with food. She pulled out a bag of salad she'd bought at the store and dished it up as a side. Then she carried the plates over to Nick. He scooted his notebook out of the way to make room for his dinner and stared at the shrimp and crab on her plate when she set it down.

She considered whether the strong scent might bother him. "If you don't like the smell of it, I can eat it later."

He picked up his burger, his long fingers consuming its surface. "It's fine," he said. Enduring smells he didn't like was one of his ways of showing her affection. "It's not that bad."

Josie grinned. "I'm glad." She walked back to the kitchen and poured them each a glass of water. "Have you figured out what you want to do about Rainy?" she asked as she returned with the glasses.

Nick shook his head. "No. I get so anxious around her. That hasn't happened before. She makes my stomach hurt."

"I wouldn't tell her that," Josie said, trying to stifle her happiness. "But your stomach hurts because anxiety and happiness are emotions that manifest there. So if you really like someone, it might be difficult to eat around them, or you might feel like you have a stomachache when you're with them." She leaned forward to gain his attention. "It just means you like her."

As she said the words, a new fear crept in. Dating was unchartered territory, and she didn't know how Nick would take rejection on top of what was at stake with the competition. What would it do to him if Rainy didn't return his feelings? And if she did, how would Nick handle the separation once they went back to their regular lives?

"I went to bed but couldn't fall asleep because I kept thinking about how I'd made a fool of myself and upset her, *and* she makes my stomach hurt, so it's probably best if I don't see her anymore. But that's the only thing I want to do." He pushed a piece of lettuce around his plate. "Should I buy her a painting?"

A laugh burst from Josie at the randomness of his question. "What? Why?"

His face crumpled in a frown. "Because that's what Julian did to show you he loves you."

Her laughter fell away. "What?" She glanced at the stunning beach scene, recalling the strain in Julian's forearms as he carried it home for her.

"He said to get her something beautiful that shows I care, so she'll think of me when she sees it. That's what Julian did, and you keep looking at the painting, so he must be right."

Josie tore her eyes from the canvas.

"I like Julian," Nick continued. "I want to talk to him. Maybe he can help me with what to get for Rainy."

"I can help you," she offered in an attempt to deter Nick from the idea. The last thing she needed was Julian coming around too often, bonding with her brother, and then making her look like the bad guy when they eventually had to leave.

Nick stabbed a piece of lettuce, falling into silence, leaving her with a prickly sensation that things might get harder before they got easier.

Chapter Thirteen

Nick was excited about the competition the next morning. He chattered on about it being the first day of scoring and how he felt like he could do this. He'd spent time in his room studying the books he'd been given and he felt confident. When Josie had gotten ready to walk over with him, he'd said he liked going alone. When she pressed him gently, telling him she wanted a chance to root him on, he explained that he wanted to have some time to himself to prepare before his group work. Everything was working out just as Josie had planned—except now she wasn't sure she liked the outcome. Feeling uneasy, she let him go and wished him luck.

While she settled in on the sofa and canceled her home-owner's insurance online, her mind raced with thoughts of her brother. She didn't like being in the dark when it came to Nick. For so long she'd had to monitor his every move to be sure his basic needs were met, and she wasn't convinced she didn't have to take care of him now. She shut her laptop and got up from the sofa, her shoulders tense.

The walls of the condo suddenly felt as if they were closing in on her and she needed to get out into the sunshine to clear her head. Trying to take her mind off things, she texted Hazel to see if she'd like to get that cup of coffee. When Hazel texted back with an immediate "Yes," Josie gathered her things, slipped the compass into her pocket like always, and left to meet her new friend.

As she walked to the coffee shop, she kept thinking about Nick taking initiative and being independent. While she should be proud of him, his hasty need for freedom spurred a whole new set of worries for her. This experience had changed him in a matter of days. He wasn't telling her *anything* when he always used to share what he was doing—good or bad. And he liked *a girl*—that hadn't happened before. His therapist was way back in Tennessee. She hadn't considered that before leaving. She probably needed to set him up with someone via telehealth so they'd be ready if he needed an appointment to talk things through. She gripped her compass, hoping for guidance she feared would never come.

She'd been impulsive with this trip, making major life decisions she was now second-guessing because the change had been too rapid for *her*. She'd been so quick to jump at this opportunity... What if Nick liked the independence, but couldn't sustain it? What if he fell for a girl but had no way to see her or navigate the relationship? And the alternative, a question Josie didn't want to consider: What if Nick was fine without her?

Her ruminating went round and round throughout the walk, her mind so heavy when she'd finally reached the coffee shop that she almost missed Hazel's wave from their same table.

"Good Lord, child," Hazel said. "What's going on with you right now?"

Josie shook her head. "Sorry. It's just... my brother." She

dropped her bag at the table. "I'll get myself a coffee. Need anything?"

"I'm okay, thanks. Fill me in when you come back."

Josie walked to the counter and perused the coffee options, pondering whether or not she wanted to tell Hazel about the whole situation. It would certainly put a damper on their coffee meeting, and she'd wanted to escape her thoughts for a bit. Hazel was so full of life that Josie would rather be pulled out of her downward reverie than drag them both low. Her mind only half on the coffee order, she settled on a lavender latte, then went back to Hazel.

"What's the problem with your brother?" Hazel asked as soon as Josie sat down.

She prepared herself for the explanation. She didn't love telling people about the fate of her family, which was why she shied away from most social opportunities. But Hazel was different, and if they were going to be friends, she needed to know.

"My parents are both dead; my mom right after my brother was born, then my dad had a heart attack three years ago. For the last three years I've been the only one who's taken care of my brother, and now he's eighteen and doesn't seem to feel like he needs me anymore," she said.

"So you're experiencing a bit of empty-nest syndrome?" Hazel sipped daintily from her mug, empathy in her eyes.

"More than that. I worry about him."

"But you said he doesn't seem to need you anymore. That's a good thing, right?"

Josie shifted uncomfortably in her seat. "I don't know. I'm concerned he might still actually need me and just not realize it. It's hard to say. He's autistic."

Hazel nodded thoughtfully.

"I just don't want to be the one who lets him fall."

"Maybe he'll soar instead."

The hope of that notion caused tears to prick Josie's eyes and she blinked them away. "I need my parents for guidance, and I don't have them. Their absence makes my grief stick around. Every day I have to parent my brother, I'm reminded that they're gone."

The barista called Josie's name and, with a deep breath, she went to get her coffee. When she returned, Hazel pulled out a photo of an attractive man in a white uniform and slid it across the table.

"I brought this to show you." She tapped the photo. "That's Charlie."

The man's dark hair was cropped short, and his smile seemed the type that would be infectious.

"Perfect timing, I suppose, given the mention of grief," Hazel said. "I hadn't finished my story and I thought you might like to see a picture of him before I told you the rest."

A sadness dimmed the usual sparkle in Hazel's eyes. Josie had had that same look in her eyes for years when she peered at herself in the mirror.

"He's handsome," Josie said.

"Yes, he was." Hazel's hands wrapped around her mug. "His plane went down on a Wednesday. Just an average Wednesday..." She tipped her head to the side and slid the photo back over. "An engine stalled during a routine training run. I was a newlywed. We'd been married only four months."

"I'm so sorry." Josie's heart broke for Hazel with this new revelation.

"What I didn't know at the time was that I was pregnant with my son Milo." She repositioned her mug on the table, her gaze remaining on it. "For a while, I was angry that I'd been dealt a hand that made me a single mother. I'd been groomed to be a wife, not a breadwinner."

"I understand questioning your fate," Josie said. Then,

little by little, she opened up more about her parents' death, her brother, and the hand *she'd* been dealt.

"At least your mother prepared you as much as she could," Hazel said when Josie had placed all her life's cards on the table. "I always thought my upbringing did me a disservice, not preparing me for life, but now I wonder if it's the world that does it to us."

Josie leaned in, wanting to absorb the wisdom Hazel had to offer. "Does what?"

"Makes us fear being alone." Hazel frowned as she ran a finger around the edge of her mug. "Most of us only know how to be ourselves with someone beside us on our journey. That's why you're struggling with letting Nick go. It's why I grappled so much in the years after Charlie died. We're taught to find the love of our life, the person to see us through thick and thin. But what about our own souls? How do we serve ourselves in a way that makes us strong? I spent about three years figuring it out, and once I began to know and trust myself, I found love again. I'm a better wife after having had that alone time."

Josie considered the idea. "I've not thought about it like that, but being alone has actually made me stronger."

Hazel smiled. "I believe the people who end up alone are the ones God has planned to make His warriors. Because once we've conquered that and found peace in ourselves, we can do anything."

Josie brightened at the thought. "Warriors? What in the world would God want *me* to do for Him?"

Hazel's eyebrows lifted, optimism shining in her eyes. "He'll show you."

Josie folded her arms and sat back in her chair. For the first time in a long time, she experienced a tiny shift of progress in herself. Knowing her life might not have been discarded in the chaos of death felt nice.

"Where's Milo now?" she asked.

A crestfallen look washed over Hazel. "I spent most of his young life helping him battle childhood leukemia. I lost him when he was five."

The news hit Josie like a sledgehammer. She'd been five when she'd lost her mom... And then, under the lens of motherhood, she considered Hazel's side of things. She couldn't imagine losing Nick. The idea was terrifying.

"Milo was too good for this world, so he didn't have to spend very long in it. Now he's with Charlie," Hazel said quietly.

As they sipped their coffees, Josie couldn't get over how confident and content Hazel had seemed the first time she saw her walk into the coffee shop. She'd said herself that she spent every day in town talking to people. Yet she'd been carrying the weight of loss the entire time. Even now, she seemed as if she were perfectly comfortable in her skin. How did she manage it? Was there some great mystery to happiness that only she knew? Or was she just the best warrior Josie had ever known?

———

After spending some time walking along the beach, Josie made her way back to the condo. The whole day she'd tried on a warrior persona like a new mink coat, shifting and jostling it to see if it fit. Viewing the world as if she were meant to be alone for a certain amount of time was a different perspective she hadn't weighed out before. She'd already proven she could manage without her parents when she was thrust into the role of Nick's caretaker at the young age of twenty. She'd handled it.

When she returned to the condo, she walked into the quiet space and sat on the sofa. She felt the absence of Nick's scribbling and turning pages in his notebook, the tapping of his pencil. She still worried about him, whether he was getting along all right with Rainy and whether he could keep up with the math competition. He was quick to doubt himself, and Josie fretted over how failure of any kind might impact him.

But as she sat in the empty room, she also thought about something else: herself. Was there really some kind of grand plan built for her life? Was she meant for greatness—a warrior like Hazel had said?

Her gaze fell on the painting Julian had bought for her once more. She walked to it, lifting the canvas to eye level. The swipes of teal and navy blue blurred at close range, the colors becoming more texture than picture. She carried the painting into the bedroom and propped it on the dresser across from the bed. She had no idea how much Julian had paid for it, and she knew he probably wouldn't let her repay him, but she didn't want to be indebted to him.

Hazel's words still in her mind, Josie pulled the compass out of her pocket and took in its gilded edges. So many times she'd hoped for guidance from her parents. She'd imagined her mother and father sending a sign to lead her, though she didn't ever seem to hear anything from them. After what Hazel had said about God's plan, perhaps her parents had been there the whole time but were hanging back, remaining silent so Josie could become the person she was supposed to be.

But who was she supposed to be?

The click of the door drew her attention to the living room. She left the bedroom and found Nick loping across the space toward the table.

"Hi," he said, although he didn't make eye contact.

"Hey," she replied, wondering why he'd shown up so early.

He didn't seem to notice her as she moved toward him. He flipped through his notebook, scanning each page with his finger. Josie worried he'd had a bad day and had retreated to the condo to scratch down more numbers, but as she watched him, something seemed different.

"What are you looking for?" she asked.

"There's a problem I'm working on, and I asked if I could come back and get my notebook. They said I could." He closed it and finally met her gaze. "I'm going back now. I'll see you tonight."

"Want to get something to eat together after you finish?" she asked.

"Yeah, sure," he replied, but his back was already to her. Then he flew through the door, leaving her alone again.

Nick's quick visit had been just enough to pull her back into her life as a caregiver, the figurative mink warrior coat sliding off her shoulders into a lump on the floor. She went back to the questions she'd been asking herself before her coffee date with Hazel, and realized that what she was good at was taking care of Nick. What if Hazel didn't have it exactly right? What if Josie's strengths *required* another person? She wanted to take care of Nick. So where did that leave her?

Just then, her phone rang. She hoped Nick was calling to tell her he needed something. When she got to it, however, Aunt Zelda's name filled the screen.

"Hello?" Josie answered. Disappointed it wasn't her brother, she went back to the sofa and sat down.

"Hi."

"Hi..." What did Zelda want? She never called. "Is everything all right?"

"Yes. I just wanted to see how you and Nick were doing."

"Good," Josie replied, figuring Aunt Zelda would prefer she spare the details. Surely she was calling for something else. Fingers crossed it wasn't money.

"That's good to hear."

"How's the house?" Josie asked.

"It's great. I'm unpacking slowly but surely. How about you two? Have you gotten settled in?"

Josie fiddled with a thread on the end of her blouse. "As settled as we can be in a rental."

"Good." There was an audible breath on the other end. "Well, okay. I just wanted to see how you were."

"All right." Josie waited warily for something to come out that would warrant the conversation.

"I'll call you again later."

She would?

"Okay."

"Bye."

Josie clicked off her phone, wondering what that was about. Had Aunt Zelda really just called to see how they were with no ulterior motive whatsoever? She stared at the phone, willing to bet her aunt would call back at some point wanting something.

Josie used to feel drawn to her aunt, thinking they could be fast friends if Zelda stayed in one place for longer than two seconds. She'd tried to call her on several occasions over the years when her dad was run ragged, asking her to visit, and every time Zelda had said she would, but then didn't show up on the day she'd said she was coming. Her aunt was the only person in their family who shared Josie's talent in art, yet Zelda hadn't once bothered to show interest in Josie or have any kind of relationship with her. The only period Zelda had spent any length of time with them was one summer when she was homeless and had nowhere else to go. Even then, she'd been absent most of her stay. Josie still remembered the anticipation she'd felt as a young girl when her dad had told her Zelda was going to visit. She had hoped to finally get the opportunity to bond with her aunt, maybe share stories during a family dinner or draw together—something. But

Zelda had come in every night after Josie had fallen asleep and was gone by morning.

When her dad mentioned that Zelda had found a place to go, Josie set her alarm early to try to catch her and say good-bye. While Zelda was walking to her van in the drive outside Josie's window, Josie knocked and waved, longing for her to come back in. Instead Zelda had stared at Josie—no smile—and then turned and got in the van. At the young age of seven, Josie hadn't been entirely sure, but she thought her aunt was crying when she drove away. She'd never known the reason, but who knew what Aunt Zelda had going on... She was a mess.

Josie tossed her phone on the sofa and shook her head, still wondering if Zelda was priming her for some big favor.

Chapter Fourteen

After completing the house sale and sending the final documents to the real-estate attorney, Josie decided to sneak in the back of the competition to see Nick during his final session of the day. Before leaving, she looked up the schedule so she'd know where to go, and was relieved to read that the participants had been divided into ten groups of five. Nick always did better in small groups. She closed her eyes for a quick second and sent up a prayer that he'd be okay.

While she was certain she wouldn't understand any of the problems he was solving, she wanted to be supportive and show him she cared, even if she did have to tell him after the fact that she'd been there. She dug her visitor badge from the folder, slipped it around her neck, and left the condo.

As she made her way to the venue, the warmth of the summer sun blanketed her skin. The air was heavier here—full of humidity and salt—but deliciously relaxing. Rosemary Beach tickled every sense: the damp air on her skin, the briny aroma mixing with the sweet scent of ice cream, and the chatter of the crowds.

Despite the festively happy atmosphere, Josie walked

along deep in thought. Her identity still in question, she couldn't shake the notion that her purpose was to be with people. That was what had drawn her to work at the diner. She didn't miss a lot about that job, but she did miss the customers. Even in college she'd decided to study marketing— an entire degree involving different ways to reach people. Though Hazel had a point that being by herself could teach her strength, and Josie had shied away from others due to her grief, when it came down to it she enjoyed connecting with others. This trip had highlighted her need to be with others on a daily basis.

Arriving at the venue, she paused to tug open the double doors, then stepped into the air-conditioned lobby. She paced through the wide hallways of the convention center, passing sculptures of sea animals and paintings of ocean scenes as she followed the signs for the Battle of the Mathematical Minds. Outside of the auditorium, a woman sitting at a long table asked her name and looked her up on the visitor roster, then allowed her to enter, reminding her to do so quietly and not disturb the participants.

Josie opened one of the doors and slipped inside, then took a moment to allow her eyes to adjust to the darkness. She found the aisle with beaded lights illuminating the path and walked down the rows of empty seating, choosing a seat in the middle, away from the group of spectators who'd settled in the front rows. Five participants were in a line on the stage, and Nick was second from the left. Bright lights shone on their faces as they stood at podiums while math problems flashed on large screens.

Nick held an electronic pen, writing numbers that showed up on a smaller illuminated display on the front of his podium. The setup looked like that of a TV game show. Instead of a host, a panel of judges sat across the edges of the stage in a V formation. On the far right of the group, Rainy was intently writing her answers in swoopy numbers—a flower in the top corner of her screen, which made Josie smile.

Josie's heart hammered as she looked back at Nick. She'd been right; she had no idea what kind of problem he was solving, but his number was one digit off from Rainy's.

"Enter your final answer," one of the judges said.

A musical chime sounded, and the five contestants put down their pens.

Rainy's podium lit up, along with one other. Nick gritted his teeth and shook his head while the judges tapped on their tablets. Josie slid down in her seat, hoping Nick couldn't see her. He didn't need any extra pressure, and if he knew she was in the audience, he'd burden himself to do well for her.

The old problem vanished from the larger screen and a new string of numbers appeared. The handwriting on the podium screens faded to blank.

"The next question is one for the physics enthusiasts," one of the judges said. "For one point, answer the following. Begin now."

Nick's eyes were glued to the screen, his lips set in a frown of concentration. Josie wanted to go up to him, to tell him it would be okay. Even with the small number of contestants, she could tell the pressure was challenging for him. Would he panic and rush off the stage to get his notebook? He picked up his electronic pen and numbers began appearing on his podium screen. He stopped, erased one, peered back up at the screen, and then a few more numbers materialized.

"Final ten seconds," the judge announced.

Nick quickly erased another number, looked up at the problem again, and jotted down one more. With only about three seconds left, he scratched through another set of numbers, hastily writing a string of digits.

"Enter your final answer," the judge said.

Nick gripped his podium, the white of his knuckles showing all the way from the stage. Josie held her breath.

The podiums lit.

Nick's stayed dark. He banged his hands against his temples, then clasped his fingers behind his head and stretched, his tension clear. Josie gripped the arms of her chair, ready to jump up and rush the stage, but that would only make a bigger scene. She forced herself to stay put.

Rainy turned toward Nick, concern written on her face.

Josie leaned forward again, rocking with the pressure. She willed Nick to take deep breaths the way he'd been taught in therapy.

The screens cleared and another problem popped up, but it was evident by the wild movement in Nick's gaze that he hadn't calmed down. Josie closed her eyes and prayed that he'd settle.

You can do this, Nick. I know you can.

"Final problem," the judge said.

Josie's eyes snapped open.

"This one is worth four points, which could tip the scales, so point-leaders, be ready."

A new problem appeared on the screen and Nick's shoulders relaxed, his eyes widening. Josie's breath caught, her entire focus on him.

The others began writing their answers.

Slowly, a corner of Nick's mouth lifted in a smirk. He picked up his pen and wrote several numbers, then set it down before the others. He seemed incredibly confident, but did he have it correct? Given his obvious certainty, what would he do if he didn't have the right answer? Josie's heart pounded as she regarded the other contestants. Rainy was still fiddling with her answer and the others' heads were down as they worked.

Nick stood, his hands motionless, waiting.

Josie swallowed, her pulse in her ears.

"Ten seconds."

Josie reached into her pocket for her compass and realized she'd left it on the dresser at the condo. Her breaths shallow, she spread her fingers on her knees, praying he got it right.

"Final answers, please."

The others set down their pens.

Only one podium lit.

Nick threw his fists in the air and cheered, and a wild breath burst from Josie's lungs.

"In an interesting turn of events, Nick Wills has won this round."

Josie covered her mouth to stifle her giddy laugh of relief.

The other contestants came toward Nick, shook his hand, and congratulated him, but Rainy hung back, studying her screen. When everyone else had left the stage, Nick went over to her and they spoke in hushed tones. Rainy seemed to be asking him questions. He pointed to her screen, and it appeared as if he were going through the problem with her.

A flutter of happiness rushed through Josie at the sight of Nick showing his affection for the young woman. In that instance, the man within him had emerged. His demeanor was mature and gentle, his approach almost tender. When he'd finished explaining, Rainy put her arms around him. Josie made out her words, "Great job." Then the two walked off the stage together.

Josie hurried to them. "Hey, Nick!" she said, getting her brother's attention.

"You're here?" he asked.

"Yes. I saw those last few problems. It was a nail-biter."

Nick frowned. "It didn't have to be. I got the non-zero number incorrect on the second one I got wrong, when I should've known better."

"Well, now you do know better," Rainy said, smiling up at him.

As they exited the auditorium, Nick led them to the digital leaderboard.

"How do you read this?" Josie asked, trying to make sense of the list of names and numbers.

"The scores for all fifty of us are tallied electronically from each session. The problems are weighted. Every day, starting today, they send home the bottom seven people," Nick explained. "The final eight will compete on the last two days."

He ran his finger down the glass, stopping at number twenty-three: Nicholas Wills. "I'm safe."

Rainy giggled, pointing out her name at number nineteen. She toyed with a delicate pink and pearl seashell necklace she was wearing.

"That's pretty," Josie said, trying to take the pressure of competition off Nick for a bit.

Rainy grinned bashfully. "Nick gave it to me this morning. He said its beauty reminded him of me, and he wanted to say he was sorry for blowing up yesterday."

"Oh, he did?" Josie immediately realized Nick had heeded Julian's advice.

"Yes." Rainy batted her eyelashes at Nick. "He told me he has a hard time sometimes and doesn't mean to direct any anger or frustration at me, and that I make him try harder."

"She understands," Nick added.

Josie's heart swelled with emotion. Not only had Nick spoken up for himself, but Rainy had understood. That was all Josie had wanted for Nick his entire life. She beamed, feeling so much lighter. Nick had managed just fine on his own.

"Are you two hungry?" she asked, trying to keep the quiver of happiness out of her voice so she wouldn't embarrass her brother with too much doting. "It's nearly dinnertime and we can celebrate the two of you making it to the next round."

"I'm *really* hungry," Rainy said.

"Let's go to The Salty Shark," Nick suggested.

Josie wrinkled her nose. "Are you sure you want to go *there*?" she asked, eager to avoid Julian. She'd hoped to enjoy a relaxing dinner with Nick and not have to think about herself for a while.

Nick answered with his typical honesty. "You know that once I find a place I like, I don't need to try anything new. And Rainy hasn't been yet. We can get her a burger if she'd like one." He turned to her. "They have great plain burgers."

Rainy snickered and threaded her arm in his. To Josie's surprise, Nick let her do it.

"And it's close." Nick pointed to the sign down the road.

With no other excuse than wanting to avoid Julian, Josie followed the two of them to the restaurant. Having beat the dinner crowd, the hostess showed them to a table for four, and in a matter of minutes they were seated on the deck in the cool gulf breeze giving a waitress their drink orders.

The waitress had barely left when the empty fourth chair turned backward and Julian straddled it, a grin on his face.

"Fancy seeing you here," he said. "Were you coming to find me?" That fondness for her twinkled in his eyes.

"It was my idea to come," Nick said. "And I followed your advice and bought a necklace for Rainy to tell her I'm sorry. This is Rainy."

Rainy shook Julian's hand.

"How'd he do?" Julian asked her, nodding toward the necklace.

"It's perfect." Rainy ran her fingers along the seashells.

Nick's chest puffed with pride while he picked up the menu. His quirks seemed to amuse Rainy.

Julian twisted toward Josie. "Mind if I join you all?"

"Don't you have to work?" she asked.

"I just got off when lunch ended. I was going to go home and work on something, but I can spare an hour or so."

"Join us, then," Nick said from behind his menu without making eye contact.

Easy for him to say.

"We're celebrating a big win," Rainy said.

Julian's face lit up as the waitress brought their drinks. "Oh, really?" Without further explanation, he ordered a bottle of champagne and then turned back to Rainy once the waitress had left. "What kind of win?"

Rainy took a sip from her glass of soda. "We're celebrating Nick and me making it to the next round of the math competition."

Nick started telling Julian about the competition and what he'd done during the day—information he hadn't shared with Josie. For the first time in a very long time, Nick was animated and motivated, outwardly proud of himself. Josie couldn't have been happier, despite a twinge of melancholy that he hadn't told *her*.

"Wow. Congratulations!" Julian said.

The waitress delivered the champagne and four glasses.

"Perfect timing." Julian unwrapped the cork and popped the bottle open. "We can celebrate with a toast."

Rainy's giggles bounced like the bubbles in the champagne that were foaming up the neck of the bottle. "We're only eighteen."

Julian's hands stilled. "Oh, yeah." He eyed the bottle. "I guess that means Josie and I will have to drink this *for* you." He filled one of the flutes and handed it to Josie then poured one of his own. "I'm celebrating something myself."

Josie set her bubbling glass on the table, the fizz dancing at the top. "What are you celebrating?"

"That project I was going home to do—I officially started my real job."

"Don't you work here?" she asked.

"Yes. And I'll have to work here for a while until I'm up on my feet. But the whole of the last year I've been planning for my career."

"What will you be doing?"

"I've been saving money since college, and my parents gave me a little nest egg they'd been building my entire life. I'm planning to live here full-time, and I've opened a beach-party supplies rental company called Stand Out Rentals. We rent everything your family needs to have a good time at the beach and stand out from the crowd—everything from beach umbrellas to bonfire necessities to beachside DJs and disco balls. I bought a warehouse space in town, and I just finished acquiring the last of the inventory I need. We've got it all."

"That sounds fun," Rainy said.

"I hope it will be." He held his glass in the air. "But we need to toast! To winning at life!"

Josie raised her champagne, suddenly feeling as if everyone was winning but her. She clinked her glass to Julian's and then to Nick's and Rainy's.

While Rainy and Nick fell into conversation about a dolphin they saw jump on the horizon, Josie swallowed the champagne like a shot, its bite making her eyes water. She reached across the table and filled her glass again. As she gulped down round two, she realized Julian had noticed.

"It's going to be that kind of night?" he asked.

She didn't answer, eyeing the waitress to try to get her attention so they could order food.

Julian leaned close enough for her to catch a delicious whiff of him. "Bad day?"

"No, I just felt like downing a glass." Her gaze fell absentmindedly on a band that had begun setting up in the corner of the deck.

When she looked back at him, a smirk had risen on his lips.

"I haven't known you as someone to chug drinks."

"Yeah, well..." She wanted to say something witty, but the truth was she didn't know why she'd guzzled the champagne. She was having some sort of identity crisis and a part of her wished she'd stayed put in Lox Creek. At least in her old life she'd known what was coming next.

Julian drank his glass and refilled it.

"Why'd you do that?" she asked over the twang of an electric guitar as the musician tuned his strings and checked his amp. She wondered how Nick would handle the loud sound, but he was too busy talking to Rainy to have noticed.

"We used to do everything together," Julian replied. "So this is a good place to pick back up, right?"

She laughed despite herself. "Binge drinking?"

Julian cocked his head to the side and rolled his eyes. "I'd hardly call having one glass of champagne 'binge drinking.'"

As she studied the menu, the musicians took their spots on their stools, strumming their guitars, switching between acoustic and electric. Nick put his hands over his ears.

Rainy pulled his fingers away and whispered something to him.

"We're gonna order dinner at the bar and then get it to go," Nick said.

"We can go somewhere else if it's too loud," Josie suggested.

But Nick waved her off. "No, no. You two stay. We're gonna take ours to the beach."

"You sure?" she asked, not thrilled with the idea of having dinner alone with Julian.

"I'll get it for you," Julian offered. "Come the bar with me." He got up and the three of them walked to the bar, leaving Josie at the table.

Only Julian returned—with two highball glasses half full of ice and pink liquid.

"What's that?" She waggled a finger at them.

He set them on the table and topped them off with champagne. "They're called conch shells because the champagne sits on top of the pink for a minute, making it look like the inside of the shell." He placed one in front of her. "If you want something to take the edge off, this works much better than just champagne."

Josie shook her head, ready to protest, but he pushed it forward.

"And it tastes like peach sherbet."

Against her better judgment, she took a sip of the sweet, fruity drink and instantly the refreshing cold of the ice combined with the peach flavor relaxed her.

Julian's eyes sparkled. "Good, right?"

Josie nodded, the tension draining from her shoulders as the three musicians onstage began strumming their guitars. Nick called her name and threw up a hand as he and Rainy carried bags of chips and salsa across the deck toward the steps that led to the Gulf.

"So I finally cornered you," Julian said with a note of excitement in his voice. "And I get to have you for an entire meal. What will I do with all the time?"

"Eat," she replied dryly, their banter coming back to her easily.

Julian rolled his eyes and shook his head, amusement showing in the curve of his lips. Then he sobered. "It's amazing to see you. I can't help but think it was meant to be."

To Josie's relief, the waitress arrived. As she scanned her menu and told the waitress her order, Julian's words swam in her head. It did seem awfully crazy that they'd run into each other after so many years. But while he ordered, Josie rationalized the idea away. They'd been planning to come to the same spot three years ago. Julian had actually been there before with Brit and Maisy, so it was only natural that if he liked the location—and what wasn't to like about Rosemary Beach?—he'd return.

"You're deep in thought," Julian said after the waitress walked away.

"I was wondering what our old housemates were up to," she said, skirting their earlier subject. She took another drink of the cocktail while the band kicked in with a beachy tune she'd not heard.

He leaned back in his chair, draping an arm across the back of the one beside him, his level of relaxation something she still had to consciously work at.

"Brit got a job in Atlanta with Emory University Hospital."

Josie gasped, delighted. "Oh, wow. That's where she'd dreamed of going."

"Yep. She was beside herself when she got the call to pack her bags."

Josie folded her arms and grinned, but a pang of guilt swelled that she hadn't celebrated with her friend. "And Maisy?"

"She's a pharmaceutical sales rep. She cleans up real well."

"That's incredible." Josie drank from her glass once more, hoping the alcohol would dull the feelings of missing out that she'd pushed away. They could still sting her without warning. She finished her drink. "Let's have another."

Before she knew it, they were talking over their empty plates hours later. She'd lost track of everything they'd talked about, her eyes growing heavy as she chatted. The waitress brought another conch shell drink for each of them. Julian had advised against it, but they'd already cast their spell on Josie, erasing her worries, and she didn't want reality to creep in, so she'd kept the drinks coming. Julian tipped the last of the champagne into each glass.

"Cheers," he said, holding his up toward her.

She followed his lead, clinking the edge of her glass to his. "What are we toasting this time?"

"Us." His gaze lingered on her as he slowly sipped the pink liquid, the band starting another song.

Josie wasn't about to ask him to define that word—"us." She was afraid of what he'd say. Never before had he referred to the two of them as a singular unit, and she wasn't sure why he'd decided to do it now. She couldn't deny the way it made her feel. Perhaps in both their cases it was the alcohol...

When he stood up, took her hand, and led her to the empty space in front of the band, Josie was certain it was the drinks.

"No one else is dancing," she whispered. Her words felt detached from her lips, as if each syllable was coming out a second after she'd uttered it.

Julian gave her a spin, the world continuing to rotate after he'd pulled her into his embrace.

"Do you hear what's playing?" He wrapped his arms around her waist, pulling her to him.

And she allowed it.

She fought to catch her breath, the memory of their time at the waterfall returning clearly. She tried to focus on the present to keep the old feelings from coming back and zeroed in hazily on the song. She struggled to recognize the beachy rendition of whatever it was.

"What's playing?" she asked.

"'Days Like This' by Van Morrison." He gave her another twirl, doing a number on her head. "Remember the time we tried to make vegetarian spaghetti and it was watery?"

She threw her head back and laughed. "Oh, my gosh, yes!"

Julian pulled her closer, his cheek at her forehead. "This song was playing that night."

"How do you remember that?" she asked.

He leaned back and looked into her eyes, the chatter of the

restaurant fading away. "When it comes to you, I remember every single thing."

She wanted to lean in and kiss him, but she knew she'd hate herself in the morning. Her life was bigger than this moment, and while she was avoiding her life right now she couldn't lose sight of that.

When the song ended, she pulled away. "Thank you for the dance."

"Anytime." His thoughts were visible in his heavy gaze.

"We should probably call it a night."

He nodded. "Let me settle the check and I'll walk you home."

CHAPTER FIFTEEN

The sunlight streaming through her bedroom window caused a sharp pain behind Josie's eyes. She swallowed against her bone-dry mouth, her tongue feeling like sandpaper. Blurry memories floated into her semi-consciousness of dancing to the band last night, Julian spinning her.

Slowly becoming aware of her surroundings, she realized she was still wearing her clothes from yesterday; the oily, cakey film on her skin evidence that she hadn't taken off her makeup either. She opened her eyes to find her shoes haphazardly strewn across the floor. Only her side of the bedspread had been disturbed, the rest of the bed covered in the turquoise and navy-blue throw pillows. She tried to focus on the wavy embroidery of one of them, but her vision was distorted.

Beyond the pillow, she caught sight of a folded piece of paper. Using the reserves of her energy to sit up, she pulled it toward her.

Josie-Boo,

Look to your left. There's a glass of water on the nightstand. You're probably going to need it.

Before finishing the note, she peered over at the small bedside table to find a full glass of water and two ibuprofens next to it. She squeezed her eyes in an attempt to eliminate the pounding in her head and turned back to the letter.

The ibuprofen's beside your water in case you have a headache—which, given the number of drinks you ordered us, I'm guessing you have.
Text me when you're ready to join the land of the living. I've got a wonderful spot to take you to. Breakfast is on me. And you and I can talk more about what you told me last night.
Julian

What she told him? She rubbed her forehead as if it were a genie's bottle, hoping the answer would surface, but her mind was blank. The only thing she could muster was the fuzzy recollection of Julian's strong arms around her, laughing, his eyes sparkling in the moonlight, not leaving her face.

As anxiety rooted within her, not having a clue of the time, she suddenly wondered what Nick was doing. Had he seen her in her state of inebriation last night? Had he gone to the competition already? What had he eaten for breakfast? Guilt for not knowing the answers swarmed her. Last night, she'd fallen back into the carefree feeling of her college days so easily. She should've known better. She'd faltered, and it wasn't like her.

Josie jumped out of bed, her feet landing on the cool tiled floor with a thud. She raced into the living room.

"Morning," Nick said from the small kitchen table in the open area between the two rooms. He'd made toast.

"Good morning." She ran her fingers through her hair and straightened her wrinkled shorts and blouse, praying he would think she'd already gotten ready for the day. "Want me to make you some eggs? You need protein."

Nick shook his head. "I was actually hoping you could give me some more money. Rainy and I are going to breakfast with a couple people from the competition. I was just too hungry to wait." He popped the last of his toast into his mouth and brushed off his hands.

"Oh, yes. Sure. No problem." She pawed for her purse on the counter and dug out a wad of bills from the cash she'd packed for their trip.

Nick got up and carried his plate to the sink, running it under the tap. "So did Julian bore you at dinner?"

The swirling sensation of moving on the makeshift dance floor, holding Julian's hands, his woodsy scent, came back again. "Bore me? No, why?" She handed the cash to Nick and he stuffed it into his pocket.

"When I got home, you were already in bed. Julian said you were super tired." Nick slipped his ID lanyard on.

"Yeah," she said, relieved she'd gotten one of her answers, and Nick hadn't seen a thing. She wouldn't let herself slip again. "I think all the change with the trip finally got to me."

Nick nodded, his mind clearly already on leaving. He slid on his shoes and made his way to the door. "I'll see you later."

"I'll come watch the competition in a little while, if that's okay."

"Okay," he said before walking out the door. Then he peeked back in. "Have a nice day."

"You too," she said.

She slumped on the counter. Growing up, she'd always imagined having a big family with lots of kids. Instead, she'd been given only one with Nick, so the entirety of her energy was wrapped up in one individual. She worried sometimes that, knowing how important family was to her, he felt the pressure of being the only person who could fulfill that need for her. She didn't want to put that kind of pressure on him, but at the same time, if anything happened to him, she didn't know what she'd do.

But now wasn't the time to think about being alone. From Julian's note, she wouldn't be alone today, and she had other fears to consider—like what she'd said to Julian last night. She located her phone on the coffee table, texted him that she was up, and asked where she could meet him in an hour.

———

Josie's white linen top billowed in the coastal breeze as she walked the cobbled pathway through the village, following the map on her phone. A few glasses of water and a shower had done her some good, and combined with the sunshine, she was almost herself again.

A woman stopped on the corner to let her dog sniff the light pole and a group of children were playing Frisbee in the grassy common area under the arc of shade trees. With the slow pace of those around her, the path paralleling the Gulf, and the warm air tickling her neck, Josie couldn't help but feel relaxed even though she had no idea what conversation she'd be walking into with Julian.

Her map route was interrupted by an incoming call and the relaxation faded very quickly. Aunt Zelda. There it was. She was probably calling with some story about needing her advance back or something equally distressing. Well, she couldn't have the money. And Josie certainly wasn't going to talk about anything like that right now. She dismissed the call and carried on, trying to absorb the serenity of her surroundings to restore her calm.

She finally reached the bistro called Seaside Salt and Chocolate. She walked past two pale blue bicycles, through the outdoor seating area, each seafoam-green table topped with a scalloped-edged, cream-colored umbrella, and up to the door. Steel drums played softly from speakers on either side of a door inset with an oval of glass that let customers peek past the swirling gold logo to the ivory counter and stunningly displayed array of pastries inside. Her phone lit up with a message, but she slid it into her pocket when she caught Julian on the other side of the door, waving her inside.

"I got us food to go," he said, gesturing to a spot at the counter where they could wait. "And I took the liberty of ordering for you." He stepped to the side to allow another patron to view the menu.

"What did you get?" she asked, trying to make general conversation when she was dying to know what she'd told him. She still had no idea.

"Quiche and coffees. I'm guessing you still like a latte."

She leaned against the counter, her fondness for him surfacing. "Yes." She offered a small smile. "And where will we eat?"

"I'll show you."

The woman behind the counter handed him a white paper bag and set two lidded coffee cups on the counter. Julian picked up one of the cups and handed it to Josie.

"Caramel good?"

He remembered.

"Yep," she replied, taking the cup.

Julian led her outside, stopping at the two blue bikes standing in the bike rack. He placed the paper bag with their breakfast in the front basket of one and then guided the other out of its spot.

"For you." He tapped a cup holder on the handlebars next to the basket.

She secured her cup and mounted the bike.

Julian climbed onto the seat of his and backed out beside her. "Follow me."

They rode down a couple streets dotted with shade from palm trees, and crossed two more blocks before turning right and maneuvering onto the bike path that snaked along the coast. The wind blew off the beach, instantly cooling Josie's sun-warmed skin. The expertly lined umbrellas in deep green and their dark wood chairs were nestled in the sand like a necklace of fine emeralds. Every time she stepped outside in this stunning town, she felt as if she'd found heaven. She could definitely understand the pull it had had on her father.

She took in the way the breeze ruffled Julian's shirt, and the tightening and release of his calf muscles as he pedaled effortlessly. He turned to look back at her and flashed his signature grin that could stop her in her tracks, causing her heart to patter. He seemed happy to see her and not overly affectionate, so whatever she'd told him last night couldn't have been so bad.

They turned onto another street and then into an alleyway. The tires bumped along the uneven route, and Josie held the handlebars tighter to keep the bike steady until she came to a halt behind Julian. He hopped off his bike, put down the kickstand, and waved an arm at the bright blue building with white trim.

"Where are we?" she asked, pulling her coffee from the cup holder.

Julian grabbed their breakfast and opened the door. "Take a look."

She entered a wide warehouse and Julian clicked on the

lights. Stacked across one side of the space were lines of closed beach umbrellas in varying shades of blue and green. Rows of beanbag-toss boards and enormous chess pieces, along with other games were arranged on metal shelves next to beach chairs.

"Welcome to Stand Out Rentals," he said. "My sign isn't here yet, but it's on the way. Most of the inventory's arrived, though." He walked farther into the large room, beckoning her to follow.

In the center of the cement floor was a small table with a blue-and-white gingham tablecloth, two beach chairs, and a small vase of flowers.

He gestured to one of the chairs. "For you."

With her cup in hand, Josie lowered herself into one of the chairs and took a sip of her warm, sweet coffee.

Julian plopped down across from her. "So how are you feeling this morning?" He set the to-go bag on the table and pulled out two paper boxes with their quiches and a couple of plastic forks.

"I'm okay. Thank you for taking me home." She didn't want to think about the pent-up emotions that might have flowed out of her under the influence of alcohol. Hopefully, her feelings weren't the conversation he wanted to continue today.

"It was no problem at all. I'd take you home any evening." He met her gaze, making her skin tingle.

She focused on opening her breakfast container. "So..." she said, keeping her eyes on the sundried tomatoes peeking through the surface of her delectable-looking quiche. "What were we talking about last night?"

"You don't remember?"

Her heart thumped at the sight of his smirk.

"No."

He leaned on his fist, his gaze on her as if he were drinking her in. "I like tipsy Josie."

"What? Why?" She tried to calm her pulse while cutting a slice of her breakfast and nibbling a bite.

"You were completely relaxed."

"I'm relaxed now," she said, noticing her shoulders were up near her ears. She worked to release the muscles, making him laugh. She loved the sound of his laugh.

"You told me what the last three years have been like for you and how stressful it's been taking care of Nick by yourself. You told me you wished you had family, and that your aunt, Zelda, was a nightmare."

"'Nightmare' is a strong word," she said. In a way she was relieved she had told him everything. But she also didn't love the fact that he knew, because she didn't want his pity. Although, as she searched his face for it, she didn't see any.

"'Absent' is a better way to describe her. She's the one person who shared similar interests with me, yet she didn't seem to care. And now, she's the only family Nick and I have." Josie rolled her eyes at the notion.

"Maybe she'll come around."

Yeah, she'll come around, all right, Josie thought, remembering the cryptic phone call.

"You know what I took away from our conversation last night?" Julian asked, pulling her from her contemplation.

"What's that?"

"You put too much pressure on yourself."

Her hands stilled, her fork hovering over the next bite on her plate. "How so?"

"You take on the junk life dishes out as if it was some divine purpose for your life, but I'll bet your dad didn't mean to leave you with all that. And he wouldn't want to see you sacrifice your life. He'd want to see *you* thrive too."

"How am I supposed to do that?" she asked. She had too much on her plate to consider doing anything for herself.

"By letting other people in."

His answer surprised her.

"You shut us out, Josie. You assumed we wouldn't want the burden, but you know what?" His smile faded and his expression became serious. "I wanted every bit of your burden. It took me ages to come to grips with the fact that I wouldn't get to see you each morning when I left for class, and I wouldn't have the privilege of trying to convince you to go out and get pizza when you just wanted to study."

She bit back tears. "It sounds good in theory, Julian, but I would've weighed you down." She waved a hand at their surroundings. "Look at this. Do you think you'd be doing any of this if you were dragging yourself to Lox Creek every weekend to see me while I worked at the diner? I don't think so."

"But would you still be in Lox Creek if you'd had your friends to support you? We could have helped with Nick. He and I could've done things together to give you a break. And we could've offered a helping hand with things around the house, getting Nick to school—whatever you needed."

Before he said anything more, she shrugged it off. "Why should you have had to? You had your whole lives to live."

"And what if I wanted you in my life? What if that was the life I wanted to live?"

"It's complicated," she replied.

He shook his head. "It doesn't have to be."

Josie nodded. They fell into silence while she went round and round with whether or not she'd made a terrible decision cutting them out of her life. As they finished their breakfast, Julian let her off the hook, and after a while they chatted about his vision for his new company.

"I'd like to be the lead outfitter for beach rentals," he said.

"I'm planning to do that by having the most inventory and incredibly prompt service. I've already had a few hits from my website."

"Are you delivering everything yourself right now?"

"Yep. Until I can get some capital, I can't hire anyone. But business is slow at the moment since I just got started. No one knows about the company yet."

Josie sipped her coffee. While so much of Julian was the same as the college student she'd left, now he seemed more mature, and she felt as if she could trust him with anything.

"I'm proud of you," she said. "This is amazing."

"Thank you."

They'd both changed over the years, but there was still an ease in talking to him that she didn't have with anyone else. Talking to Julian held the same comfort as coming home after a long day at work. She was glad she'd found him again. At the same time, she had no idea what would happen next.

Chapter Sixteen

On her way to see Nick at the competition after leaving Julian that afternoon, Josie's phone rang. It was Aunt Zelda again. She knew she should probably get it this time. With a steadying breath, she stopped and sat on a wooden bench on the perimeter of the common area at the condos and answered.

"How are you?" Aunt Zelda asked.

Her aunt had never seemed to care one day of her life how Josie had been until this week.

"Fine. What's up?" She didn't have time for insincere pleasantries from Zelda. Best they get right to the point.

"I was just calling to find out how you and Nick were doing..."

Josie heard a sniffle and her breath stopped for a tick. She'd only heard Aunt Zelda's sniffle one other time. Her thoughts raced back to that fateful day when she'd called her from her dad's phone.

"I thought maybe I'd drive down to see you," Zelda continued.

Josie scooted to the edge of the bench, her spine straightening with suspicion. "Why?" *Here it comes*, she thought. *Something's gone wrong.*

"No reason. I was just going through everything here at the house, and I came across so many things from your dad's life that I hadn't known about. Did you know he has a collection of books on Thomas Edison?"

"Yes," Josie said, her gut tightening at the mention of her dad. "He loved to read, and he was captivated by Thomas Edison. He swore the man had divine insight."

"I never knew that."

Well, you wouldn't, would you? she wanted to say, but she stayed quiet.

Zelda continued. "And, right before he died, he was researching the area where you're staying. He had a full itinerary written up for a trip with prices of accommodations... and phone numbers for private investigators in the area."

That gave Josie pause. While she knew of her father's recent interest in the Gulf Coast, she'd not been privy to any actual plans to visit. And what in the world would he have been investigating?

"It's made me realize how much I've missed. And now he's gone, and I feel like I didn't get a chance to know my brother as an adult."

Josie's shoulders fell and she suddenly felt terrible for having jumped to conclusions about Zelda, but her aunt's actions in the past hadn't given Josie any reason to trust her. She never seemed to care for anyone but herself. Her tone this time, however, felt real. And Josie recognized it: the pain of loss. Now immersed in her brother's things, Zelda felt his absence, the same absence Josie had been feeling every day for the last three years.

"When would you like to come?" Josie asked, already hoping the additional person wouldn't impose on Nick. He was used to it being just them in the condo, and she didn't want to cloud his mind with anything other than the competition.

"I'd have to clear it with work first, but I could probably drive down in a few days."

"So work's going well?" Josie asked, still amazed that her aunt had kept a steady job.

"So far, so good."

Josie sensed a slight hesitation after Aunt Zelda's answer that made her wonder if her aunt had something more to say. Maybe Josie had trusted Zelda's sincerity too soon.

"Well," Zelda infiltrated the silence on the line. "I should let you go. I'm sure you're busy."

Josie stood. "Yeah, I'm actually on my way to see Nick's next session."

"How's he doing?"

"He's hanging in there. He made it through the first round of cuts." She skipped across a crosswalk quickly before the sign turned.

"Wow."

"Yep."

It wasn't as if she had a lot to chat about with her aunt, and Zelda probably knew that too, because she said she had to go and hurried off the line. Josie returned her phone to her pocket and made her way to the venue, glad she was still a few minutes early.

The setup was the same as it was the day before, the same woman at the table, the closed double doors. But there was one difference: to her dismay, Nick was standing against the wall, his hands on his knees as he breathed deeply, a coping skill he'd learned to use in therapy. The woman at the table eyed Josie helplessly.

Josie went to him. "Nick, what's wrong?"

"I'm going to be one of the seven," he breathed between inhalations.

She leaned down to try to get eye level with him. "The seven?"

"The people cut today—I'm going to be one of them." He hung his head lower, his body rising with the next breath. "Why am I doing this? I told you it was a bad idea."

"What happened?" she asked, putting her hand on his back.

Nick righted himself and let another breath through his lips slowly. "Before each session, they give us practice problems to work with our partner. Today they're all the same kind of problem. I had no idea how to do them and Rainy did."

"Okay," Josie said, trying to come up with some kind of answer for him. "When you didn't know how to do the problems, what did you do?"

"I told Rainy I'd be right back, and I came out here." He grimaced. "I'm overwhelmed."

"I'm proud of how well you handled yourself," she told him. "Once you're feeling calm enough, we can try to troubleshoot the situation."

"There's nothing to troubleshoot," he said, tipping his head back and rolling it on his shoulders.

"Wait a minute and back up." Josie looked at the clock on the wall. "We have fifteen minutes until the session. You're a super-quick learner. Could Rainy teach you how to do it?"

He shook his head. "I don't know. I've never seen that math strategy before."

"You owe it to yourself to try. You've come this far. Give it everything you've got." She took him by the shoulders and looked him in the eye. "I have no doubt that if it's possible to learn it in fifteen minutes, *you* can. You're an incredible mathematician. I believe in you."

Nick slumped. "All right. I'll ask Rainy to show me. But I'm not making any promises."

He turned toward the door, but Josie grabbed his arm.

"Wait."

He stopped.

"You don't need to make *me* any promises. This is for you, remember? This is for *your* future."

"Are you sure about that? Because *you* urged me to apply. I was perfectly fine living in Lox Creek."

Josie gaped at him, the minutes silently ticking away. "We'll talk about this tonight. Just try your best."

"Don't come in," he said. "It's too stressful already. If I know you're in there, it'll just make it worse."

"Okay. If you don't want me to come in, I won't."

"Thank you."

Nick went through the double doors, leaving Josie in the open corridor. She peered at the woman who was checking badges, and the woman quickly looked down at her list. Feeling defeated and a bit overcome herself, Josie turned around and made her way out of the venue.

As she walked along the street bustling with tourists laughing and chatting merrily on their vacations, she was lost in thought, wondering if this whole thing had been Nick's way of showing her he cared when, really, he'd wanted nothing to do with it. Didn't he realize he could use his talents and do so much more with his life? And if he found a job in mathematics, he might *enjoy* his work.

She barely noticed the crowds as she meandered through them, her mind troubled. Had she pushed him when she shouldn't have? If so, what could she have done to help Nick see that this was all for him? Everything she did was for him.

Slam! The next thing she knew, she'd nearly knocked into someone. Grabbing the woman's arm to steady her, she realized it was Hazel on her daily walk through town.

"Oh, I'm so sorry, Hazel," she said, checking her over to be sure she was okay.

"My goodness, child. What in the world had you so deep in thought just then?"

"I'm not sure," Josie said, not knowing where to start.

"I have some free time. Let's go sit by the water, shall we?"

"Okay."

They walked along the trail that led to the beach, arm in arm. Josie tried to clear her head. It seemed as if she couldn't catch a break. But it also felt as if Hazel was always there when she needed her—like a guardian angel.

"How do you always look so composed?" she asked the older woman.

Hazel let out a quiet chuckle as they slipped off their sandals on the edge of the path just before the boardwalk. "Years of practice."

"I feel like I can't get a foothold on life," Josie admitted while striding beside her new friend on the warm boards. "I take one step forward and two steps back."

"Ah, that's the dance, isn't it? The goal is to make that step forward as big as you can so the two steps back can't quite carry you to where you were."

They paced down the winding wooden structure, the salty wind pushing against them. The green beach flag, signifying a calm day on the water, flapped in the wind.

Hazel stopped walking and Josie turned to find out why.

"When it's time to take that next step forward, Josie, you've got to *leap*. Leap with all your might. Follow what's in here." She tapped herself on the chest.

Josie's father's voice floated into her mind: "If you follow your heart, you'll never lose your way."

"Prepare yourself and then *jump*," Hazel continued. "With both feet, hurl yourself forward." A friendly smile on her lips, she began walking once more.

As they made their way down the steep staircase to the sand below, Josie weighed out Hazel's suggestion. Most of her steps forward had been calculated, but if she gave herself credit, she had made one big leap.

"I sold my childhood home and came to the beach without a job or any real direction. Is that the kind of leap you're talking about?" she asked.

"Yes," Hazel said, excited. "Wow."

"But that leap hasn't turned out the way I thought it would."

Hazel held a finger in the air. "Not *yet*."

"I don't think it ever will." Josie hopped down into the cool sand.

Hazel frowned. "Did you make the decision with your heart?"

"Yes," Josie replied.

"Then it will work out. You'll see."

"I don't believe that." Josie held her hair back as they made their way down to the lapping water, its crystal-clear surface sparkling in the sunlight like a bowl of glitter. "I think I could mess up the best leap."

"*I* think you haven't had enough perspective yet to know that you aren't messing up a thing." She reached her hand into the foam by their feet. "Take this water. It suds in my hand. The suds don't do anything." She flicked the bubbles onto the sand and dipped her hands in once more, scooping up the Gulf water. "And this just looks like clear water." She wrinkled her nose and let it fall back to the ebbing tide. "The foam, the water—nothing special." Then she clutched Josie's arm and walked back a few paces. "But take in everything as a whole."

Josie scanned the navy-blue water on the horizon and the brilliance of the turquoise as the same water made its way inward, finally flowing onto the sand in shimmering clarity.

"You can't see the beauty of the water when it's in my hand because it's too close. You have to step back to really understand its magnificence. Life is the same way. When you're too close to the situation, it's just foam and clear water. But, later, the vibrancy will reveal itself. Your leap *will* lead you."

"I wish I could see the world the way you do, Hazel," Josie said, feeling a little better that at least Hazel could see something great in her decision, even if she couldn't. "Life would be a whole lot easier."

"Ah, one day, you will."

With all her heart, Josie hoped that was true.

CHAPTER SEVENTEEN

As Josie typed on her laptop back at the condo, she inhaled the lime scent of the fresh grouper tacos that she'd picked up on the way home. A swell of renewed optimism had taken over after she'd talked to Hazel.

She'd researched short-term rentals near Rosemary Beach and reached out to a few, then decided to search for homes for sale in the area—just for kicks. While she wasn't sure if she could ever live in Rosemary Beach, she loved the thought of living close to Hazel, and she certainly didn't mind the surroundings. Living there might also give her and Julian more time together.

She bit into her taco and pulled up the house listings page, then typed in her price range. She clicked Search.

Zero results?

Josie checked she hadn't mistyped anything. Her entry looked fine. She hit Search one more time, just to be sure. Again, the site returned zero results. She upped the number to $100,000. Nothing. Deleting her parameters entirely, she searched for Rosemary Beach to see what came up.

When the results appeared, her mouth fell open. She set

down her taco and scanned the prices of the homes for sale in the area: $5,195,000. $3,185,000. $8,875,000. She sat at the condo table, stunned.

Those numbers couldn't be correct. Julian must have found a way to make it work, right? Unless he was using that nest egg his parents had saved for him to pay for a rental. The difference was that he had a business to get off the ground in hopes of sustaining his lifestyle, and Josie had nothing. Her only work experience was waitressing, and she doubted very seriously a job somewhere like The Salty Shark would support her and Nick in this area.

She did another search for apartments. Most were priced by the night to accommodate vacationers: $300 a night. $600 a night. $800. It didn't matter. From the looks of the real estate, Josie certainly wouldn't be living there on a waitress' salary, even with her own nest egg.

Nick walked in the door, and Josie shut her laptop. "Hey, how'd it go?"

With a shrug, he sat at the table, then pulled his notebook toward him. He opened it to one of the problems he'd been solving and scrutinized it.

"Was Rainy able to show you how to do the math for today?"

"Yeah." He eyed her tacos and scowled.

Was he holding on to the notion that Josie had done all this for herself?

"So... Will you be going back tomorrow?" she asked.

"There were forty-three of us and seven got cut. I'm one of the thirty-six remaining contestants."

"That's amazing!" Josie clapped a hand over her gaping mouth.

"I don't think I'll be going back tomorrow, though."

Her hand dropped to her lap. "Why not?"

"You said this was for me, right? But I don't want it."

"What? Why? You're brilliant, and this gives you a chance to be rewarded for your intelligence when no one in Lox Creek gave a hoot about your talents."

He shrugged again.

She stood and leaned on the table. "You deserve more than Lox Creek can give you, more than I can give you. Look! You made it to the top thirty-six mathematicians in the contest. That says something about your knowledge, doesn't it?"

Nick was already jotting numbers in his notebook.

"Do you hear what I'm saying?"

He set his pencil back down. "This is day four of a ten-day competition, and I barely made it. How am I supposed to keep going when I'm stressed out on day four?"

Josie recalled Hazel's words. "Today is just a tiny piece of the whole puzzle. Get all the pieces in front of you before you make your decision. Today is only one kind of math, but tomorrow might be the math you're greatest at, and the day after that might be even better. You should take a leap and see every day before you decide it isn't for you."

He frowned, thoughts behind his eyes. "There is one thing that has been on my mind, making me reconsider," he said.

"What's that?"

"Rainy."

Josie smiled. "You like her, don't you?"

"Yes." His brows pulled together as if he were trying to make sense of his emotions. "The things that make me different don't bother her. They make her smile."

"That's wonderful. Maybe *she's* worth staying for." Josie wanted that for him so much. She prayed Rainy was a miracle sent from heaven just for Nick.

Nick frowned. "She's from Maryland." With a loud exhale, he picked up his pencil and flipped to a new page in his notebook. "How about we just have dinner?"

Josie looked down at her cold tacos. "Okay," she said,

picking up the plate and dumping it into the trash. "What do you want to eat?"

"Eggs and toast?"

"Your favorite," she said, the familiar breaking through the slight tension in the air. "Okey dokey."

They settled into their usual, comfortable silence, and Josie went into the kitchen. While Nick read over the numbers in his notebook, she pulled the eggs from the refrigerator, hoping with everything she had that Nick would take that leap Hazel had talked about.

———

After dinner, Nick retreated to his room, and Josie went into hers and got ready for bed. She showered, combed her wet hair, and applied lotion to her sun-warmed skin. Then she stared at her new painting on the dresser, the day's events still on her mind. Her compass sat on the dresser as well, standing out among the seashell décor. She picked it up, then lay on the bed on her belly as she studied the old piece.

The brass had been worn with time, and the hinges were slightly bent. On the back, a swirling engraving around the edge gave her a glimpse of what the front cover of the casing must have looked like. She closed her eyes, hearing the echo of her father's voice in her mind once more while she gripped the old compass: "If you follow your heart, you'll never lose your way."

"That's not true," she whispered into the silent room. "I love Nick. He's my heart. I followed what I thought he needed, and I'm not so sure I was right. My new friend Hazel tells me I'm too close to the situation right now, but I don't know if I believe her." Tears welled in Josie's eyes. It was rare that she let her emotions surface. Perhaps she was tired, but there in the quiet of the night, she felt very alone.

"Daddy," she whispered louder. "Mama?"

She brushed a runaway tear from her cheek and steeled herself to get through the night. As she lay in bed, she tried to rationalize why she was falling apart tonight. She'd built herself to be stronger than that. It felt as if she was working so hard to make things better, but only treading water.

Help me, she called up to her parents. *Tell me something.*

With a heavy heart, she gripped her compass and buried her head in her pillow to stifle her sobs, the way she'd learned to do as a girl.

CHAPTER EIGHTEEN

Early the next morning, the ping of a notification woke Josie. Barely able to open her swollen eyes, she pawed at the nightstand for her phone and checked the time: 4:45. She'd forgotten to silence it before she fell asleep.

Once her eyes had adjusted enough to make out the smaller characters on the screen, she looked through the notifications of spammy sales emails that had disturbed her slumber and saw that she'd missed a call from Aunt Zelda after eleven.

She rolled her eyes and lay back on her bed, wondering how she could have slept through the phone ringing last night, but a random email notification was enough to wake her this morning. And why was Aunt Zelda calling her so late anyway? Since she hadn't left a message, Josie assumed Zelda was okay, but this new interest her aunt was taking in her was unsettling.

She let her mind wander as she tried to find sleep again. She worked to relax each muscle, beginning with her neck and moving down her body to her toes. The more comfortable she made herself, the less aware of her surroundings she became. When she finally drifted off, she was suddenly back in the empty lot at home. Her dad was walking toward her, his arms stretched out and wearing that wide smile that took up his whole face. He looked younger. No, not younger. He was happy—he radiated happiness.

"I missed you," he said, wrapping her in his strong arms. "You doin' okay?"

She shook her head as the tears came and buried her face in his chest, inhaling the spicy cedar and vanilla scents she hadn't been able to enjoy for three years. A tiny voice in the back of her mind told her she was dreaming, but she refused to listen and hugged him tighter.

"Why don't you draw anymore?" His deep voice was in her ear. "You're so talented." He lifted her chin with his finger, and in that moment she felt filled with love. "Follow your heart," he said. "It will lead you. And I'll make sure you know when you're going in the right direction. You're going to finish what I started."

Finish what he started?

He pulled back and stepped aside. She wanted to reach for him, but stopped when her mother stepped into view. The vision of her clouded with Josie's tears, and she frantically blinked them away to savor the sight. Her mother's skin was milky, her lips a rose pink. Her dark hair was in loose curls, and she wore a white sundress over her thin frame.

"Mama?" Josie whispered, yearning for her.

"Hi, baby." Her mother drew her in and held her. When she let go, she locked eyes with Josie. "I need you to know that you were always my girl. And I've been with you the whole time. You couldn't hear me, but I used to sing you to sleep when Daddy wasn't there."

Josie swallowed the lump in her throat, her heart aching for the young girl she'd been.

"I need you to do something for me," Mama said.

"Anything." Josie could hardly get the word out.

"I need you to go out there and shine your light. Your

flame is only a flicker when it has the potential to be a bonfire."

Josie shook her head. "I don't understand. What do you mean?"

"Shine," Mama said. "You can't truly love others until you love yourself."

Before Josie could ask anything else, her parents faded away, along with the lot, and she was suddenly aware of the sheets beneath her. She squeezed her eyes shut, frantically trying to get the dream back, but the more she struggled, the more awake she became, until she couldn't deny it anymore. She opened her eyes to the golden light peeking over the horizon, making its way through the window, settling on the ledge and across the floor.

Her mind in a frenzy, she tried to recall everything her parents had said in the dream. Her dad had asked specifically why she didn't draw anymore, and he'd told her to follow her heart. Mama had said to go out there and shine her light. As a girl, she'd been happiest when she was drawing. And it was those days and nights that had been easiest for her, running home in the golden hour. Perhaps tapping into her younger self would help her regain some of the joy she hadn't felt in so long.

———

Nick had been quiet on his way out this morning, but he'd asked if he could go alone to meet up with Rainy. Josie was glad he'd decided to give the competition another chance. Still, his silence made her nervous. And she worried about Aunt Zelda's recent bout of chattiness and what she could be up to.

The dream also kept playing out in her mind. In her awakened state, she knew it was just that—a dream—because her dad's message hadn't made any sense: "You're going to finish what I started." But she couldn't shake how real it had felt. And Mama's words kept repeating while she puttered around the kitchen: "You can't truly love others until you love yourself."

She considered whether to check in on Nick or call her aunt back, then remembered she wanted to find a new sketch-book. After breakfast and two cups of coffee to combat her exhaustion, she put on one of her new sundresses and headed out to the shops.

The streets were bustling with tourists ready to start the weekend. Josie made her way past a group as they stopped to chat. She shielded her tired eyes from the bright sun, giving her a view of the bike racks full of the town's signature beach cruisers. She stepped onto the crosswalk, along with two other women in bright dresses who jogged from one side of the street to the other when the traffic cleared, their arms full of shopping bags with fancy boutique names scrawled across them. Josie peered down the row of shops, past families that had gathered outside to wait for cafés to clear enough for them to go inside. None of the storefronts looked like an art shop or a place she could get a sketchpad.

She turned to investigate the other direction when she caught Hazel across the street, leaving the coffee shop in her usual routine. Josie jogged to the other side, waving her down.

"Hello!" Hazel called as she walked alongside a well-dressed man about the same age, who was holding a paper coffee cup and a small take-out bag. When they neared Josie, Hazel gestured to the man beside her. "This is my husband."

The man was wearing a pair of pressed shorts and a linen shirt with a generous number of buttons undone, making him look as if he'd just stepped off a yacht while on vacation.

"This is Josie, the woman I told you about," Hazel said.

Josie shook the man's hand. "Josie Wills."

"Lovely to meet you, Josie. Hazel's been glowing since she met you. I'm Randolph McDonough."

The name immediately registered, and Josie placed him from the glossy photo in Nick's folder. She paused to take in the face of the man who had provided her brother with such an incredible opportunity. She resisted the impulse to tell him how much it would mean to them if Nick were successful; it was as if the man held their golden key in his hand.

"You created the Battle of the Mathematical Minds competition," she said to cover up her previous thoughts.

Randolph's eyebrows lifted, but he maintained a curious look. "Yes. You know it?"

"My brother's a contestant."

Hazel lit up with the news. "You didn't tell me you were here for Battle of the Mathematical Minds."

"I can't believe I didn't. I suppose it didn't ever come up," Josie replied.

Dr. McDonough leaned in. "Speaking of the competition"—he wriggled the bag in his hand—"I'm on a coffee break and I should head back. The next session begins in about ten minutes." He kissed his wife on the cheek. "See you tonight. And, Josie, it was nice meeting you."

"Same," she said.

As he walked away, he called back, "What's your brother's name?"

"Nick Wills."

"I'll keep an eye out for him." There was a protective note to his tone, and a swell of relief took over Josie. He lifted his coffee into the air in a wave.

"I was doing my usual walk around town and Randolph had a free minute, so we grabbed coffee. Now I'm free as a bird. What are *you* up to?" Hazel stepped off to the side to allow a golf cart full of beachgoers to cross in front of them.

"I was actually looking for a new sketchbook," Josie said,

forcing herself to let go of the previous exchange with Dr. McDonough.

Hazel's eyes widened. "You draw?"

Josie nodded.

Hazel's expression brightened. "Oh, I know just the place. I'll show you." She led the way down the sidewalk, motioning for Josie to follow. "I've been wanting to go for ages. And it'll cool me off; this humidity isn't helping things." She patted her styled hair.

Feeling lighter already in Hazel's presence, Josie followed. "How did you meet your husband?" she asked, curious after Hazel's story of her first marriage.

Hazel led them down a winding street of smaller shops behind the busy square.

"I met him three years after losing Charlie. Randolph had just taken a job as a statistician at an international company based in New York. I was modeling there at the time. We met at a fundraiser; he was a friend of a friend."

Josie remembered reading about Dr. McDonough's stint as a statistician from his bio when she was learning more about the competition. His first placement was with a Fortune 500 company.

"How did you know you were ready to love again after Charlie?" she asked.

"Randolph adored both me and Milo, but it was more than that. I'd become a warrior." She winked at Josie. "I knew when I'd learned to love myself first that I could love someone else."

Josie sucked in a breath.

Hazel paused in the shade of a magnolia tree. "What is it?"

Wanting to keep the dream to herself, like a rare family jewel, she replied, "You sounded a lot like my mother just then."

Hazel smiled and carried on walking, and Josie looked at her with fresh eyes. She felt alive when she was with Hazel.

Josie stopped at an outdoor display of dresses that caught her eye. She pulled at the hem of a pink one to get a better look.

"I miss my mom. Remember in the coffee shop when I told you she'd passed? I was only five when she died, and I've missed her every day since. I used to cry myself to sleep at night." The words spilled from her lips, surprising her. She let the dress go and turned to her new friend.

Hazel put her hand to her heart. "You poor dear."

It was almost as if her mother had had a hand in bringing Hazel into her life. As if Mama knew she needed a mother figure.

"You lost your only child, and I lost my mother—we're the perfect pair," Josie said.

"Maybe we can help fill the void in each other."

"Maybe," Josie agreed.

They continued down the sidewalk, passing others out shopping.

"I'm delighted to have you around," Hazel said.

"I feel the same way when I'm with you."

"I've always wanted more children, so you're a blessing. I'm so happy I came over that day in the coffee shop."

Josie smiled. "Why didn't you have more children?"

"Randolph and I tried but it wasn't in the cards. I was open to adoption after Milo died—being adopted myself— but my life got so busy... I looked back years later and wondered where the time had gone."

"You're adopted?" Josie asked.

"Mm-hmm. My adopted mother was a breath of fresh air, my mother—like an angel. Through the years I've always felt as though my birth mother had given both my mother and me a gift by letting me go, but I still wonder where I came from.

175

My adoptive mother never told me, and I never pushed because guilt swarmed me for wanting more than the absolutely perfect childhood I'd had."

Josie could understand what that struggle was like.

Hazel gestured toward a shop with art supplies in the window. "Here we are."

Their conversation faded on the summer air and a fizzle of excitement took hold as they walked into the shop. The walls were full of paper of every style and weight, shelves displayed paints and markers in rainbows of colors, and aisle upon aisle offered everything Josie could ever need, from chalk pencils to portfolios. In her young life, she hadn't been able to afford much in the way of art supplies, and she used to ogle over her friends' notebooks and fancy pencils. This was an adult version of paradise.

"I love this shop," Hazel said as if she'd read Josie's mind. "I used to paint watercolors with my father, but I haven't in ages." She plucked a paintbrush from a bucket on the shelf and ran her finger over the bristles. "I should probably do more of that."

"I stopped sketching too," Josie said, delighted to find out that Hazel enjoyed art as well. She sent a silent nod to her mother, nearly sure, now, that she must have sent her new friend. "This morning, I felt like starting again."

"We could start together." Hazel dropped the brush back into the bucket and pulled out another one, waving it in the air as if to say she'd found her purchase.

With enough savings to afford her favorite supplies, Josie picked up the thickest sketchbook she could find, in her preferred nine-by-twelve size. It had a pale pink leather case and a ribbon sewn into the spine to mark the page. She flipped it over and sucked in a breath when she saw the seventy-five-dollar price tag.

Mama's words from her dream whispered in her ear: "Your

flame is only a flicker when it has the potential to be a bonfire." For the first time in her life, she decided to invest in herself. Josie tucked the sketchbook under her arm and walked to the next aisle where she found a brass sketching pencil. It, too, cost more money than she'd ever spent on herself, and she gripped it tightly as she walked to Hazel.

"Ready?" Hazel asked, holding a large canvas and an armful of paints.

"Yep." Josie held up her two items that felt like treasures.

After they paid, Hazel turned to Josie and said, "Why don't we grab lunch?"

"All right."

"Do you have time to bring your things back to my house after? You haven't had our key lime pie yet. The chef made two and there's no way Randolph and I can eat it all. I could pour us a glass of wine or make us some coffee to go with it, and we could work on our creative endeavors." She lifted her shopping bags with an excited wiggle of her perfectly lined eyebrows.

Josie considered her options. Nick had asked her not to come this morning, and he still had four or five sessions remaining for the day. Her only other agenda items were to sit somewhere by herself or return Aunt Zelda's call.

"I'd love to," she replied.

CHAPTER NINETEEN

The million-dollar mansions Josie had seen dotting the coast during her real-estate search were nothing compared to the McDonough property. She should've guessed when she climbed into Hazel's Mercedes-Benz S-Class 500 that she was about to be blown away, but her vivid imagination hadn't conjured anything quite as spectacular as the sight before her.

"This is incredible," she said.

"Thank you. I've always thought it too big for just the two of us, but Randolph likes it."

Josie was appreciative of her friend's modesty.

Hazel pulled the Mercedes to a stop. Josie stepped onto the slate tiles of the circular drive and stared at the sprawling estate in front of her. She followed Hazel onto the front porch, which was the size of her house back in Lox Creek. White rocking chairs and wicker furniture padded with coordinating overstuffed cushions were expertly arranged in conversational patterns. Paddle fans whirred above them. The expansive double doors with beveled glass reflected the blue sky. Hazel opened them, letting Josie inside.

"What are you in the mood for—coffee or wine?" Hazel asked as she ushered Josie down the corridor, past a cascading staircase, and into the kitchen. The back wall of windows overlooked the sparkling gulf and what seemed to be, given the absence of vacationers, a private beach.

She put her bag of art supplies on the floor and took a seat on a barstool at the family-size marble bar while Hazel washed her hands under a gold faucet.

"Coffee sounds good," Josie replied.

"Coming right up." Hazel retrieved the ingredients from a pantry hidden behind cupboard doors that matched the rest of the light-wood cabinetry. "Is an iced latte okay?"

"It's more than okay," Josie replied, distracted by the incredible view of pristine sand that looked as if it had been raked—had it? Even the water seemed brighter here.

Hazel dished out two slices of key lime pie from the fridge, handing one to Josie. Then she went over to a commercial-grade espresso machine and started on their lattes.

"Why do you go to the coffee shop when you have all that?" Josie asked, gesturing to the machine.

"Coffee tastes better with people," Hazel said with a grin.

"You have a point."

Hazel pulled a couple of glasses from the cabinet. "Feel free to take your pie to the back porch. I'll meet you out there."

Josie carefully picked up her plate and walked to one of the four sets of oversized French doors flanked by white gauzy curtains. She opened a door, letting herself outside, and had to stifle her gasp. What she hadn't seen until she was on the porch was the yard below. Outlined in artful landscaping, it was dotted with pots of pink flowers and sleek wooden loungers surrounding a huge swimming pool with built-in seating and a swim-up hot tub on one end. She hadn't seen anything like it.

Under more paddle fans, she sat on one of the wicker chairs, running her hands along the cool, weather-resistant fabric. She peered at the outdoor kitchen on one end of the porch and wondered if parties there rivaled Gatsby's. Suddenly inspired, Josie stood.

"Here we are," Hazel said, balancing the two glasses and her pie and setting the items on a low table. She handed Josie her drink.

"Thank you," she said. She placed it next to her pie, too inspired to try it just yet. "I had an idea just now. Do you mind if I grab my sketchbook and draw something for you?"

Hazel clapped happily. "Oh, yes. Go get it. I can't wait to see."

With a buzz of exhilaration, Josie went back inside, grabbed her bag of supplies, and returned. She pulled the beautiful sketchbook and pencil out of the bag, still in disbelief that she'd bought such wonderful things for herself. With a deep breath, she opened the book and drew her hand down the blank page, the pencil sliding along the paper with ease.

Hazel took a seat and sipped her coffee, interest showing in the straight line of her posture.

Josie drew another mark and then another, until the picture in her head began to take shape on the page, as if some magical force moved her hand, creating the image. She shaded in shadows and added smaller lines to frame the areas of light, zeroing in on the folds of dresses and the shimmer of sunlight off the martini glasses. When she'd finished a rough outline, she turned her sketchbook around to show Hazel her elegant drawing of partygoers around the McDonoughs' pool.

Hazel threw a hand to her chest. "Oh, my, Josie. That's stunning. I'd love to keep it and frame it."

A rush of exhilaration Josie hadn't felt before swelled inside her at Hazel's praise. "I'm not finished," she said, unable to hide her delight. "I'll get everything filled in and then you're welcome to have it."

"You're so talented."

Once again, Josie thought back to her dream from this morning, Hazel's words mirroring her father's this time. "Thank you."

She felt as if her parents were with her, guiding her for the first time, and she wondered if they'd been waiting for her to step into her authentic self. She picked up her latte, savoring it while the breeze blew off the Gulf, cooling her. She took a bite of the crisp, tart pie, the tanginess of the lime mixing deliciously with the cream. Something inside her told her to take a mental snapshot of this moment, because given the freedom and complete release she felt, this day might be the start of something incredible.

"I definitely want to see it when it's done," Hazel said.

Contentment swam through Josie. She closed her sketchbook and inhaled a satisfied breath of salty air.

They fell into easy conversation for the next few hours, but the whole time Josie's mind was spinning with all the locations she wanted to visit with her new sketchbook. When Hazel offered to drive her home, Josie asked if she could drop her off in town instead. The first place she went was the grassy square in the center of the village.

She settled on a bench at the edge of the lawn, opened the leather cover, and turned the page, the white paper nearly blinding against the summer sunlight. The soft pull of her pencil felt like coming home to the stream out back, the solitary strokes a tether to her past. She sketched the fringe of one of the umbrellas shading a café table nearby, every line bringing her back to a piece of herself she'd long forgotten.

A woman walking by stopped to see what she was drawing. Looking over Josie's shoulder, she said, "That's lovely. You're so talented."

Josie thanked the woman as her father's voice from the dream came through once more. It was the second time she'd heard his words today, and she hadn't realized how much she'd needed to hear them.

She continued sketching the scene at the café, improvising characteristics of people once they'd moved along, her pencil able to catch their essence and her mind filling in the rest. She drew the roofline of the small building, the striped awning out front, and the swirling pattern of the logo on the café door.

For the next hour or so, Josie was lost in the image, adding details like the uneven cobblestones in the sidewalk, and the dark and light appearance on the picture window. When she'd finished the scene, she signed the corner and carefully ripped out the paper from her pad. Then she took it into the café and offered it to the guy behind the counter.

"This is incredible," the manager said after her employee had called her over to view it.

"Thank you. I thought you might like to have it," Josie said.

"You're just giving it to us?"

"Yes," she replied, elated by their response. "I'm a little rusty, and I was just practicing."

The manager's eyes bulged as she peered at the paper in her hand. "If this is your 'rusty' work, I can't imagine what the rest looks like." She handed the sketch to the employee to take to the back room. "I'm going to frame it and put it up in the café."

Josie threw her hands across her mouth to stifle the sheer joy from the day. In that moment, she felt truer to herself than she had even back in college. After telling the manager good-bye, she nearly skipped out of the café.

She walked along the busy streets, looking for another spot to draw. Everything called to her: the shingled rooflines, the delicate feathering of the blooms on the Pampas grass along the manicured edges of the shoreline, the movement of hundreds of flip-flops along the pavement. Before she could decide on her next subject, her phone rang. It was Aunt Zelda. Figuring this was as good a time as any, she answered it.

"Hi," Aunt Zelda said.

"Hi," Josie returned.

"I was planning days when I could come down, and I thought tomorrow might be good. It's the weekend, and I'm not working. And I could put in for a week off."

Josie frowned, slightly annoyed. In order to afford two weeks at the beachfront condo, she'd had to sell her childhood home to Aunt Zelda. Now Zelda got the house *and* expected a free trip to Rosemary Beach? While that wouldn't be a terrible ask from a regular family member, Zelda hadn't really proven that this was anything more than a free trip for her. She'd never wanted to see them before.

Josie's mind raced with what to tell her. If she had to come, she could come on a Saturday; Nick wouldn't have the disruption during the competition since there weren't any sessions on the weekend. That would give him a day to get used to having Zelda there before he had to be on his game again.

"That sounds good," Josie said through her teeth, still wondering what she'd do to entertain the woman. She barely knew her.

"Okay, great," Aunt Zelda said. "I'll put in at work. I should arrive tomorrow around dinnertime."

"All right."

A weighty silence hung between them.

"Well, I'll see you tomorrow, then," Zelda said.

"See you tomorrow." Josie said goodbye and carried on down the street, stopping at the ice-cream parlor. As she sat down on the bench seat across from it and opened her sketch-pad, she was consumed with Aunt Zelda's odd request to visit.

She couldn't for the life of her figure out what her aunt was up to.

"Hey!" a familiar voice called from down the street.

Josie looked up to find Julian jogging her way, wearing a baseball cap turned around backward, and his cheeks pink from the sun. He plopped down beside her and draped his arm across the back of the seat, causing her breath to catch.

"Whatcha doing?" he asked, leaning in to view her empty page.

"I was about to sketch the shop over there." She waved at the ice-cream parlor.

"Don't let me interrupt."

"Oh, you aren't at all," she said, her happiness to see him winning out over her desire to explore her creative side.

Julian grinned. "I used to love watching you draw."

"I've only picked it back up today," she admitted. "I haven't sketched anything since I left for home to take care of my brother."

Julian gaped at her. "But you're so talented."

The hair on Josie's arms stood up and she called up to the heavens, *Okay, I hear you*. The idea of her dad urging her on gave her a new sense of purpose. If it was entirely a coincidence, she allowed herself to believe her parents were really there, sending messages through the people in her life. The idea comforted her.

"What are *you* doing right now?" she asked, changing the subject.

"I had my first customer! I just set up two umbrellas, a couple chairs, and a ladder-ball toss in the village of Watersound."

"That's great," Josie said.

"Yes. And hot. What do you say to me getting us both an ice cream?" Before she could answer, he added, "They have this one flavor that's vanilla with caramel swirl—I know you'll love it."

He had her at "caramel swirl." She closed her sketchbook and slipped it back into the shopping bag. "I'd like that."

"Be right back." Julian hopped up and bounded across the street. A couple minutes later, he returned with two massive cones and handed her one.

She gratefully took it and licked around the edge to keep the drips from escaping down the side, the Florida heat already impacting the ice cream. She relished the sugary, ice-cold taste, the perfect antidote for the high summer temperatures.

Julian wiped his forehead with his wrist. "It's so hot."

"I know," she agreed. "The heat soaks into your bones."

"When I was setting up the furniture, the water was calm. Want to change and go swimming?"

She took a bite of her ice cream to avoid answering right away. The last time she'd been swimming with Julian was at the waterfall back in college. This time, she wouldn't have the interruption of Brit and Maisy to save her from doing something impulsive. While everything inside her told her to say yes, the fact that she'd be leaving soon bothered her. Deep down, she knew if she let Julian in, she wouldn't want to say goodbye again.

"It's just swimming," he said, but there was more in his gaze, and she thought maybe he, too, wondered what came next for them.

Perhaps it was the buzz of happiness from drawing again that made her want to seize the day. Either way, she found her heart winning out over her head.

"Meet me outside my condo in about fifteen minutes?"

A tiny smile twitched at the edge of his lips. "Done."

Before she knew it, Josie was back at the condo, shimmying off her shorts and slipping on her new red bikini. With every movement, she drew parallels to that day at the waterfall. Yes, she had on a new bathing suit and she was about to jump into the water with Julian, but that was where the similarities ended, she reasoned. They'd both changed since then, the innocence of their youth long gone. She was a totally different person now—she had adult responsibilities, and Nick's future to think about—but there was something intoxicating about giving in to her feelings for Julian. Maybe it was the spark of hope, the tiny dream that things could still, somehow, be different.

She pulled on a button-up shirt to cover her bikini, grabbed a beach towel from her suitcase, and slipped on her flip-flops. Then she headed out the door. When she got to the bottom of the steps outside, Julian was already waiting for her.

"Hey," he said, looking way too attractive in his T-shirt and board shorts, the wind tousling his hair. This lifestyle definitely fit him. He threw his towel around his shoulders just as he'd done that day three years ago, and she inwardly flinched at the way it forced the memory of his arms around her to surface. "Ready?"

The pair walked across the parking area to the boardwalk leading to the beach. When they got to the other side of the white sand dunes, the water beyond the break was as clear as a sheet of glass, the sun sparkling off the surface as if it had been sprinkled with diamonds.

"This is ours," Julian said, gesturing to an umbrella, two chairs, and a small table between them.

"How nice." She draped her towel along the back of one of the wooden chairs.

"One of the perks of my job." He grinned at her, his gaze lingering on her longer than it should have, making her heart patter. As if he could read her thoughts, he gave her one of his flirty grins and nodded toward the Gulf. "Let's go."

They walked into the lapping waves, the water crisp and refreshing on her skin. The Gulf was so translucent she could make out a school of minnows swirling around her feet. To her surprise, Julian took her hand, leading her farther out until they were submerged to their chests. He dipped under the surface, then came up and shook the water off his head. She swallowed to keep her emotions in check.

"What is it about us that we ended up in the water again?" he asked, the look in his eyes telling her he remembered.

Her pulse quickened. "I don't know."

"It's a lot better when I don't have a botany assignment hanging over my head."

She laughed, feeling as if she hadn't missed a day with him. "Sometimes, it's hard to believe it's been as long as it has."

He spread his arms, pushing the water away, and floated closer. "A lot's happened in that amount of time."

"That's for sure."

He was near enough for her to see the water glistening on the ends of his wet hair.

"The entire time I've wrestled with something I never got to do." He pushed against the small waves again, completely invading her space as her pulse now drummed in her ears. What should she do? Her mind and heart were at war once again, but something had shifted, and if he tried to kiss her, she'd absolutely let him.

"What's that?" She swallowed and relaxed, ready to accept his advances.

But instead, a brotherly mischief filled his eyes, confusing her. She'd seen it countless times before—like when he'd dropped water balloons on her while she was sitting out in the grass or when he'd slipped ice down the back of her shirt just before class started. She was still processing the look when his strong arms wrapped around her and lifted her out of the water easily, the blue sky hurling toward her. In seconds, she was sailing through the air at high speed, her tummy flipping with the movement until *splash*! She sank under the water.

When she emerged, Julian was laughing as he swam to her, then wrapped his arms around her once more.

She pushed her drenched hair back, trying to catch her breath. "What did you do that for?" she asked, half laughing, half startled.

"To get you out of your head and loosen you up. So it wouldn't be such a shock when I did this." He leaned in and pressed his salty-sweet lips to hers.

She didn't protest—she couldn't anyway. The feeling of them together was too delicious. It was as if his touch pulled her from the very bottom of the darkness inside her. He made her feel like a woman, his desire for her clear, yet his playful side reminded Josie that her youthfulness was still within her. A light that had been extinguished turned back on and shined inside her. Julian's hands gripped her waist, his lips moving on hers urgently, as if he'd been waiting to kiss her for three years and couldn't hold back.

They slowed to a gentler pace, and he pulled away, his gaze on her as if to receive the verdict. The truth was, she couldn't think straight. She wanted to promise him that they could move beyond this moment, but the reality was that she wasn't yet able to stand on her own two feet. And she had Nick. At this early point in his new career, she didn't want to force Julian into a family, whether he welcomed the burden or not.

"Should I toss you in the water again?"

"Hm?" she asked, breaking free from her thoughts.

"There's a lot going on inside that head of yours."

She sucked in a deep breath. "Yeah, there is."

His fingers caressed her sides affectionately. "Care to divulge what?"

She knew if she laid it all out he'd say it would be fine, because that was how he was. But would he be fine? Would helping her get Nick to his next stage of life and taking on responsibility for their small family be fine? Would supporting her when she couldn't afford a life in upscale Rosemary Beach be fine? And if she believed him, would *she* be all right under those circumstances? She'd only just started to explore the sides of her she hadn't unearthed in years. She wasn't sure who she was yet.

"Not going to tell me?"

"It's not that I won't tell you. I just have some things to work out before I jump into anything."

"Whatever it is, you don't have to handle it all by yourself, you know."

She wasn't sure how Julian could help her figure out her life.

"We'll take it one day at a time." The playful sparkle returned to his eyes. "Now that you know what you're missing, I give it two days. You'll have everything worked out by then."

She squinted at him skeptically. "How are you so sure your kiss was any good?" she teased, knowing he could see right through her.

"If it was anything like what I felt on my side, it had to be life-changing for you."

She laughed, but she knew exactly what he meant.

The rest of the evening, all Josie could think about was that kiss. When Nick came home, he told her he'd made it through another cut. They celebrated with a soda and some cookies out on the balcony. He didn't stay out long before he told her he was exhausted and retreated to his room. She watched the sun dip behind the condos, pressing her lips together to conjure up the feeling once more. Then she went to bed. And for the first time she could remember, she fell asleep without a moment to worry.

Chapter Twenty

"We have the whole day to ourselves before Aunt Zelda arrives," Josie said to Nick over breakfast. "She said she'd be here around dinnertime."

"I don't know why she's coming," Nick said as he worked out some numbers in his notebook.

"I'm not sure either, but we have to do our best to make her feel comfortable while she's here."

He looked up from his page. "Why? We barely know her."

Josie's chest tightened because he was right. She had no idea what her aunt was up to, and if Zelda did anything to upset Nick and his performance in the competition, she'd never forgive her.

"Like it or not, she's the only family we've got, so we need to be open, since she's reaching out to us." Josie leaned into Nick's line of vision. "She's Dad's sister, and he always tried to include her. He would expect the same from us."

Nick shrugged and went back to his math, the conversation fizzling. There wasn't much else she could say because she agreed with Nick's indifference.

Josie got up from the table and put her plate in the sink. "So. It's your day off. What are we doing today?"

"I think Rainy and I are going to the beach with a few people we've been hanging out with at the competition."

"Oh?" Josie ran the water at the tap to rinse her dish. "You didn't tell me you'd made other friends. That's good."

"Yeah." He kept writing in his notebook, paused to study the page, then turned to a fresh sheet. "Their names are Sam, Richard, and Cammy."

"That's wonderful. Do you need me to pack you any snacks or anything?" Would he know to apply sunscreen and then to reapply every few hours? The sensory repercussions from a sunburn could impact him for days. "I could put a bag together with some sunscreen and towels—"

"I'm good," he said, cutting her off. "Sorry."

Josie walked over and sat down at the table. "What's going on?"

He shut his notebook and looked at her, the words visibly building within him. "I am fully capable of taking care of myself."

She folded her hands, trying not to show her emotion regarding the subject. "Are you?"

"Yes. Legally, I'm an adult. I can get to the beach with my friends by myself."

"I'm happy to hear that." She chose her words carefully. "Do you know how many minutes you can be in the sun before you get a sunburn?"

He frowned. "No," he said pointedly. "But I can look it up."

"Great. Why don't you look up that as well as what level of sun protection you'll need. Thirty? Fifty? Waterproof?"

"Sometimes I feel stifled by you."

His words felt like a slap in the face. She'd given up everything to care for him, including her own wants and needs. The idea that she suffocated him sent her reeling. What else had he wanted her to do? She'd only been trying to take care of him the way he deserved. And this was how he felt about her efforts?

Josie only *wished* Mama had been there to dote over her and make sure she had the correct amount of sunscreen. Her elbows on the table, she leaned on her clasped fingers, trying to keep the tears from spilling from beneath her lashes.

"I don't mean to be overbearing. I just want to do right by you."

"I know," he said. "I just feel that I can manage on my own and be okay."

A piece of her broke in two at the thought of him leaving her. "Well, if you really want to do that, let's see if we can take some steps to ensure you're ready for the responsibility."

"Okay. So how do we do that?"

She had to be careful to give him his freedom while not setting him up for failure. Until this trip, Nick hadn't shown any desire to do things on his own.

"Let's start with you taking care of yourself at the beach today. You need to figure out what's required, what you're planning to eat, whether you should bring snacks and drinks, if you need any money, and what else you'd like to have with you. Once the competition is done and we know your next steps, we can go from there."

"Okay," he said, pushing his notebook to the side. "I'll go pack for the day."

The act of pushing his notebook away told her he was feeling confident in this moment. Her fear that the day of his independence might be nearer than she'd thought pecked at her. Who was she if she wasn't Nick's caretaker? He was the last of her immediate family, the final direct tie to her mother and father.

She loved him so much. Could *she* live without him? Her

throat tightened, the tears coming, and she scrambled to hold back her emotions so she didn't put any pressure on Nick. She'd learned from his counseling that it was natural for teenagers to push away from their caregivers. It was the next step in their independence, and something she and the therapist had been hoping for at some point, but now she wasn't certain she could handle it.

———

Once Nick had gone, Josie let the tears come. She lay on the bed and sobbed as if all the emotion from the last three years had waited for that moment. She tried to tell herself she should be happy for Nick's progress, and if he did move out on his own one day, she could find somewhere to live nearby and still see him regularly.

But she knew she wouldn't get to take care of him. She wouldn't get to peek in on him late at night to be sure he was covered up when the house was too cold. She wouldn't need to search the grocery store high and low for Lays potato chips, stocking up on them just for him. She wouldn't get to have their quiet time at the kitchen table every morning.

When she'd cried herself out, Josie got dressed. She tried to refocus and think about what brought her joy. She picked up her sketchpad and pencil, and envisioned different places she could draw to clear her head.

Her father's voice floated into her mind again: "You're so talented." It was as if he wanted to be sure she wouldn't forget. All those times she'd been to the empty lot to talk to him and Mama, had they heard her? It certainly was a nice thought.

"If you're actually here, Dad, if you're helping me through my life, can you show me some grand gesture to prove it? Can you make it rain in here or something?" She looked up at the bright white painted ceiling. "No, better not. I don't want to lose my security deposit."

She stood in the middle of the room, searching for something out of the ordinary, a cosmic answer to her request. Her compass, sitting on the dresser, came into focus. She picked it up, waiting for the needle to spin by itself or something. But nothing was out of the ordinary. Feeling closer to her dad anyway, she slipped it into her pocket.

Josie let herself out of the condo and headed back to the quaint streets of Rosemary Beach, finding a spot along the green to people-watch. She smoothed out her sundress, sat on one of the benches lining the square, and opened her sketchbook. Zeroing in on a woman and her small child chasing a ball, she began her piece with the soft silhouette of the woman's dress and the delicate shape of her ankles. She followed the woman's figure up above her shoulders where she captured the lift in her chin as she laughed.

Immersed in her sketching, she hadn't noticed the couple observing her.

"Excuse me," the man behind her said.

Josie stopped sketching and twisted around to face him.

"Are you, by chance, the artist who drew the sketch in the café over there?" He pointed to the place where she'd left her drawing yesterday.

"Yes," she said, thrilled he'd been able to tell.

"It was meant to be." The man's smile widened as he looked at his wife.

"Meant to be?" Josie asked.

The man turned back to her. "The owner had it displayed."

The woman leaned in, beaming. "My husband and I were telling the manager it was too incredible not to be framed."

Elated, Josie set her pencil down and gave the couple her full attention.

"The manager said someone had dropped it off yesterday as a gift and that it was being framed this afternoon," the woman continued, "but it was too beautiful not to be displayed right away."

Until now, Josie hadn't shared her talent with the world, and she couldn't deny her delight at hearing that her work had been so well received. She'd only meant to pass it along; she hadn't expected it to warrant a frame, let alone a conversation. Her gaze flitted to the bright blue sky. *Dad? Did you and Mama have something to do with this?*

"It's stunning," the woman said. "You're incredibly talented."

A burst of exhilaration pelted Josie. *Or so I'm told*, she thought with a nod to her dad, praying the mention of her talent was no coincidence. If there was one person who would be able to send a message from the heavens, it would be her dad—he could do anything. *Make it grander*, she teased him in her head. *You can make something bigger than this happen; I know it. Send me an undeniable sign.*

"Are your drawings for sale?" the woman asked, bringing Josie back to the conversation. "I'd love to commission one."

"Oh, I haven't sold any before," Josie replied, surprised the woman would be willing to offer any money at all for one of her drawings.

The woman's eyes widened. "You've never sold one of these? I assumed you had a studio somewhere. I've been on my phone, trying to find a gallery in the area that might be yours so I could come by."

Josie shook her head, the idea of her own studio was something she hadn't ever considered—not even in college. She'd never given that much weight to her drawings.

"I just have my sketchbook."

Her husband cut in. "She offered to buy the drawing in the café, but the manager said it wasn't for sale. So she took a photo of your signature to see if she could locate the artist, and here you are, like fate."

"What would your time be worth if I were to pay you right now for one?" the woman asked. "Would you have time, by chance?"

Josie reached into the long, square pocket of her sundress and caressed the compass, trying to figure out what to say to the woman.

"I could pay you five hundred dollars to do a sketch for me. It's worth at least that. Would that be appropriate?"

Josie clenched her teeth to keep the shock from spilling out of her lips in a wild gasp. Someone would pay her five hundred dollars for one drawing?

"I hope I haven't insulted you with my offer," the woman said.

"Yes," Josie replied. "Not that you insulted me," she added quickly, trying not to stammer. "Yes, five hundred would be... plenty." She flipped to a new page in her sketchbook, turning the wide paper over and repositioning the book on her lap. "Is there something specific you'd like me to draw for you?"

The woman put her arm around her husband. "Robert proposed to me on a bench like that one at a beach in North Carolina." She nodded toward an empty bench at the edge of the green. "Our bench got swept away in a hurricane, and when we returned, something new was built in its place. So I always find benches everywhere and tell him they're all for us."

"Oh, I love that," Josie said, already immersed in their story. She looked at the lone bench, imagining what it would be like to share it with someone she loved. How wonderful it would be to sit beside someone and know that she was his forever.

Clearing her throat, she concentrated on the task at hand, noting the curl in the iron base to begin her sketch. She dragged her dark pencil along the page, shading, moving with the arcs of the object as if she were reacting to some kind of inner music only she could hear. The couple's love story moved her, giving her lines a softer edge as she filled out the buildings behind the bench. She paid close attention to the beds of flowers, each individual bloom standing out as if to pronounce the significance of the bench for the couple.

With every stroke, Josie felt release, as if some dormant part of her had been awakened and she'd only now been able to set it free. Wide wings of creativity expanded and filled her up from the inside. She could almost feel the cold earth beneath her youthful bare feet again and hear the gurgling of the brook out back of her old house. Drawing was a direct connection to who she truly was, who her soul had intended her to be.

"Oh, my gosh," the woman said, her words breathless as she leaned over Josie's shoulder. "That's more beautiful than the one at the café." She squealed with excitement.

When Josie had finished, she carefully tore the paper out of her sketchbook. "I wish I had a tube to put it in," she worried aloud.

"It's all right," Robert said. "We're just staying right there." He pointed across the street.

Her face alight, the woman dug into her purse then handed Josie a wad of cash. "This is the best use of my vacation money! I couldn't have asked for anything better." She hugged it gently to her chest. "Thank you."

"You're so welcome."

Josie felt lighter knowing that whenever she felt down, drawing would be her reprieve. She placed the cash in her pocket, closed her sketchbook, and decided to return to the condo to put her payment in a safe place.

CHAPTER TWENTY-ONE

J osie wanted to explain what had just happened with her drawing to someone who would understand, so she called Hazel while she sat on the small balcony at the condo.

"I can't believe it! I made more money in thirty minutes than three days' pay at the diner where I worked back home."

"It's incredible how talent will do that," Hazel said. "You're giving in to your natural abilities, which is what we're meant to do."

Josie propped her knees up, putting her feet in the chair and hugging her legs. Everything felt better here, compared to where she'd grown up. There was so much sunshine. Back home, she'd had to chase the sun, staying out all day until that final hour when her eyes adjusted to the low light, the orange-and-pink stripes in the sky dipping below the horizon. Here, it felt as if it was always bright, always radiant with happiness.

"Using my talent makes me feel so good," she admitted.

"Of course it does. It's what you were wired for."

"Five hundred dollars," she said again, still completely in awe that the woman had invested that much in her ability.

"It's amazing what people will spend on what they love," Hazel said.

Julian's gesture came to mind and plunged Josie into silence.

"You okay?" Hazel asked.

"Someone bought an oil painting for me right off the street the other day, just like the people bought *my* sketch."

"Oh, really?" The uptick in Hazel's tone gave away her interest.

"Yeah. In a way, it feels like a full-circle moment."

"And who bought a painting for you?"

Josie paused, unsure how to define her relationship with Julian. The mere thought of him caused a calm to settle over her, taking her back to a side of herself she'd thought didn't exist anymore.

"A guy from college," she said, the description not doing him justice.

"It's almost as if his actions were foreshadowing what would happen to you. As if God was letting you know of some big plan for your life. He might be a special person... He sounds like it, anyway, if he's buying you paintings."

"I hadn't thought of it that way."

"Speaking of art... You've inspired *me*! I've been painting again since we bought our supplies."

"That's wonderful."

"I'll have to show you my latest piece."

"I'd love to see it."

Josie gazed at the bright blue sky above, wishing she'd see her dad there, smiling down at her. It would be just like him to have had something to do with Julian showing up in her life again. It was good to have Julian back.

She was so glad she'd met Hazel as well. With Zelda never around, she hadn't had the luxury of a friend who shared her love of art. Josie had made it through the hardest times alone and become a warrior, like Hazel said. Now it was as though she were being sent people she needed to help her through whatever the next stage of life brought. And she couldn't be more grateful.

———

Nick looked pink from the sun when he came in late that afternoon, but Josie refrained from saying anything. She'd barely seen him during the trip, and she didn't want to spend their few moments together nitpicking his sunscreen application strategy.

"How was it?" she asked.

Nick poured himself a bowl of chips, then cracked open a soda. "Fun."

Josie sucked in her lips to avoid disclosing her absolute surprise. Nick had rarely found anything *fun* back home.

"What did you do?" she asked, trying to sound relaxed when she wanted to jump for joy that Nick was having a good time. At the root of everything she did was the hope that he'd find happiness in life.

Nick sat at the table, moved his notebook to the side, and popped a chip into his mouth. "We swam in the water, which was nice because it got the sand off my feet."

Josie smiled and sat next to him, stealing a chip.

Nick playfully pulled the bowl away. "Get your own."

"Maybe I will." She got back up and walked to the other side of the kitchen island, taking a bowl down from the cabinet.

"I want to ask Rainy on a date," Nick said.

Josie stopped unrolling the bag of chips and looked at him. "Oh?"

"Yes." Nick nodded once, as if he was acknowledging that

he'd made the decision just then. "I make her laugh and the sound of it makes me happy."

"Where do you think she'd like to go?" Josie resumed filling her bowl with chips, folded the bag over, and returned to Nick.

"I don't know. She seems content anywhere."

"Yes, she does, but maybe you could think of a place you both might enjoy. Maybe somewhere that would make her laugh a lot."

Nick's eyebrows pulled together in thought as he drank from his soda can. "I have no idea."

"Maybe you could talk to her, ask her questions about things she might like and feel her out."

Nick cocked his head to the side. "Feel her out?"

"Get a feel for what she likes."

"I'm not sure what to ask."

"You could invite her to dinner, and I could ask her some questions."

Nick's eyes widened. "No, that's fine. I'll figure it out." He crossed his long arms on the table. "Dating is much more difficult than I expected."

Josie laughed, the memory of Julian's arms around her floating into her mind. "Yes, it is."

———

That evening, Nick had gone off with his friends to a mid-competition social gathering put on by the Battle of the Mathematical Minds. His willingness to attend was another big shocker. Nick hadn't voluntarily joined in on anything social in Lox Creek, and it made Josie wonder how much earlier he'd have come out of his shell if he'd been with like-minded people.

The event was actually great timing, considering Aunt

Zelda would be there any minute. Josie would much rather get her aunt settled before Nick came in. Zelda would have to sleep on the pull-out sofa in the living room, and their quarters would be cramped. Nick seemed to be acclimating so well in Rosemary Beach, and the last thing Josie wanted was to disrupt his day with a change in dynamic.

While she knew change was a part of life Nick had to cope with, it felt like a tiny gift from above when things fell into place easily. And she didn't want anything to spoil this time for him. She really wanted him to see how far he could get in the competition, how far life could take him, and then she'd worry about his skills for managing change.

Sadly, life didn't work that way. Zelda was en route, and there was nothing Josie could do about it.

She checked the clock on the oven timer in the kitchen, arranged the cheese and crackers she'd laid out for her aunt one more time, wondering if she should put the cheese back in the fridge, and then peered out the window at the parking lot. In typical form, Zelda was about an hour late and Josie only had a short time before Nick would be back.

She tried to give her aunt grace, guessing the traffic could be heavy in the major cities along the route at that time of the evening, but she couldn't help the niggling feeling that her aunt was late because she lived in her own little world sometimes and didn't seem to think about anyone else. She'd been late to Josie's father's funeral. How was that possible? He was her older brother.

Just as Josie was about to slip the slices of cheddar into a plastic bag, there was a knock at the door. She opened it to find her aunt looking frazzled, standing beside two suitcases. The odd mixture of emotions Josie had always seen lurking in Zelda's eyes was present. It made her wonder if the time alone wasn't really what her aunt had wanted all these years. Maybe she just didn't know how to be social and now she was trying.

"Come in," Josie said, helping Zelda with her bags.

Zelda stepped inside and looked around, her thoughts clearly elsewhere, making Josie a bit nervous. What was her aunt going to say? Had she lost all her money? Was the house more than she could manage? Was she planning to leave again? The questions swirled in Josie's mind as she shut the door and ushered her aunt into the living area.

"How was the drive?" she asked, not knowing what else to say.

Zelda didn't sit. She seemed full of nervous energy. "It was fine." She walked around, dragging her finger along the seashells on the shelf by the television. "It's so beautiful here." She pointed toward Josie's bedroom. "Mind if I have a look?"

"Not at all."

Zelda walked into the room and pressed down on the fluffy bedspread as if testing its spring. Then she surveyed the room, stopping at the painting Julian had bought for Josie.

"Wow. This is incredible."

"It's by a local artist," Josie said, glad to have common ground. "The man's work stopped me in my tracks on a walk the other day."

Zelda faced her. "You always did have a love of anything artistic."

"Yes."

Josie wanted to point out that the gene didn't seem to spread easily in the family and Zelda was the only one who might have been able to foster Josie's artistic inclinations, but she thought better of it. Perhaps that was why Josie was so bitter. Artists seemed to see the world in the same way, and Josie had always felt like an outsider. She'd wanted nothing more than to talk about light and color and shape, but her dad and Nick didn't have a deep understanding of it. Her father tried, but when Josie talked about the varying shades of purple she could see in the shadows on the floor or how she loved when the light shined on part of their brick wall in the kitchen, making the grout appear to have silver flecks, he just couldn't see what she saw.

Zelda seemed to be trembling now, her fingers quivering by her sides.

Not knowing what to do next, Josie led the way back into the main room.

"Are you hungry after your drive? I made a plate of snacks." Worst case, they could nibble on crackers together to avoid the lack of conversation, although Josie would prefer her aunt reveal what was ailing her before Nick walked through the door.

"Oh, yes. Thank you." Zelda went to the sink and washed her hands, taking all the time in the world to lather, rinse, and dry them.

Just observing her tension put Josie on edge. "Is everything okay?"

Zelda's gaze snapped over to her. "Yes, yes. Everything is fine. Why?" She balled up the paper napkin she'd used to dry her hands and hunted around the kitchen.

Josie opened the cabinet housing a small trash can.

Zelda didn't look up from the cabinet. Something was definitely on her mind. She went to the snacks, piled a few cheese slices onto a cracker, and popped it in her mouth.

"Would you like something to drink?" Josie offered. "I have lemonade."

"Yes, lemonade would be wonderful."

Her aunt built another cracker stack. The nervous energy she put off was making Josie's heart race.

Just then, Nick walked through the door, followed by Rainy.

"Hello," he said. Nick seemed unfazed by Zelda's presence, but why should her sudden appearance have any significance to him when she hadn't spent any time with him either? He picked up his notebook from the table and slid the pencil into the spiral.

"Hi, Nick." Zelda waved at him across the bar separating the small living space from the kitchen.

"Zelda, this is Rainy, Nick's friend from the competition," Josie said after giving the girl a little wave.

Zelda nodded. "Hello, Rainy."

Rainy let out her usual giggle and said hello before readjusting her glasses with a squinch of her nose.

Nick held his notebook against his chest. "Rainy and I are going to the beach."

"Oh, all right." Josie was relieved to avoid Nick's involvement in Zelda's drama. She needed to get to the bottom of her aunt's behavior before Nick spent any time at the condo. "Want any munchies to take with you?" She slid the plate of cheese and crackers closer to his side of the island.

"No, thank you. We ate dinner at the event." Nick opened the door once more and allowed Rainy to exit first.

In an instant, they were gone, carrying the lighter atmosphere with them. The condo was quiet once more, and Josie busied herself with getting two glasses and filling them with lemonade. The silence thickened.

She handed the lemonade to her aunt, taking in her familiar green eyes. Striped through Zelda's gray hair were remnants of brown locks like Josie's. Her aunt's peachy complexion was almost a perfect match for her own. This woman was Josie's only family, and yet she barely knew her. It tore at her.

"Would you like to sit on the balcony? It's really nice out there," she offered.

"Yes."

There was a catch in Zelda's voice that they both noticed. They locked eyes, but Aunt Zelda covered the emotion with a smile.

Josie took her lemonade with her and opened the French doors, stepping out into the glorious evening sunshine. She lowered herself into one of the Adirondack chairs and turned toward the soft breeze, letting the salty air work its magic to soothe her.

"How's the house?" she asked, fishing for an answer as to her aunt's motivation for visiting. Nostalgia could have made Zelda curious about the rest of her family, but given her aunt's state, Josie was nearly certain something bigger was at play.

"It's fine," Zelda replied after settling in the other chair.

Josie waited without responding, hoping she would elaborate.

"I just thought it would be a good idea to come see you."

That wasn't quite the clarification Josie had been hoping for. Her aunt had said, "*you*." Why her specifically? What about Nick?

"A good idea?"

"I'm not doing a great job explaining, am I?"

"No, not really." Josie folded her hands and put them in her lap, waiting.

Zelda cleared her throat and wriggled tensely before resting her arms on the chair. "I sat at that house, all alone, thinking. I never got to tell you how great your mom was."

A bolt of surprise at the mention of her mother bounced around Josie's insides like a pinball.

"You didn't get long enough with her," Zelda continued.

"No, I didn't," Josie agreed, unable to say more regarding Mama to a woman who so clearly didn't know anything about nurturing someone. While Josie wanted to believe Zelda had experienced some great epiphany, she couldn't be convinced by a few thoughtful anecdotes.

"And then your dad…"

When Josie swam out of her thoughts, she realized her aunt was crying.

"Tell me what's going on," she demanded.

Aunt Zelda dragged the back of her hand under her eyes. "I'm sorry," she said with a sniffle. "It's..." She gazed into Josie's eyes as if she were hoping Josie could somehow receive the message telepathically. "I just wanted to see you." She let out a long sigh, then offered a weak smile and laid her head back on the chair, closing her eyes.

Josie waited for more, but nothing came. A seagull squawked overhead, and Zelda didn't move. Clearly, she wasn't getting anything more out of her aunt right now.

"I haven't been sleeping well and I'm so tired," Zelda said, her eyes still closed. "Do you mind if I go inside and take a nap? Maybe after I get some sleep I'll be a better houseguest."

"I don't mind."

Zelda opened her eyes and sat up.

Josie stood and went inside, leaving the door open. Zelda followed.

"You can sleep in my room for now."

As Josie worked to get her aunt's things into her bedroom, she couldn't help but worry about how Zelda's mood might impact Nick. With the second half of the competition ramping up, he definitely didn't need any of this to distract him. Not to mention that Josie barely saw Nick now, and any chance she had to spend some one-on-one time with him was very likely gone.

Saying yes to Zelda's visit had been a terrible idea. She grabbed her compass from the dresser and slipped it into her pocket—she'd need it.

Chapter Twenty-Two

With Aunt Zelda asleep this morning and Nick at the beach again with Rainy, Josie was going stir crazy sitting in the condo, so she decided to take a morning walk to settle her mind.

Mama? Dad? If you two are here with me, I need your help. She strolled down the quiet cobblestone streets of the town, most of the shops still closed at the early hour. *Dad, you know your sister better than any of us. Tell me what to do with her.*

Josie tilted her head up to the sky—already bright blue and full of billowy clouds under the long summer days—wishing she could hear her parents' voices, and not in a dream. She wanted their guidance while she was awake and fully able to absorb the message. It felt as if the whole world was on her shoulders.

She looked up and saw Julian at one of the outdoor tables at the café with an empty plate and some papers pinned down by his laptop. It appeared as if he also had the world on his shoulders.

"Hey," she said as she walked up to him. Just seeing him

made her earlier issues with Zelda fade away. He was a light in her soul, even when he wasn't his usual happy-go-lucky self.

His features immediately lifted when he saw her, as if she, too, were some sort of magic elixir for his stress. "Hey." He gestured for her to take the empty seat across the small table. "Want a coffee?"

"Maybe in a minute," she replied. "You looked very thoughtful just now."

"Yeah..." His smile faded as he peered at his laptop screen before closing it and scooting it to the side.

"Want to talk about it?" she asked.

He shook his head. "I don't want to bother you with my issues."

While she didn't really need to take on any more burdens, she hadn't seen Julian appear so troubled before, and she had to admit she wanted to help him through whatever it was.

"Please," she said, the warm early sun shining on her face. "Tell me."

He put his elbows on the table, folded his hands, and leaned on his fists, clearly considering.

"It's okay," she urged.

"It's just work."

"At the restaurant?"

He shook his head. "No." He let out a heavy sigh.

"Your new business?"

He waved a hand at the condos lining the street across from them. "All these people and nobody wants chairs and umbrellas, it seems."

"You're not receiving orders?"

"It's really slow. I keep poring over everything, and I can't figure out why the other companies seem to be doing better. I guess they've been around longer." He shook his head. "I don't know."

"Maybe we could analyze the market and how you're

getting the word out. That's what I studied in college, remember?"

He drummed his fingers on his laptop. "Yeah... But we won't solve it today." He shrugged it off and smiled at her. "You're here. Distract me from my troubles. How was yesterday?"

She blew air through her lips. "Not much better. My aunt came to visit."

"*The* aunt? As in the 'nightmare'?"

Josie nodded.

"Why did she come?"

"She isn't saying." Josie pursed her lips. "I have no idea why she's here."

"Where is she now?"

"At the condo. When she finally started talking to me yesterday, she got teary and nervous and said she was tired and needed a nap, so I let her sleep in my room." Josie tried to focus on the kind expression on Julian's face to relax her.

Their eyes met and she could have sworn he was sending her a silent message of adoration. Her heart filled with joy because she felt the same way for him.

"I was going stir crazy already and had to get out," she said.

Julian stacked his papers and stuffed them in his closed laptop. "Well, I'm at your disposal. What do you want to do?"

The shops began to open around them and vacationers were slowly emerging for breakfast and walks on the beach.

"Oh, I don't want to bother you."

He leaned across the small table just enough to allow his woodsy scent to catch on the breeze. "Believe me, you don't bother me."

She considered the fact that he'd just told her he was worried about not having any customers. She could tell as she'd walked up that it troubled him. Yet he didn't seem to allow it to ruin his day. How did he do that?

"You're so easy going."

The corner of his lips turned upward and her skin tingled with the memory of his touch, and she had to work to get it out of her head. What was this between them? It hadn't taken any time at all for her old feelings for him to resurface. And now the thought of leaving him again made her chest ache.

When she emerged from her thoughts, Julian was grinning at her.

"What?"

He chuckled. "You're always in your head." He stood and tucked his laptop under his arm. Then he stepped to her side of the table and held out his hand. "Come with me."

"Where are we going?"

"I'll show you."

He dropped off his laptop at his car and they walked down the street to a kite shop on the edge of the town center. The shopkeeper was arranging his display outside when they walked up. After greeting the man, Julian pulled the door open and let her go in first.

Looking at the fancy nylon kites immediately channeled memories of the old lot back home.

"My dad used to fly kites with me," she said. "He, Nick, and I would stay outside all day." She ran her fingers over the long, brightly colored tails that draped to the floor, the wooden dowels holding them together along with the strong stitching on the edges of the fabric. "I would get such a thrill when I'd wake up to the howl of the wind blowing past my bedroom window because I knew we'd be flying kites that day." She put her hand in her pocket and toyed with the compass, missing her dad. Then she turned to Julian. "What made you bring me here?"

"I want to show you something kites can do. Pick your favorite," Julian said.

"They're expensive."

"It doesn't matter."

He reached for her hand again—a gesture she didn't mind, although she knew that with every touch it would be harder to say goodbye at the end of her trip. They walked around as bouncy summer music played above them, and perused the different kites in various shapes and sizes.

There were box kites and hexagons, kites shaped like animals and others in the shape of diamonds. At the back of the store, one in particular caught her eye. It was flat and triangular with a swirling pattern of reds and oranges against a dark background, reminding her of the sun when it dipped behind the hills back in Lox Creek just before she had to be home for dinner.

"That one."

"Okay." Julian asked the clerk to pull down their kite. He paid for it, and they carefully carried it through the shop, barely getting the massive thing outside the door. "Let's take it to the beach."

As they walked the path to the boardwalk, Julian carrying their new purchase, the tails flapping in the wind, Josie slipped her hand into her pocket and clutched her compass once more, feeling closer to her father. He'd like it here.

They made their way down the wooden path that led through the seagrass and over the sand dunes. Then they stepped onto the soft sand and kicked off their shoes, the cobalt-blue stripe on the horizon giving way to the bright teal water. The sun had begun its ascent and cast a golden glow along the white sand.

Julian faced her. "At the café just now, it occurred to me that you're like this kite."

She squinted at him. "How so?"

He held it out, the thick nylon fighting against his hold. "You're always in your head, working so hard to stay in one place, to be the right version of what you should be." He wiggled the kite, the edges bending, causing the muscles to show in his forearms as he attempted to hold it in its spot while he positioned the wooden spool in his other hand.

Josie zeroed in on the tautness in the fabric and the bend of the dowels as the wind pushed against it, and she understood. She knew that kind of tension; she felt it every day.

"But if you just let life lead you"—he let go of the kite and with the force of a rocket, it flew out of his hand, sailing straight up into the sky—"you'll fly." He handed her the spool.

His words settled on her, and she held the wooden reel, the kite pulling against her strength in the coastal wind, dipping and bobbing, swirling and soaring. Her hair blew behind her shoulders, her bare feet in the silky sand. In this moment, she felt free like the kite. She considered the other things that made her feel free: her sketches, the glorious sunshine, Julian.

Julian had always been the one to fly by the seat of his pants. While she loved that about him, she wasn't the same. Her circumstances didn't allow her to be.

"And what happens when the wind stops blowing?" she asked. But the thing was, she already knew, so she answered her question. "The kite will fall to the ground, broken." She held the spool out to him.

He stepped behind her, putting his arms around her, placing his hands over hers on the spool.

"Yeah," he said into her ear, giving her goose bumps. "But if you're in the right place, the wind doesn't stop, and if, on the off chance it does, there's someone to catch the kite before it breaks." He leaned around her and kissed her cheek.

She'd never allowed Julian to catch her before. She'd

always tried to handle it all on her own, and she had done a pretty good job, but it would be nice to let him help.

The kite dipped again, tugging her to the side. When she bent over to move with it, the compass fell out of her pocket.

"What's that?" Julian lifted it out of the sand. "Oh, I remember. It was your dad's, right?" He took the spool from her and jammed it into the ground, covering it with sand to keep it from blowing away, the kite soaring above them. With the bottom of his shirt, he wiped the sand from the compass.

"Yes, it's my dad's."

He blew on it, the last few grains falling from the surface, and inspected the side where the hinges were. "Was there a cover?"

"Somewhere. I'm not sure when it got lost."

He handed it back to her. "It's nice."

"Thank you." She slipped it back into her pocket, wondering if her dad could see them now. What would he tell her to do? He'd certainly know the answers. If only he could show her. If he could, he'd definitely have to do it in a big way, she decided firmly, or she worried she might miss it.

———

Josie wasn't sure what she would've done if Nick had left her alone all day, but with Zelda there, she didn't have to worry about it. Zelda had found a deck of playing cards in the living-room cabinet and they'd decided to take them down to the picnic table outside. They'd been there playing all afternoon.

"Your dad suggested I visit this area once," Zelda said from behind her hand of playing cards as a passing seagull cast a shadow across their game of rummy. "I see why he was so enamored with it. It's beautiful here."

"He recommended Rosemary Beach to me when I was planning a summer trip back in college." Josie laid down three kings. "He had anywhere in the world he could dream to visit —why here, specifically? And why would he suggest it to *both* of us?"

"I have no idea." Zelda drew a card, but it was clear her mind was elsewhere.

"Why do you think he was looking up investigators?"

Zelda shook her head. "I have no earthly idea." She seemed just as baffled as Josie.

"Are you sure that's what he was looking up?" Josie asked. None of it made any sense.

"I found a handwritten list of three businesses, and when I searched online for the names, they were private investigating firms, all based along the Gulf Coast." Zelda set down a run of cards, leaving her with only two remaining in her hand.

They were playing the game, but their focus was on one another.

"What could he be investigating? He'd never been here?" Josie asked. She drew a card and added it to her hand, then turned toward the water, hoping the wide expanse beyond the dunes would manage to send her an answer.

"I'd never even heard of this place until he mentioned it. We have no ties here whatsoever. I'm at a complete loss." She drew a card and laid another run on the table. "Rummy."

"I guess we'll never know," Josie said. She gathered up the cards and they went in to make dinner.

The whole time she cooked, Josie wondered what business her dad had had at Rosemary Beach. The question lingered into the night and followed her to bed. As she drifted off, she hoped he'd find a way to tell her. If it was important, she knew he would.

CHAPTER TWENTY-THREE

Josie arched her back as she rolled over and looked through the window. The sun was just beginning to rise. After stretching her tight muscles, she sat up and yawned. She'd awakened late last night when Nick had come in, but she didn't get up. With the second half of the competition starting back up today, he'd gone straight to bed.

Josie got up, made her bed, and tiptoed past Zelda into the small kitchen area to brew a cup of coffee. Her mind was still spinning with the things going on around her. She couldn't shake the fact that Julian had decided to take her to a kite store of all places. Had that been a sign from her dad that he was there?

A part of her felt as if her parents had led her to Rosemary Beach this summer, and she couldn't help thinking it wasn't an accident that Julian had been there too. It would be just like her dad to give those things to her. Yet she still had the lingering question of why he'd been researching—*investigating*—the area. What had he wanted to do here? Did he have unfinished business of some kind? What could it be? His message from her dream floated into her consciousness:

"You're going to finish what I started." Her skin prickled with the thought that maybe the dream made more sense than she realized. But how was she supposed to know what he'd started? Maybe she was just trying too hard to make the dream real.

Movement on the sofa stopped Josie in her tracks. She turned around to find Zelda coming toward the kitchen area.

"Good morning," her aunt said as she settled on a barstool at the counter. She stretched. "I was exhausted."

"I figured you were," Josie said, loading the coffee maker. "I didn't want to disturb you." She pulled down two mugs without asking if her aunt wanted any, preoccupied with the fact that she had to face her this early. The woman's mere presence brought back nothing but memories of her father's death—the only time Zelda had been remotely present in Josie's life. She filled one of the mugs and slid it across the counter. "Why are you here?" Josie finally asked.

Zelda gripped the mug with both hands, her lips parting as if there was something she wanted to say but wasn't ready to, which only served to frustrate Josie further. Lifting the mug to her lips, her aunt took an excruciatingly long drink before answering.

"I wanted to see if there was any way I could make up for lost time."

Josie wondered if this could be the only reason. She'd heard Zelda's tears through the phone. Why would simply wanting to catch up make her aunt cry? Maybe being in the house with her brother's things had moved Zelda and made her realize the time she'd lost. Perhaps this truly was a change of heart and Josie was being too hard on her. Forcing her shoulders to relax, she stared into her aunt's green eyes, looking for a clue as to another motive, but the only thing she saw was sadness.

Trying to embrace Zelda's newfound interest in her life, she asked, "What would you like to do today?"

The tears that seemed to be waiting for the smallest thing surfaced in her aunt's eyes. She blinked them away. "Anything you like."

"We could take a walk on the beach and then go watch Nick," Josie suggested.

"That would be nice."

Josie grabbed her coffee, went around to the other side of the bar, and sat next to Zelda. The proximity felt unusual, but her desire to make things work with her aunt won out over the discomfort of their new situation. Maybe this was a turning point for them. And maybe it was up to Josie to make the first move. She just hoped Zelda's motives were good.

———

After getting ready for the day, Josie and Zelda saw Nick off and then left the condo and walked along the beach. Making their way down to the small breaking waves, the wet sand smooth and compact under her feet, Josie tried to imagine what life would be like with Zelda at her side.

Zelda's physical similarities to Josie's father were undeniable, and Josie felt closer to him with her there. She prayed her aunt wouldn't break her heart by unleashing something she'd been holding in. Josie wanted to believe she just wished to visit, and she wanted to have her aunt around, to find out more about this woman who seemed so similar to her. Having her there made Josie feel less alone.

She sent another silent message to her parents. *I keep asking and hoping you can hear me. If you're trying to tell me something, I'm going to need you to make it pretty obvious what you want me to do because I have no idea.*

Josie stepped into a small wave as it gurgled at her toes and looked around for a sign, something huge to tell her that her parents were with her, but nothing came. Receiving messages from the other side was a ridiculous notion, but still the silence let her down every time.

Aunt Zelda tucked her hair behind her ear. "I've enjoyed being with you."

Josie smiled, but she was still deciding if it was a good thing to have seen her aunt.

"You know, I've spent many years on my own." Zelda lifted the hem on the flowy skirt of her sundress to avoid a wave crashing into it. "For a long time, that was what I needed." She bent down, plucked a seashell from the sand, and held it out to Josie.

Josie studied the bright white of the thin shell, wondering how something so delicate had made it through the washing of the waves unharmed.

Then Zelda commanded Josie's attention once again. "Even though I needed the alone time, I feel like I've missed out... on so much."

Yes, she had. And she'd neglected to *help* her family. When Josie's mother died and Josie had needed someone the most, Zelda hadn't been there. But at least she seemed to have realized she'd missed important milestones. It was something to build on. Could that understanding have been the source of her unease when she'd arrived?

"I didn't get to make many memories with my family," Zelda said, skipping the shell across the water.

Josie took her hand. "Maybe we can start now."

Her aunt's eyes welled with emotion.

"Why don't we go into town for lunch?"

"Okay," Zelda said, wiping away her tears.

They walked back down the beach, rinsed off their feet at the public water station, and sat down at a café for a quick lunch. Zelda was quiet most of the meal, but offered some small talk about the beach and a few shops she'd like to visit before she went home. This time, Josie didn't press her. They had their whole lives ahead of them to open up. They spent the rest of the afternoon popping into shops until it was time to see Nick. Josie wanted to catch his final competition of the day.

"Want to come with me to see my brother?" she asked.

Zelda's cheeks, rosy from the sun, lifted with her smile. "I'd love to."

————

After retrieving Josie's visitor's badge from the condo, Josie and Zelda headed to the venue. Josie led her aunt down the main hallway to the event space, where they stopped at the table to sign Zelda in, quietly entered the auditorium, and claimed two seats at the back. The contestants' scores were illuminated above them, and Josie sucked in a breath of excitement to see that Nick was leading by a mile.

"The other day when I came, Nick really struggled," she whispered to her aunt. "But it looks like he's winning this round."

"That's great," Zelda said softly.

"Final ten seconds," the judge announced.

They'd caught them right at the closing question. The contestants were scribbling madly at their podiums, heads down, lips pursed in concentration.

"Enter your answers," the judge said.

There was a hush on the stage as they set down their pencils, their screens lighting up.

"Nick Wills, you are the winner of this round."

Josie jumped up with a squeal, causing Nick to look out into the audience. She snapped her lips closed, hoping she hadn't upset him by being there. To her complete surprise and delight, he waved at her. She wrinkled her nose at him affectionately and waved back before dropping into her seat, feeling content.

"You've done such a wonderful job raising him," Zelda said.

Even though Zelda barely knew what Josie had or hadn't done for Nick, no one had ever told her that before, and it was nice to hear.

"Thank you," she said, a lump forming unexpectedly in her throat. The fear of Nick leaving her one day surfaced again. She coughed quietly into her fist to clear it and focused on her brother up front.

As the contestants left the stage, Josie and Zelda went back to the hallway to view the leaderboard. Nick and Rainy had both made it through day six. Nick was now in the top twenty-two contestants, with two more cuts to go before he could reach the top eight.

"You made it!" Josie said, bouncing toward Nick and Rainy as they came down the corridor toward her and Aunt Zelda.

"Yes," Nick said before giving Zelda a nod hello.

"He was on fire today," Rainy said, smiling up at him.

"Well, the questions today were based in number theory and mathematical analysis. Those are my strong points."

"It was impressive," Rainy said.

Nick's cheeks flushed, and Josie knew he was completely smitten by Rainy. She adored seeing Nick in love.

While she had no idea what the future held, for the first time in a long time, it felt as if things were looking up.

CHAPTER TWENTY-FOUR

Aunt Zelda's behavior continued to confuse Josie. When it came to being with them, her aunt seemed to go from zero to one hundred and then back to zero. Tonight, after spending the day together, she'd said she wanted to take a drive, and she hadn't invited anyone. She'd been gone for over an hour.

Despite her aunt's odd behavior, Josie was pleased to have some alone time with Nick. Even if it was only because Rainy was out with a few girlfriends she'd met at the competition. Since they hadn't had a chance to have pizza together last week, she decided to give the dinner another try. Nick was at the table flipping through the strings of numbers he'd written over the months. He hadn't been writing in his notebook as intensely the last few days. Instead, he'd been observing his writing quite a bit. Was he coming through his grief and finding hope?

"Whatcha thinking about?" she asked as she slid a frozen pizza into the oven and set the timer.

"Rainy."

"Oh?" *How sweet*, she thought. The girl had really impacted him.

"I haven't figured out what she likes yet."

"You, apparently." Josie sat down next to him.

Nick grabbed his pencil and started writing numbers in his notebook, his nerves clearly getting the better of him.

"I can tell you like her," Josie nudged.

He gripped his pencil, his knuckles turning white the way they did when his emotions had surfaced too quickly for him. He set his pencil down and put his hands in his lap.

"What am I supposed to do?" he asked.

"What do you mean?"

"I have four days left with her." He clasped his hands together. "Part of me wants to tell her I can't let her leave, but the other part wants to let her go."

Josie tried to make sense of his statement. "Why would you want to let her go?"

"Because I don't know what to do after four days. I can't figure out where to take her outside of the Battle of the Mathematical Minds party. I'll probably screw it up."

Josie leaned forward, waiting for him to meet her eyes. "It's hard to know what to do when you really like someone. You want to show them how much you care, and it's difficult to figure out how to do that." She couldn't help but think of Julian as she explained. In a way, she was in the same boat as Nick. They were supposed to leave in four days and she, too, faced having to say goodbye. And she had absolutely no plan for what to do next.

"I want to stay with her more than I want to leave," Nick said.

"Why don't you tell her that? Maybe the two of you could figure it out together."

"I can do that?"

"Of course you can. That's how relationships work—you

share your burdens and you help each other." Her mind flitted back to Julian once more.

"I'll text her and see if she wants to talk tonight."

"She'd probably like that."

The oven beeped.

"Pizza's ready." Josie stood and went into the kitchen, her mind still on Julian, wondering if she should take her own advice.

———

Later that evening, after Nick had gone to meet Rainy, Zelda returned with a take-out box. Her eyes were bloodshot and she seemed to be wrestling with something.

"I bought Chinese. Want some?" she offered.

"No, thanks. I ate with Nick." Josie clicked on the TV. "Where'd you go?"

"I just took a drive down the coast."

The two women sat in the living room with a movie playing, and Zelda didn't elaborate. Josie used the moment to speak to her parents. *Please, tell me what to do with Aunt Zelda. What's going on with her?*

"I have two fortune cookies," Zelda said from across the room. "Want one?"

"Sure," she replied, more to be agreeable than anything else. She got up and took the wrapped cookie. "Thanks."

Zelda unwrapped hers and read the fortune. "'In everything you do, have passion.'" She shrugged. "They never make any sense for me."

Josie read hers. "'Wait and see.' Yeah," she said, dropping it on the table. She broke the cookie into a few bite-size pieces and popped them into her mouth one by one. "What does 'Wait and see' mean?"

From the kitchen, her phone pinged with a text. She was

relieved to have something to do, so she jumped up to get it. Hazel was inviting her over tomorrow to show her the water-color she'd painted, and she wanted to tell Josie about something she'd found. The most interesting part of the text, however, was that she'd told Josie to bring her compass.

Incredibly curious, Josie texted back that she'd love to visit. She was glad for the light her new friend had brought into her life.

With Zelda still quiet, Josie said, "I think I'm going to head to bed early." She yawned and then texted Nick to be home in the next half hour.

"All right." Zelda gathered up her trash and stuffed it into her take-out bag.

"Just knock if you need anything."

Zelda stood with the bag of trash and faced Josie. "Okay. Thank you."

It seemed as if she wanted to say something more, but she didn't, so Josie turned around and headed into her room. Her fortune might be right. "Wait and see." She'd have to wait and see what would happen with Zelda for sure.

CHAPTER TWENTY-FIVE

Zelda was still sleeping when Nick left for the competition, so Josie wrote her a note to let her know she'd be back in a bit. As Josie walked through town toward Hazel's house the next morning, the sun was already strong. The beaches were being set up with umbrellas and chairs, and the sidewalks were full of people on bicycles, golf carts, and families pushing strollers.

She was taken with how quickly she'd become familiar with the area. In a strange way, it felt more like home than Lox Creek, and she'd only been there a matter of days. Here, she felt like a whole person. She'd been able to reconnect to her childhood with her drawings, she'd gotten to expose Nick to new things that they wouldn't have done back home, she'd reconnected with Julian, and she'd met Hazel.

There was a pep in her step at the thought of Hazel. Josie really enjoyed the woman's company. At this point, Hazel was like family. While Josie had always wished for a big family, she was willing to settle for a really great friend, and she hoped she could still keep in touch with Hazel once the competition was done.

Hazel was sitting on the massive front porch at the top of the curved staircase waiting for Josie when she arrived. Josie waved to her, taking the steps as quickly as she could.

"It's so lovely to see you," Hazel said when Josie reached the porch. "Come, come." She stood and ushered her inside the grand house.

They made their way to the living room and Josie was offered a seat on the linen sofa. Instead, she was drawn to the substantial white-washed mantle. Above it was an incredible sunset painting of the beach in various shades of oranges and yellows, reminding her of that time of evening when Josie used to run home through the woods as a child.

"Do you like my new creation?" Hazel asked, peering at the landscape.

"It's magnificent." Josie turned her head to get a better look at how the pastel colors mixed with the more vibrant ones. "My mother used to call this time of day 'the golden hour,'" she said, feeling her mother in that moment. Maybe because of Hazel's maternal nature—she wasn't sure. "That would be a great name for this painting," she said, turning toward Hazel.

"'The Golden Hour' is a beautiful name for it." Hazel studied the painting, an indecipherable thought lurking beneath her gaze. "This isn't the only reason I asked you over. I found something that might just blow you away."

"What is it?" Josie asked.

Hazel offered her a seat on the sofa again. "You might need to sit."

This time, she did.

Hazel moved toward a decorative dish on the table, taking an object from it. She then sat next to Josie with the item in her fist.

"Did you bring the compass?"

"Yes." Josie pulled it from her pocket and held it out, the brass needle inside jiggling with the movement.

"Where did your father get it—do you know?"

"I don't. He never told me."

"Well, do you believe in fate?"

Josie stared at the compass in her palm, deciding on her answer. "I can't say I used to, but this trip has made me wonder. It seems to be bringing me full circle in a lot of ways. Like I was meant to come here."

"Well, we're about to test fate."

"What do you mean?"

"I was cleaning out an old box of my father's, looking for his paintbrushes, and I found this." She held up the object she'd been holding—a circular brass piece. "I immediately thought of the compass you showed me." She turned it around and the pattern on one side of it looked awfully familiar. "May I?" Hazel reached for Josie's compass.

Holding her breath, Josie kept her eyes on Hazel's hands as they gently set her brass piece on top, lining up the small hinges. The two sides snapped together, and Josie looked at Hazel wide-eyed, every hair on her body standing on end.

Her dad's voice came back to her: "You're going to finish what I started." What had he started? Sifting back through all that she'd experienced here, she recounted every single step, but what surfaced was the idea that she'd asked her parents to do something big to prove they were there, and the big thing she'd been waiting for had been wrapped up in the small events.

It could have been anywhere, but the math competition had been here. She'd met Hazel on a whim. Nick had found real friends for the first time in his life, even her fortune cookie now made perfect sense: "Wait and see."

"Do you know why, when you looked at me that day, I

actually got up and came to sit with you at the coffee shop?" Hazel asked.

Still struggling to get a breath, Josie shook her head.

"Something in my gut told me to. I saw you were busy on your computer, but I went over anyway. And we became friends. Fate." She handed Josie the compass. "And now this. It reminds me of those friendship lockets where the two friends each have half of it. I wonder if that's what happened with this. Could your father and my father have somehow known each other?"

"I have no idea," Josie said, peering down at her keepsake, now whole. Since childhood, she'd held on to this compass, never giving the missing front a single thought. But now, it was as if that piece in particular was more important than the compass itself. Had her father known about this? Could this have anything to do with why he'd been researching this area?

"Given our ages, my dad would be a generation above your father. How would they know each other?"

Josie toyed with the broken hinges. She popped the front off once more and inspected the inside, looking for an answer. On the back of the lid, she made out a tiny engraved sentence. She squinted to read it.

Love will guide you.

She remembered what her father had told her when he'd given her the compass: "If you follow your heart, you'll never lose your way." In simpler words, "Love will guide you." What hadn't he told her?

"I've been through everything in that box and there's no explanation," said Hazel.

Josie pored over her father's words: "I've always wanted to visit the Gulf Coast." At the time, she'd assumed he said it because he'd never had a vacation of his own, but now, with the new knowledge of him actually researching the area, there was obviously some other reason he'd wanted to go. It was he who'd suggested Rosemary Beach back in college. Had he known the other half of the compass was here? Did it hold some kind of larger significance?

"Your father didn't say anything about someone named Rodney Wills? That's my dad."

Hazel shook her head, her lips forming a pout. "Not that I can remember. That name doesn't sound familiar at all."

Josie searched Hazel's face for answers, but she couldn't find any.

"I think you should keep the cover of the compass," Hazel said. "It obviously belongs to you."

The two women sat in silence. If Josie hadn't already felt close to Hazel, now she felt bound to her. "I wonder if we'll ever know what this coincidence means," Josie finally said.

Hazel shook her head. "I'm glad that, of all the people it could've belonged to, it was yours."

"Me too."

With a soothing sigh, Hazel smiled at Josie. "I'll get us both something to drink."

"Thank you." Josie slid the compass into her pocket and sent a silent message to her dad: *You've got some explaining to do.*

———

Josie had stayed with Hazel longer than she'd expected. They'd continued to talk until the lunch hour when Hazel had offered her a meal. Now late afternoon, her phone quiet, Josie wondered what Zelda was up to—she hadn't texted or anything. But she'd have to check on her later. It was time to go see Nick.

Her mind was heavy with the revelation of the compass

piece, and Josie didn't want to face Zelda. While she had considered that Zelda could have answers, given her aunt's absence in her life, she doubted it, and Josie wasn't sure if she was ready to let Zelda in on her thoughts about such an intimate object. She needed time to figure out what, exactly, she wanted to ask her aunt, if anything at all. For the time being, she wanted to keep the tether to her father to herself, the way he'd intended it, so she texted Julian and asked if he felt like going with her to the venue to see Nick. He told her he'd meet her there.

When she walked up, Julian was already waiting for her, leaning against the side of the building with an affectionate grin on his face. A tiny ache began to form in her chest. In three days she'd have to figure out what she and Nick were doing next. She'd received two emails regarding available short-term rentals in the area, but neither was in her price range. She could afford the rent temporarily, but she feared she'd eventually have to say goodbye.

She and Julian entered the venue and sat in the back of the auditorium. At this stage of the competition, the math was so specialized that it didn't even look like math anymore. Josie had no idea what the announcer was talking about; none of the words sounded like English. Nick was busy scratching his head, his brows pulled together, a frown on his lips as he wrote frantically at the podium. After the final answer, Nick and three others, including Rainy, had gotten the problem correct.

"Your brother's really smart," Julian whispered.

"Yes."

"That's incredible."

"He's a cool kid," she said. "I've really seen him blossom here. He hasn't needed me hardly at all since he's been around peers who share his interests."

She didn't want to think about what would happen after the competition if Nick didn't win it. She'd put him in a tough spot because now he'd had a taste of living life around likeminded people. Would he be okay in a different city? What would he do if he didn't get a scholarship for college? And then if he *did* win, could she handle letting him go? And could he manage on his own?

The time for another math problem came to an end, and Nick and Rainy got the answers correct. They were neck and neck.

Josie and Julian were quiet as they watched the rest of the session. Julian's company felt good. He didn't have any motivation to be there apart from wanting to be with her. She liked that. And she enjoyed being with him. They just fit. It was an indescribable feeling realizing that he was someone she could spend loads of time with and not get tired of.

When the session finished, Nick had scored in the top three contestants. Rainy was also among the top three.

They met him out in the hall at the leaderboard. He and Rainy had made it to the next round.

"Great job, man." Julian clapped Nick on the back, the touch clearly startling him.

"Thank you," Nick said.

Rainy looked up at him, her eyes full of adoration. "We made it through another round."

"I know," Nick said, smiling at her. "It's a good thing you're smart."

She giggled. "Why?"

"Because it means you aren't going home yet. And I get to see you tomorrow."

Rainy blushed and played with her skirt.

"Well, bye," Nick said too abruptly, his cheeks also rosy.

"I'll see you tomorrow," Rainy said. With a final smile and a wrinkle of her nose under her glasses, she went off, catching up with a group of contestants while Nick walked outside with Josie and Julian.

"Can we sit somewhere and talk?" Nick asked. "I'm having a crisis."

"You are?" Josie asked, her mothering instincts immediately kicking in.

He didn't answer.

They went to an empty bench and sat.

"I still don't know what to do about Rainy," Nick said, his knee bouncing. "I keep acting like I'm okay, but when I'm alone, I'm doing deep breathing and working in my notebook, and inside I'm not okay."

"What don't you know about Rainy?" Julian asked.

"I want to ask her out, but I don't know where she'd like to go."

The corner of Julian's mouth twitched upward. "It doesn't matter where you take her."

Nick's eyes rounded with this information. "What?"

"It's what you do when you're there. Hold her hand. Tell her she looks beautiful. Be honest about how you feel." He glanced at Josie.

Nick rubbed his lips together, his forehead creasing, clearly trying to make sense of Julian's answer. "But if I'm honest, I might scare her away."

"Why?" Julian asked.

"Because if I'm being entirely truthful, I'd tell her I can't wait to see her every day, and I don't know how I'm going to be able to leave her, and I might follow her and try to live close to her because I find her fascinating."

Julian broke into an enormous smile. He patted Nick on the shoulder. "I think you should tell her exactly that. But maybe instead of *following* her, you could tell her you'd like to stay close to her."

Nick nodded. "Oh, yes. That's a good point." He twisted his fingers. "Where do I tell her all this?"

"Take her for a walk on the beach," Josie suggested.

"I want to show her how much I like her. My feelings are bigger than the beach." He turned to Julian. "Could you help me come up with a date?"

"Sure. I know lots of places. But what if we..." Julian leaned in and whispered in Nick's ear.

"I would be okay with that," Nick said.

Julian put a finger to his lips, motioning to keep quiet.

"What are you two up to?" Josie asked.

"Don't worry about it," Julian replied with a twinkle in his eyes.

Nick leaned back on the bench and seemed much more relaxed. "I'm relieved you came today," he told Julian.

"I'm glad too. It was a nice break from work. Did Josie tell you I own a rental company?"

Nick shook his head. "You rent houses?"

"No, I rent beach chairs and umbrellas. But I haven't been renting much of anything, if I'm honest." Julian leaned forward with his elbows on his knees.

Nick bent over, lining his face up with Julian's. "You aren't renting anything?"

Julian shook his head. "I can't believe it. I sank my entire savings into this idea, rented a place I can barely afford, bought a huge warehouse and all the furniture..."

"Why did you do that?" Nick asked.

"I thought with all the tourists, we'd get started with a bang, but it's more like a fizzle. We've got the best of the best in inventory, but it's not profitable yet and I'm impatient. The other companies are controlling the market and I'm struggling to get noticed."

It seemed unfathomable to Josie that Julian would ever struggle. He had such a good head on his shoulders, and he was right, the beach was brimming with tourists. A beach rental company seemed like a wonderful idea.

"Your success is like physics," Nick said.

Julian turned to him. "Physics?"

"Yes. Physics is how energy and matter interact. You want your tables and chairs to move, right?"

Julian squinted at him as if not following.

"You want to take the furniture from the warehouse and place it on the beach, but to do that, you need orders. What energy are you using to get those orders?"

"I have signs up by the warehouse, and I have a website."

A light went on inside Josie's mind. "The energy Nick is talking about is marketing."

Julian shook his head. "I can't do much marketing. I don't have a huge budget."

"You don't need one." The couple of marketing classes she'd taken in college started to come back into focus, the old Josie she'd left behind finding her voice. "You could put a QR code on a flyer to go in every rental house and condo in Rosemary Beach. You can make those online for free and print them cheaply. Call every rental company and cottage and condo owner you can get your hands on. Try to get an ad in the free local magazines. That QR code could take renters to a form on your website where they could rent their beach needs. Then Stand Out Rentals would deliver it to their location that day or the next, depending on how much advance notice you need."

Julian's eyes widened. "That's genius."

"To beat your competition, you could also add something the other companies don't have."

He leaned forward into her personal space, his interest clear. "Like what?"

Josie's mind was whirring as quickly as it had when she'd started drawing again, the buzz of creativity filling her.

"What if you offered something like a date-night package option? Blankets, wine, baskets of fruit, cheese... You could set up fire pits with ingredients for s'mores in areas that allow that. You might be able to partner with a local market or café to handle the food orders. They could give you, say, three charcuterie options."

"I love this. You're an angel." He put his arm around her, pulling her into him and kissing her cheek. "Will you work with me on it?"

"Of course." Excitement bubbled at the thought of getting to use her marketing skills. More ideas kept coming to her now she'd started thinking about it. More thrilling, however, was the idea of getting to spend more time with Julian.

CHAPTER TWENTY-SIX

Zelda was already tucked into her sofa bed, her eyes closed, when Josie and Nick got home that night. And in the morning, when Josie had gotten up to see Nick off, her aunt had still been asleep.

Josie asked Nick if he wanted her to spend the day watching the competition, but he said it would make him too nervous to have her there all day. He preferred for her to come at the end of the day the way she'd been doing. She told him she'd be there and wished him luck.

As she quietly prepared breakfast, she was still trying to decide whether to bring up the piece Hazel had found. She concluded she should—Zelda might have information about the compass that Josie didn't know, and even if she didn't, Zelda was family, after all.

Her aunt finally roused. "It smells delicious in here." She folded up the bedding and put the sofa back in place without saying another thing.

"I made eggs and bacon. Would you like a cup of coffee?" Josie asked when Zelda came into the kitchen. "I'm making some."

"Yes, please." Zelda had only been up a minute or two and she already had that pensive look on her face.

Josie had had enough of this mysterious act. They weren't going to get anywhere unless Zelda divulged whatever seemed to be bothering her so much. Trying to give her time when she'd first arrived, Josie had remained quiet, but this was getting ridiculous. If Zelda wanted to wallow in her anxiety alone, she could've done that back in Lox Creek.

Josie stopped preparing the coffee, mid-scoop. "Will you please tell me what's going on? Is it something I've done?"

Zelda blinked a few times, evidently startled by the question. "No, no. You've been nothing but perfect."

"Then what is it? I can see there's something wrong. Tell me. We're family."

Zelda closed her eyes, her chest rising and falling with her breathing, as if she were trying to center herself. Then she looked at Josie.

"You might want to sit down for this."

Josie set the bag of coffee on the counter and went around to Zelda's side. Her aunt motioned for her to take a seat at the table.

Zelda blew air through her nostrils, her lips pinned together as if she were gearing up for something big, and placed her hands in her lap. The drama caused Josie's heart to race.

"There's a trait in our side of the family that seems to repeat itself."

This was the first time in Josie's life that Zelda had said anything about family. She was on pins and needles waiting to hear what her aunt had to say.

"My mother got pregnant when she was very young. She told me about it her whole life, warning me of the perils of young love." She shook her head, her gaze rolling up to the ceiling with a huff. "But still, I followed in her footsteps and found myself pregnant with no job, no husband to help, and nowhere to live." Her eyes filled with tears and her hands began to tremble.

"Oh, my gosh," Josie said.

"I finally understood what my mother—your grand-mother—felt. The guilt that I'd created this child, this wonderful soul, and couldn't give it the life it deserved was too much for me. I knew I couldn't be the mother my little one needed."

"So I have a cousin somewhere?"

Zelda shook her head, tears flowing down her cheeks. "Your mother struggled to get pregnant. She and your dad had tried for years. She'd done everything right. She'd read all the books and made sure her diet was flawless. She kept her stress low by playing music in the house and dancing with your dad. She tried not to let their struggle to conceive impact her, but I know it did. She told me once that she prayed every night for God to give her a child. She said she'd promised God she wouldn't let Him down."

This didn't make any sense at all. What did her mother's struggle have to do with anything?

"I knew she'd be a better mother than I could be. So I offered up my baby girl."

All the blood ran out of Josie's face and limbs, leaving her cold and clammy, her breath unable to come. She peered into Zelda's eyes—the same green eyes as hers—until the tears came, blurring her vision. Questions began to surface through the haze of astonishment. But she could only form the first one.

"You're my mother?"

"Yes," Zelda said with a groan of grief.

"Who's my father?" Josie asked, finding the rest of her words. She knew when she asked that whatever name Zelda said would mean nothing, because her dad would always be her dad, no matter what.

"His name was Paul Hughes. He didn't know."

"Why didn't you tell him?"

"I knew him in high school. He joined the army after we graduated, and he was already in another state by the time I realized I was pregnant. He was sent to Afghanistan in the early days of the war. He called me when he could and wrote letters, but it was so difficult over there that I didn't want to burden him with such a huge thing as having a child he couldn't see or help me raise. I told myself I'd explain everything once he came home. But I didn't get that chance. He was killed in combat only days after deployment."

Josie sat silently, absorbing this jarring information, trying to wrap her head around it. She'd never know her biological father. And she had grandparents she hadn't met. She'd never felt motherly love from Zelda. And she'd never know if she was anything like her birth father. The revelations raced through her at warp speed, making her dizzy.

Initially, she was livid with Zelda for not telling her, and angry at the world for taking the man who'd given her life. Then resentment rose at the deception from everyone around her.

"Why didn't anyone tell me?" she asked.

"Your mother adopted you with one condition. I demanded she wouldn't tell you."

"Why?" Josie asked, the word coming out in a whisper.

"I wanted you to grow up thinking your mother was perfect, because she was." Zelda wiped her tears away with her fingertips.

As the information began to settle on her, Josie realized that Zelda and this Paul person had given her life, but her mother and father had nurtured her. They taught her about the world, and even though she shared no blood with her mother, she knew that they were still bound by love. Love connected them all.

As the bombshell was taking hold, Josie was suddenly skeptical. This was Zelda. She hadn't been around enough for Josie to trust her. Now that her father wasn't there to speak up for himself, Zelda had decided to tell Josie their secret? What if there was something else her aunt wanted, some other motive?

"How do I know you're telling the truth?"

"I have no reason to lie."

"But you didn't seem to care about us. You said you'd come to see us so many times and you didn't. You weren't there for Mom's funeral. You didn't show any interest in me until now."

"That's not true." Her aunt blinked madly, tears still brimming in her eyes. "I couldn't come around because every time I saw you, I selfishly wanted you back, and the pain of losing you was too much to bear. So I ran. I spent my whole life running. I couldn't face seeing your pain when your mother died because I knew how much you loved her, and I couldn't comfort you like I wanted to. I constantly felt that I couldn't measure up to her. I doubted I would ever see that love in your eyes. I spent the entire week of the funeral unable to get out of bed." Zelda put her face in her hands. "I'm so sorry," she said, and then fell into a fit of sobs.

Josie sat there, stunned, her life as she knew it now in complete shambles.

"And Nick? You said my mom couldn't have kids."

"She finally got pregnant, and we couldn't believe it. When she died, we wondered if God had been trying to protect her by making it so difficult to conceive."

"So Nick isn't my brother," she said, feeling faint.

"Yes, he is. You were officially adopted, so he is your brother, he just isn't your full-blooded brother." Zelda leaned into Josie's view, her eyes swollen and red. "I didn't know how to tell you, and I know you think poorly of me, but I've been mustering the courage to break the news since your father died."

Josie wiped the tears that were spilling from her eyes.

"When you lost your father, I knew you needed someone to lean on, and that I should tell you. Right after, I worried that divulging it would only make things worse—you were dealing with so much... Then I struggled to find the right time. I know how much family means to you. Your dad told me when he tried to get me to come visit. And I want you to understand, while I've been a terrible aunt, deep down, I've been your mother from afar." She broke down again.

Josie was still hurt that they'd kept the truth from her, that her aunt—her *mother*—hadn't worked harder to be stronger, but she couldn't even put herself in Zelda's shoes. She couldn't imagine what she must have gone through. Slowly, Josie began to surrender to her new reality. At the end of the day, Zelda had loved her enough to give her the best she had—a new family.

She put her arms around her birth mother.

Zelda reciprocated, squeezing her as if she was afraid she'd lose her if she let go.

As Josie held on to Zelda, the dream from the other night came back to her. Mama had said, "I need you to know that you were always my girl." Had it been a message for her and not just a dream, or had Josie somehow subconsciously known? Was all this meant to be?

Josie and Zelda stayed together the rest of the day, getting to know each other in their new roles of mother and daughter. Josie had been so busy taking in Zelda's incredible news that she'd forgotten about the compass matching Hazel's piece. It had seemed so significant yesterday, but now the idea that her father had known someone in Rosemary Beach didn't feel as consequential, and she let it go.

Later that afternoon, she tried to regain some semblance of normal. Zelda had urged her to decide where she and Nick would live after the competition.

"You're always welcome in Lox Creek," Zelda said. "I'd love nothing more than to have you and Nick with me every day, but I think there's more out there for you."

Josie knew she couldn't take Nick back to Lox Creek. He had so many better opportunities to find. She sat next to Zelda on the balcony of the condo with her laptop, searching for possible living arrangements. She filled out another form for short-term housing. Throughout the day, one question kept surfacing: How was she going to tell Nick everything she'd learned today? How would he take it? She emailed his counselor back home, asking for the best way to approach the situation. He'd managed the other changes during their trip with ease, but this was different.

Josie closed her laptop. "I'm wondering how to tell Nick. I'm worried about how he'll take the news."

"You don't think he can handle it?" Zelda asked.

Josie rubbed her temples. "I don't know."

Zelda looked into her eyes and smiled. "May I share something with you?"

Josie focused on her.

"When your dad died, I wondered how in the world you'd handle all of it. I followed you around and checked in on you, driving past the house to make sure everything seemed okay. But it didn't take me long to realize you were more than okay. You have been amazing. You could handle so much at such a young age when I couldn't accomplish half of what you were managing." She took Josie's hand. "I didn't give you enough credit. Maybe we can expect Nick to do more as well."

Josie had let him go while he was here, and he'd done wonderfully. He'd made friends and spent time with Rainy. He'd kept himself together under pressure. Maybe Zelda was right, and he could handle more than she was giving him credit for. Maybe she just hadn't wanted to let go.

"Can we at least wait to tell him until after the competition?"

Zelda nodded. "Of course."

CHAPTER TWENTY-SEVEN

Nick had made it to day nine of the competition—
the top eight of fifty contestants. With each day he
seemed calmer and surer of himself. This morning,
he'd had another breakfast without opening his notebook, and
he actually smiled on the way out the door. He'd seemed
excited when he told Josie he was meeting Julian after the
competition. She asked if she should join him, but he'd
said no.

With Zelda still asleep, Josie went to the balcony with her
coffee and sat in the sunshine. The warm rays were a nice
distraction from the heaviness of the previous day. She closed
her eyes to try to clear her mind. Her world had been turned
upside down, and when she'd awakened this morning she was
still trying make sense of it all. What would she call Zelda?
How would she act around her now? Could they have a relationship?

Nothing else in her life could calm her like the shushing of
the Gulf and the squawk of the seagulls. With renewed
purpose, she tried to focus on something lighter. She searched
online for Julian's company, Stand Out Rentals. She copied

the address of the website and opened the graphic design software she'd installed back in college. She got to work designing a card with a QR code to hand out to hotels and rental companies, and decided to take some photos of the warehouse to incorporate into the images.

Closing her computer, she went to the bathroom to get ready for the day, the excitement of surprising Julian with her marketing materials fueling her. Zelda hadn't stirred on the sofa, so Josie wrote her a note. As she left the condo and made her way down the side streets to Julian's warehouse, she let the adventure of this new opportunity overshadow the fear and confusion still swirling around the revelation that the two people she'd known her whole life as Mom and Dad were not her biological parents. A twinge of distrust pecked at her, and she still wasn't sure she wanted to believe Zelda. Was she in denial?

She arrived at Stand Out Rentals and pushed the questions out of her mind. Her lungs filled with a breath of happiness when she saw the blue-and-white swirling sign now installed above the sliding doors. The windows were dark; no one was there yet, just as she'd hoped. She held up her phone, zoomed in, and took a photo. Then she walked around the building looking for artful angles and eye-catching images to give her options once she got back to her computer.

Photography was similar to finding objects to sketch. She looked for shimmers of sunlight or darker shadows that created drama. She paid attention to the way a scene made her feel and then tried to capture that feeling in her photo. Whenever she worked on something creative, all the other things in her life faded away. She'd forgotten how therapeutic the act could be.

But once she'd gotten the photos she'd come for, and she began the walk back to the condo, her mind returned to Zelda's revelation. It was the most important news of her life.

Still not wanting to believe it, she went back over her aunt's words, trying to find a hole in the story.

Then, when the thought hit her, she stopped cold right in the middle of the sidewalk. Zelda *was* lying. She'd combed through her aunt's words and, yes, there was something that didn't add up.

Zelda had said Josie's grandmother had warned her about getting pregnant at a young age like she had. Josie counted on her fingers, double-checking. Her grandmother was twenty-eight when she had Josie's dad, and Zelda was younger than her father. So her grandmother wasn't *that* young when she first got pregnant. Why would she warn Zelda not to get pregnant at twenty-eight?

But slowly something else began to emerge from the fog of confusion, like the pinprick of light from the first evening star, its illumination getting brighter as Josie began speculating. Here mouth fell open. *No…*

She picked up her pace until she was in a full sprint toward the condo. She needed to talk to Zelda right away. She bounded up the stairs to her unit two at a time, then burst through the door out of breath. Zelda was at the coffee maker filling her mug.

"Is everything all right?" she asked.

Still panting, Josie sat down at the table, getting her racing thoughts in order.

Zelda lowered herself across from Josie, confusion swimming on her face.

Josie pulled out the compass and slid it across the table. "Do you know what this is?" she nearly demanded.

Zelda seemed frozen in her spot as she stared at it. Her smile dropped, her eyes widening in surprise. Hands suddenly shaking, she laid her fingers on the compass and pulled it toward her. She opened the door on the front, and the piece came off in her hands where the hinges had been broken. Zelda's lips parted as she gazed at the two pieces.

"My mother gave this to me. And I gave it to your father to pass down to you, since I couldn't do it." She picked up the front cover. "But I didn't give your dad this piece," she said, holding it up.

"You didn't?" Josie asked, her heart pounding.

"Where did you get it?"

"From a woman I met at the coffee shop last week. We've spent some time together. It was in a box of her father's things."

Tears spilled from Zelda's eyes.

"My mother told me that she didn't have anything—she was so young and poor. She found this compass at a pawn shop just before she gave up her first child for adoption. She told me she'd pulled the two pieces apart and asked the adoptive parents to keep the side with the inscription, 'Love will guide you.' She kept the other side, hoping it would somehow lead her back to the child she was giving up."

Josie covered her mouth in complete shock that her hunch had been right. Hazel was adopted—she'd said so herself. Had Hazel been who her father had been trying to track down? Had he found out somehow that she was here? She recalled the dream: "You're going to finish what I started." Josie had asked her parents to give her something big. Well, she just got it.

Through her fingers she said, "I might have found your sister. Her name is Hazel McDonough."

Zelda sucked in a breath. "What?"

"Yes." Josie pulled out her phone to text Hazel to ask if she and her aunt could come over, but then she stopped. "Maybe we shouldn't tell her just yet."

Zelda's face crumpled. "Why not?"

"Dr. Randolph McDonough, the founder of Battle of the

Mathematical Minds, is Hazel's husband. What if we tell Hazel now and Nick wins the competition? Would it be an issue if it came out that he was a relative of Dr. McDonough's wife?" Josie put her phone away. "We have two days. Let's wait."

————

When Julian called to ask if Josie would go on a double date with Rainy and Nick, Zelda said she didn't mind being alone; she'd enjoy spending some time on the beach. Josie couldn't wait to leave her troubles behind if only for one evening, spend some quality time with Nick, and see Julian again.

As she walked down the stairs of the condo, she felt as if she might burst, holding in everything she'd learned in the last two days. She wasn't telling Nick about Zelda, and now she prayed she didn't run into Hazel, because if she did, she'd certainly struggle to keep this new information under wraps. Her whole life had been turned upside down.

She couldn't stop thinking about how Hazel had been drawn to her that day in the coffee shop. Now she wondered if it was because she was family. They shared the love of art, and Josie looked up to Hazel and was mesmerized by her. She felt lighter as she considered the fact that she now had an aunt she loved, one who filled the shoes she'd always hoped Zelda would fill.

And Zelda had a new place in Josie's heart. She understood her absence more and felt for her. She'd spent so much time alone, running from Josie in an effort to give her a more normal life. The sacrifice had been incredible, and Josie had a new appreciation for her.

When she got down to the parking lot, Nick, Rainy, and Julian were waiting for her.

"We're celebrating tonight," Rainy said as Josie walked up

to them. The girl's blue eyes were wide behind her glasses, her face alight.

Josie met Julian's affectionate gaze and gave him a smile to say hello before turning her attention to Rainy. "Oh? What are we celebrating?"

Rainy's eyebrows bobbed as she looked up at Nick. "Want to tell her?"

"Rainy and I had a good day."

Rainy bounced excitedly, clapping her hands before wrapping her arms around Nick and giving him a squeeze. She let go and danced around the parking lot. Nick hid his surprise well and let out a chuckle.

Josie couldn't help herself. She threw her arms around her brother. "That's amazing! Congratulations to both of you."

Nick seemed to stand taller, and she noticed the slight air of confidence in his features. It was absolutely wonderful to see.

Turning her attention from Nick and Rainy, she observed that Julian was holding the handlebars of a pink bicycle with a basket on the front.

"For you," he said, rolling it closer.

Rainy went to the steps and pulled a lavender bike from a group of three that were leaning against the railing, leaving two dark blue ones. She mounted it and rode it over. Nick and Julian grabbed the other two.

"Follow us, ladies," Nick said, mounting his bicycle.

He wobbled a bit, but he straightened himself out and rode up next to Julian, the two men leading the way. Rainy and Josie rode just behind them on the side of the street where the pavement crumbled away to a trail of sand just big enough for two bikes. They pedaled along the edge of the tree-lined road, through the slips of sunlight shining through the trees, until they reached the long stretch between Rosemary Beach and the next village. The salty summer air felt cooler with the speed of the bike, now that the intense heat from the day was subsiding. The ride was soothing for Josie's heavy mind.

When the traffic died down, Josie maneuvered next to Julian, and he flashed her a devious grin. "Are you trying to race me?"

"Definitely not," she said, but pedaled a little harder to push in front of him.

Nick leaned across his handlebars, watching them.

"But if I wanted to, you know I'd win," she teased, pulling out ahead a bit more.

With swift movement of the pedals, Julian overtook her, but then quickly slowed to be by her side.

"You giving up that easily?" she asked.

"I don't want to rush a single bit of this night," he replied, his gaze on her, giving her stomach a flip.

They rode down the sidewalk and over the walking bridge that straddled the deep-blue saltwater lakes. The sun sparkled off the surface, dancing in the water's movement as if it were cheering them on as they passed.

When they finally arrived on the other side, Josie followed Julian's lead, and they stopped at a pink beachside shop lined with bright silver buckets of fresh flowers with a chalkboard sign that said, *Make your own bouquets.* More bundles of wild-flowers arched above the double doors that were propped open with conch shells.

They parked their bikes in the bike rack at the edge of the small parking area.

"I'm going to wait here," Nick said to the group, standing by the bikes. "The smells of all the flowers are too much for me."

Julian led the two women to the door. "I told Nick we could do something else, but when I mentioned this he was insistent that you and Rainy would like it."

"They will," Nick called.

Julian grinned at Josie, and Rainy wrinkled her nose playfully at Nick.

"I'll wait outside with your brother," Julian said.

She and Rainy went into the shop.

"This is gorgeous," Josie said, tipping her head up to take in the glass chandeliers that illuminated the stands of fresh flowers and shimmered over bundles arranged on distressed beech-wood tables with satin ribbons and glass vases in every shape and size. The sweet scents of roses and gardenias wafted around them when they moved through the shop.

"I love it," Rainy said, as they strolled from table to table. "I'm going to try to pick flowers with the least amount of scent so they don't bother Nick."

Josie's heart squeezed. "That's really kind of you."

Rainy smiled, squinching up her glasses, and gave Nick a wave through the door. Then she blew him a kiss and the surprise on his face was priceless, making Josie laugh.

"Choose as many as you like," Nick called through the open door before retreating to the bikes.

The woman behind the counter handed them each a long basket lined with parchment paper to carry as they browsed the incredible array of flowers.

"You're really kind to my brother," Josie said.

Rainy glowed and turned her attention to a bouquet of roses. "I like him a lot. He's different from anyone I've ever met. He's so honest." She giggled.

"Yes. He certainly is." Josie placed a bundle of baby's breath in her basket, her heart full.

"I'm from Maryland," Rainy said, a tiny falter in her usual spunkiness.

"Nick told me."

Rainy nodded. "My parents didn't want to let me come alone, but they had to work, and they knew that I really wanted the opportunity. I begged to come, and they finally agreed. I have to call them three times a day to let them know everything's all right." Her love for her parents was clear in the sparkle in her eyes.

"What do your parents do?"

"My dad works for a plumbing company and my mom's a receptionist for an insurance agency. They only get a certain number of days off each year. This trip would've used up the entirety of their leave, and they want us to visit my grandmother this fall." She plucked a flower from one of the baskets and held it under her nose. "She's been battling health problems, so they didn't feel like this would be a good time to skip seeing her. I wouldn't want to miss out on spending time with her either."

"I totally understand."

"I used my savings to rent a hotel room and my parents helped me buy a used car as a graduation present. I can't believe it made it the whole way here."

"I definitely get that," Josie said with a laugh. She liked Rainy. "Our backgrounds aren't that different."

"Nick told me he didn't fit in at school. I had a similar experience. Not many girls in my school were interested in math like I am. They should be." She gave a firm nod as if to emphasize the point. "I spent a lot of time by myself, and my parents worried about me. That's why they let me come. They were hoping I'd find people like me. I definitely did!"

"You and Nick have a lot in common then."

Rainy gazed out the window at him. "I've never found anyone who challenges me like Nick does. And he's the nicest person I've ever known."

Josie smiled, full of pride for her brother. "I think he probably feels the same about you."

Rainy blushed and then stepped away to peruse a group of yellow flowers just as Julian walked in.

"Nick and I really put some thought into this," he said

when he stood beside her. He pulled a daisy from one of the buckets and offered it to Josie. "He's a great kid. You've done a wonderful job with him. He told me so himself."

"He did?" She accepted the flower and set it in her basket, gazing up at him.

"Yep. He told me that being around Rainy makes him calm and he hasn't felt that with anyone else except you. He told me you used to sing to him at night and that it was hard for him when you went away to college."

"Wow." She swallowed the lump in her throat and peered through the door at her brother, waiting patiently as Rainy chose her flowers. She knew this exercise at the flower shop was his way of doing something to show he cared. She was so thankful he'd found someone who could understand the kindness he had for others.

It felt as if a weight had been lifted from Josie as she built her bouquet. Talking with Rainy and knowing Nick's feelings helped her believe everything else would be okay because they had each other.

When they finished, Josie and Rainy carried out their bouquets, wrapped in paper and tied with pink and seafoam-green satin ribbons, and set them in the baskets on their bicycles. Nick pulled his bike from the rack, radiant with satisfaction. His hands were still, his cheeks pink, a small upturn to his lips. Josie hadn't ever seen him so content. Whatever happened with the competition, they'd done the right thing in coming.

"Where to next?" Rainy asked, taking off her sweater and draping it inside the bike's basket beside her bouquet.

"We'll lead the way, won't we, Nick?" Julian gave him a wink, the two sharing some sort of secret.

They rode on through the town to another shop. This one was made of white stucco with lantern-style lamps on each side of a sleek door.

"Bring your flowers," Nick told them when they'd parked at the bike rack. "I'll wait out here."

"I'll take them in and then come back out with you," Julian said.

Nick nodded, and the three of them went inside the cool, shiny space.

"Welcome to The Perfumery," a woman said, coming around the glass counter to greet them. "These guys have planned a pretty big day for you two—you must be very special ladies."

Rainy grinned at Josie and then blew another kiss to Nick through the window. A small smile formed on his lips.

"Today, we're going to create a unique perfume just for you, based on the flowers you chose." She stepped toward Josie. "May I see?"

Josie and Rainy held out their bouquets.

"Wildflowers, my favorite," the woman said.

"Do you have any unscented soaps?" Rainy asked the woman.

"Of course. We have a line of sensitive skin bath products on the wall."

"Thank you." Rainy moved to the line of free-and-clear soaps and bath salts.

"Have a seat." The woman offered Josie and Julian a couple of stools at a long table full of jars and droppers. She went around to the other side and pulled a tray of empty bottles in different shapes from under the counter. "You can take a minute to decide on the bottle for your scent."

Josie chose a flat bottle that was circular in shape. As the woman talked about the different scents, Josie's thoughts turned to the individuals around her. Julian and Nick were two of her favorite people, and she couldn't imagine what she would do without either of them. And Rainy had been such a lovely surprise for Nick. The competition would end tomorrow, and the morning after they were leaving the condo—where to, she still had no idea. But one thing was for sure, there was definitely no way she could go back to Lox Creek.

She thought back to the conversation she'd had with her boss, Helen. "Neither of us expected you to stay as long as you have."

Josie hadn't understood the message fully until now. She'd been in the cocoon of a small town and college, then wrecked by grief, and she hadn't been given a chance to see anything outside of that. Maybe it was good that she and Nick didn't know where they'd end up. Perhaps they should see more places.

But then there was Julian. He'd started a business, he needed her help to get it up and running, and he certainly wouldn't be able to travel with them. The thought of leaving him again made her feel as if she were suffocating. But she pushed it aside to enjoy the moment with him.

———

Josie fiddled with the bouquet she'd placed in a glass of water once they'd gotten back to the condo. Zelda had spent a while with her before taking a bath and then setting up her bed on the sofa. Nick came out of his room and leaned on the counter.

"Today was fun," Josie told Nick, rearranging another flower in the makeshift vase. "You and Julian planned a wonderful date."

"Thank you," Nick said.

Zelda turned off the lights in the living room, climbed under the blankets, and closed her eyes. Josie poured her and Nick a late night lemonade and they took it to the table. Josie was so thankful for the few minutes with her brother. She hadn't gotten many moments with just him lately and she missed spending time with him.

"Where's your notebook?" she asked quietly, hoping Zelda hadn't done anything with it.

"It's in my suitcase," Nick replied. "I haven't needed it, so I packed it."

Josie tried to keep her composure, but she was thrilled for him. No matter the outcome tomorrow, this trip had changed them both for the better. But she did wonder why he hadn't expressed concern about the competition ending. It seemed like such a shame that he and Rainy would have to leave each other.

"Have you made any plans to keep in touch with Rainy after the competition?" she asked.

Nick sat across from her and wrapped his wide hand around the glass of lemonade. "I spoke to her on the phone about it while I was in my room. We decided we both want to stay here in Rosemary Beach," he said before taking a sip. "She already told her parents."

"What did they say?" Josie asked.

"They said they wanted to see what happens with the competition first. If she doesn't win, she already has a scholarship with a college near her hometown. She told them she can take remote classes, but they still want to wait."

"I think it's a good idea to wait and see." Josie sipped her lemonade.

"Neither of us really wants to win anymore. We just want to be together."

His change in demeanor over the last two weeks was bigger than any prize, and while she'd love nothing more than to have him win a scholarship for a four-year school, she was willing to bet he'd be just fine no matter what he ended up doing. *Follow your heart.*

"I want to live here," he said again.

Josie set down her glass. "I've thought about it too. But we can't afford to live here."

"We can figure it out. Didn't you say that? We can live in a tent if we have to, right?"

"Not long term. I only said that with the two weeks in mind."

"I'm willing to do anything for Rainy. Even if it means sleeping in a tent forever."

Josie looked into her brother's eyes, and for the first time since he was a child, she saw life in them.

"I know what you mean," she said, her thoughts moving to Julian. She had to find a way to stay.

Chapter Twenty-Eight

Nick had asked Josie to let him go alone to the final day of the competition. As usual, he'd told her he was way too nervous about it to have her in the audience, but he seemed conflicted about something today as well. Perhaps it was simply the pressure of the final day. She wanted to support him, but he wouldn't have asked her not to go unless he really didn't want her there, so she'd spent the morning with Zelda.

"What are you up to?" Zelda asked from the other chair on the balcony, looking up from the novel she'd been reading.

Busily typing on her laptop, Josie replied, "I'm creating some marketing materials for Julian." She'd been finishing up compiling her photos and images online, playing with fonts, trying to match the Stand Out Rentals signs. She'd built an entire marketing package, and she couldn't wait to show Julian what she'd made. She'd texted him to say she had a surprise for him and wanted to see him as soon as possible tomorrow.

Zelda faced the sun. "It sure is lovely here, isn't it?"

"Yeah." Josie dragged the final photo of the sign over to

the template she was using. The image took her back to the time she'd spent with Julian at the warehouse; then her mind went to the memory of that day with him at the beach and their kiss.

"I'm getting a glass of orange juice," Zelda announced, yanking Josie from her daydreaming. "Want one?"

Josie closed her computer. "Sure, thank you. Would you want to do something together today?" For the first time, she didn't feel uneasy around Zelda.

"I'd like that. What should we do?"

"I have an idea." Josie stood and headed inside. She was actually excited to spend some time with Zelda.

———

As she waited for Zelda to get ready, Josie sat on the sofa, her sketchpad in her lap, lost in her thoughts. She hadn't felt this whole in a very long time.

She pulled out her compass and read the inscription on Hazel's side: *Love will guide you.* That was certainly the truth. She'd found nothing but love since she'd arrived in Rosemary Beach, and her love for Nick had gotten her there. Zelda's love for her had finally brought them together, and Nick was stronger than he'd ever been after loving himself enough to believe he could compete with some of the best mathematical students in the nation, *and* after falling for Rainy. Josie had also found Julian again, the one person who'd always been able to turn her head.

"Ready," Zelda said as she stepped into the living area.

Josie grabbed her purse, and they walked to the door. They'd decided to buy Zelda a sketchpad, then go to the beach and draw, and Josie couldn't wait to work creatively together for the first time.

"What are you planning to sketch while we're out today?"

Josie asked as they went outside and took the stairs to the ground floor.

"I'd love to find a few seashells," Zelda said.

The coastal wind was heavy today, blowing against them and feeling like a warm hug. "That sounds perfect. I've decided I want to draw the sand dunes and the weathered wood of the boardwalk."

"I can't wait to see it."

Zelda's acceptance and encouragement was unexpectedly emotional, and Josie blinked away the wetness in her eyes. They left the condo's parking lot and walked the few streets to the art shop, then settled on a spot on the shore. A green-flag day, the crystal-clear water was almost still, shimmying in tiny whooshes onto the pearly sand. Beyond the break, the Gulf showed off its vibrant greens and deep blues Josie never got tired of, the sun reflecting off its surface in a spectacular show.

Cross-legged in the sand, Josie twisted around with her back to the water, so she could have a good view of the dunes. The breeze was constant on the shore, and she tucked her hair behind her ear to keep it out of her face while she opened her sketchpad to a clean page. She dragged her pencil lightly across the width of the paper to map out the edges of the dunes. Then she added wisps of seagrass.

Zelda was off combing the beach, bending down every now and then to pick up shells. Once she had a good handful, she returned and sat on the sand next to Josie. She placed a delicate shell in front of her and opened her own sketchbook, then started outlining the edges of her little treasure.

She peered over at Josie's drawing and began sketching the dunes around the shell as if the drawings were two halves of the same scene. Zelda's style was a bit finer and her lines lighter than Josie's. It was interesting to see how the same talent manifested itself in each of them. What had always been a solitary endeavor for Josie was a partner activity today, and it felt completely natural.

————

That evening, with their sketches laid out on the kitchen table, Josie and Zelda sat on the sofa while Josie waited anxiously to hear the outcome of the competition.

No matter what happened, Nick had made it to the final day. She couldn't believe it. But then again, a part of her could. She'd always known Nick had potential, but she hadn't given him enough credit for his ability to grow and adapt. They'd experienced a ton of change the last few weeks, and he'd handled all of it.

When Nick and Rainy finally arrived, both were beaming with happiness, Rainy nearly falling through the door as she giggled at something Nick had said.

Josie stood and smoothed out her shorts, trying not to look as eager as she was. She didn't want to make too big of a fuss in case they hadn't won, but their positive behavior gave her the go-ahead.

"Did one of you win?"

"No!" they said in unison before doubling over laughing.

Josie gaped at her brother. Nick was *laughing*. The sound was heaven.

Nick put his arm around Rainy. "We both lost. A guy named Gerald Simpson won. He says he's going to MIT."

"And you two are happy about this?" Josie looked at Zelda, who shrugged.

Nick dropped onto the sofa. "Yes."

Rainy followed. "I already have college plans and I can work from anywhere." She batted her eyelashes at Nick and nudged him. "Tell them."

"Tell me what?" Josie asked.

"Dr. McDonough said he'd like to give me my own scholarship outside of the competition. Once I choose where I want to go, he's going to meet with admissions personally to explain my talents. And he also wants to mentor me."

Rainy added, "He said he sees something in Nick, and if Nick wants to stay around town, he can work directly under Dr. McDonough while they find an online program for him."

Josie's eyes widened in utter shock. "You're kidding."

Nick shook his head. "No. I'm not kidding. I'm meeting him Monday to talk about abstract algebra."

"But we have nowhere to sleep tomorrow."

"Yes, we do," Nick said. "I told him about our situation, and he said we can live in his guesthouse until we find a place. It has four bedrooms, so there's room for Zelda if she wants to stay a few more nights."

Zelda and Josie both gasped, tears of joy pricking her eyes. Did Nick realize what this meant? Relief tingled through her body. Her big gamble—selling the house, running off to Florida, putting Nick through so much change—had paid off. He'd found a *future* with Dr. McDonough, whose mentoring would be invaluable to him. Nick could build a career learning from a top mathematical mind and doing what he loved.

"I'm blown away, Nick," she finally managed.

She was delighted for her brother, but this meant something big for her too. It meant she could spend more time with Julian.

She sat on the sofa to take it all in. This was the moment when her life changed for the better. It was the end of the last chapter and the beginning of the next.

———

After their excitement had settled a bit and Rainy had gone back to her hotel, Josie and Zelda sat Nick down and told him Zelda's secret as well as their speculations about Hazel.

Nick listened intently, appearing unruffled by it all. He folded his hands on the table and his attention darted between the two women. "So I'll be working with my uncle?" he asked.

Josie eyed Zelda, surprised that was Nick's first question.

"Yes," she replied. "But are you concerned that I'm not your biological sister?"

Nick frowned and shook his head. "No. Genetics are just a sequence in our DNA chains—why would that matter? You were still there for me my whole life, and you're here now. What's the big deal?"

Josie burst into a smile. Sometimes she loved the way Nick saw the world. If she were being honest, she felt exactly the same about him. It didn't matter how they were connected. Just as she'd thought about her mother, love was at the root of everything. Nothing else mattered except love.

"We're going to talk to Hazel to confirm what we think about her adoption," Josie said. "Would you come with Zelda and me to tell her?"

Nick nodded. "Sure. May I bring Rainy?"

"Of course."

As she texted Hazel to check that the late evening hour was okay to come over, a memory floated into Josie's mind of the days she'd gone to the lot to talk to her parents. She'd told her father she wanted to believe her parents were with her, guiding her, just like the compass said. All she'd wanted was family. Now here she was, surrounded by one. *Love will guide you.* She had to wonder.

———

With the sun setting, casting an orange-and-yellow glow through the window, Josie sat at the McDonoughs' dining-room table with Hazel, Randolph, Zelda, Nick, and Rainy, the compass in the center.

"We think we might know why your father had that part of the compass," Josie said.

Hazel drew the small instrument toward her and scrutinized it. "Do tell. I'm dying to know."

Josie swallowed, trying to figure out the best way to say it. She gestured to Zelda. "Why don't you tell Hazel what your mother told you?"

Zelda laced her fingers together, her gaze moving around the table as if she were taking in her new family. Then she told her story.

Hazel listened, her eyes attentive. Her expression was soft, interested, and composed. With every word Zelda spoke, Hazel seemed more invested, as if she'd been waiting her whole life for these answers. Side by side, the resemblance between the sisters was clear.

"This is unbelievable," Hazel said once Zelda had finished the story. "My whole life, I felt guilty for wanting to know... I had a wonderful childhood, doting parents, and I lacked nothing. Yet there was this tiny whisper asking where I'd come from that was always there." She turned to face Zelda, emotion clear in the tears forming under her lashes. "We seem to have the same green eyes..."

Zelda smiled. "The trait is strong in our family. My brother had them, and so do Josie and Nick."

A tear escaped down Hazel's cheek. "My son, Milo, had green eyes." Hazel took Randolph's hand and clutched it tightly as she explained to Zelda what had happened to her son.

Never before had Zelda appeared so grounded, serious, absorbed in the moment. And it only occurred to Josie then that Zelda was finally getting what she'd always wanted as well. All three women were surrounded by blessings, their deepest wishes granted at once.

"So we share the absence of a child as well," Zelda said. "While I didn't lose mine to a terrible illness, I had to spend my life without her." Zelda offered Josie a meaningful look before explaining that she was Josie's biological mother.

"We have so many similarities..." Hazel shook her head, clearly still in disbelief.

"Zelda is also an artist," Josie said. "Just like you and me."

Hazel's lips parted as she sucked in a tiny gasp. "Unbelievable." She blinked over and over as if trying to get her mind around it all. "I'm not sure if I need any more proof at this point, but should we get a blood test or something just to absolutely confirm it?"

"If you want to," Zelda replied.

Hazel lit up, her eyes glimmering with happiness. "Well, family or not, none of us has to spend a single minute away from the others anymore."

Dr. McDonough clapped his hands. "Yes, Hazel has been dying to have family around, and it's as if you all were brought to her by some miracle."

"That's why I spend time in the coffee shop," Hazel added. "I feel so alone when Randolph is off working. I've only ever been a good housewife, and I've been struggling for where I fit." She placed her hand on Josie's. "I was so excited when you wanted to go to the art shop that day. You helped me connect with who I am."

"Josie took me to that shop too," Zelda said.

Hazel beamed in response to the connection.

Dr. McDonough stood. "This calls for a toast. I'll get us some champagne."

An electric buzz enveloped the room as Hazel got Nick and Rainy glasses of lemonade while Randolph opened a bottle of Moët & Chandon, the cork giving a hollow celebratory pop, followed by a burst of fizz. Hazel brought out four crystal flutes and her husband filled them with champagne.

When they held up their glasses in unison, Josie imagined the tinkling as applause from above. She'd asked her parents to show her something big, and it seemed they'd delivered.

I don't think I had to finish what you started, Dad, she sent into the air. *I think you're busy finishing this one yourself.*

It was a wonder that they'd all been brought together, and she was nearly certain, now, that her father was behind it. Something deep down told her that as long as her parents were watching over them, everything would be okay from here on out.

CHAPTER TWENTY-NINE

"So this is the QR code that takes people to the website," Josie said as she and Julian stood at a counter in the crisp air of the warehouse the next morning. She pulled her gaze from his affectionate stare and tapped her computer screen. "And here you can add the different rental packages. I suggest giving them fun names like 'Life's a Party' or 'Dream Date.'" She minimized the screen to get to the next slide.

"Are you wearing your new perfume?" Julian asked, moving awfully close to her, off task, as if he already sensed the good news she'd yet to divulge.

Wanting to tell him everything in person, she'd tried to hide her excitement on the phone when she'd called him this morning to pin down a time to come over. But she'd struggled to keep her emotions in check. Her inability to stop flirting when he said something funny had been her downfall. She was nearly sure by the light chuckle on the other end of the phone that he already knew she was crazy about him. Her mind went back to that day on their college hike, the first time he'd tested the waters, and then to the day they'd spent at the beach... their kiss, his lips moving on hers.

She'd come to tell him everything that had happened the day before and how she was planning to stay a while in Rosemary Beach—Nick and Randolph were taking their bags to the guesthouse already. She'd also planned to tell Julian how much she adored him. But he didn't know yet, so he was still taking things slowly to see how she'd handle his advances.

"Yes, I'm wearing my new perfume," she finally answered, biting back a smile, enjoying this little game of being all business. She tapped her screen to keep him on task. "I found a few local printers for hard copies," she continued. "You should also be on social media platforms. I couldn't find any accounts under Stand Out Rentals, so I created some for you." She clicked through the various platforms, showing him the initial posts she'd put up with the photos of the warehouse and a couple sketches of the furniture she'd made and uploaded. "You could do a few giveaways to get people interested."

"You are an angel," Julian said, his stare swallowing her. "This is amazing."

She smiled at him, trying to control the flutters in her stomach. She wanted to grab him and kiss him, but his advances were adorable, so she continued to play along. If she didn't, she'd fall right into his arms, and she actually did think it would be good to get the business out of the way so they could enjoy the rest of the day once she gave him the news.

"How's your website converting? Have you checked your analytics?" she asked.

He made a face. "Uh... analytics?" His gaze moved along the side of her neck.

She gestured to the computer. "Do you mind logging in to the back end of your website for me?"

Julian reached around her with both arms as if he were

hugging her, taking her breath away while he typed in the address and entered his login information.

Josie clicked a couple buttons, checking the numbers, while trying to slow her pounding heart.

"You could enter some keywords here," she said, but her explanation faded into silence as Julian moved her hair off her neck and leaned in, kissing her skin.

"Thank you," he whispered, pressing his lips to her shoulder. "What keywords should I use?" The question was on task, but everything else about him wasn't. His hands found her waist and he turned her around.

She attempted to force thoughts through the haze of emotion.

"Cat got your tongue?" he asked, his lips finding hers in one gentle movement.

"We're supposed to be working."

"I am." He kissed her again, making her laugh.

"This isn't work."

"Yes, it is," he whispered in her ear, giving her goose bumps.

She used all her mental energy to pull back. "How do you figure?"

"Because I'm *working* on making you understand that I'm crazy about you."

He stood and scooped her up and threw her over his shoulder, running around the floor, her laughter echoing in the airy warehouse, then he set her back on her feet and took her hands in his.

"I need the marketing help, that's true. But I know you're planning to leave, and I want to convince you to stay. Nick and I can share a room and you can sleep on my sofa if you need to. I'd love to have you on my sofa." He made a playful growl and pulled her close, making her laugh again.

She sobered and looked into his eyes. "I am head over heels

for you, and I'm staying," she said. Then she told him about Nick and Dr. McDonough's offer, about Zelda and Hazel, and Nick's opportunities.

But as she told him all of it, a small piece of her still worried that something might come along and get in the way of her happiness. She wasn't used to happy endings.

"I don't have enough emotional space left to play games, though. I've got to find where I belong so I can really start my life. I feel like I've been treading water for three years."

"I'm not playing any games. I've been in love with you for years, and I'm tired of waiting." He held out his arms. "I'm all yours." He took her hands and pulled her to him. "Stay with me, Josie."

She wrapped her arms around him. "I'm yours, too, if you'll have me."

Julian picked her up and gave her a wild spin, then kissed her once more. When their lips met, it was as if everything in her life previously had prepared her for this joy, because all she'd been through had helped her appreciate the absolute thrill of this moment. She knew she'd be okay if Julian was by her side. She had everything she'd ever wanted, and it was time to start living *her* life.

Epilogue
Eight Months Later

I n the McDonoughs' guesthouse, nestled between the magnolias and pines, Josie cuddled up with Julian on the sofa. Randolph had taken Nick on his private jet to the National Museum of Mathematics in New York for Nick's nineteenth birthday, and they were due back late tonight. Josie had planned a birthday surprise for tomorrow with Rainy, Hazel, Zelda, and a couple of his friends from the math competition whom Rainy had helped her contact.

Through the bay window with a view of the backyard, the sun was scarcely visible, its golden light outlining the trees as it disappeared behind them. Not since those youthful days as a child had Josie felt more content than she did right then. Even if she was quite tired from the whirl of the last eight months.

After her marketing push, Stand Out Rentals had hardly been able to keep up with the demand for the remaining summer months. Then all fall and winter they'd been busy with marriage proposal orders and s'mores package deliveries, and now they were preparing for the massive spring-break crowd. Julian had hired five people and bought two vans to help with delivering the inventory. He'd also hired Josie to do part-time social media and PR.

With the money she'd made from that, a portion of her savings, and a monetary gift from the McDonoughs they wouldn't allow her to refuse, she'd been able to open her own art gallery in town, which she'd named The Golden Hour to honor her mother. It was a tiny space with white walls filled with framed sketches of sunsets and scenes from both Rosemary Beach and her childhood. The front wall boasted one very large set of French doors that opened to the cobblestone streets. She'd kept the furnishings minimal, like her drawings —mostly distressed beech-wood tables with a couple plants in varying shades of green to give a pop of color to the place.

She'd put her natural marketing skills to work for her gallery as well, and she could hardly keep it stocked of drawings. After the launch party, they were selling quicker than she could sketch new ones and keep up with commissions.

But she had more time these days than she once did. Randolph had taken Nick under his wing, and she'd never seen her brother so independent. She realized how much he could grow once he was able to use his strengths. He was unstoppable. And in love. When he wasn't with Randolph, he was with Rainy, who, thanks to the McDonoughs pulling some strings, had moved into a basement apartment in the beach cottage of a retired couple in town. She'd gotten a job at The Salty Shark to pay the rent while she took online classes. It felt as if she had been sent just for Nick. Rainy adored him.

Zelda and Hazel had become fast friends, and Zelda visited frequently, driving back and forth from Lox Creek. The sisters were currently remodeling Josie's childhood home and adding on to provide a mountain vacation spot for the family. Whenever Josie needed a break from work at the gallery or the warehouse, she headed to Hazel's to weigh in on paint colors and carpeting samples. The three artists were in their element when it came to home décor.

On one of the trips to Lox Creek to help with the remodel, Josie had stopped in to see Helen and Ruth. She gave them each one of her sketches, and Helen had cried and told her how proud she was of her. News of the renovations had carried around their small town, and the women at the diner had been following the changes to the house, overjoyed to see the fresh perspective and new life breathed into the town.

Cuddled up with the man she loved, Josie thought about all the surprises she'd received this year, and she was brimming with gratitude.

Julian, who'd been flicking through the TV channels but not stopping on one long enough for Josie to get into the show, checked his watch. Just when she'd begun to wonder why he seemed so fidgety, he got up off the sofa and held out his hand to her. "Will you follow me outside?"

"Right now?" she asked from under the blanket.

"Yeah." He grinned.

She stood and linked her fingers with his. "What is it?"

He walked her from the back of the house to the front door leading to the courtyard between Hazel's house and the guesthouse.

"Close your eyes."

"What are you up to?" she asked, as she complied.

"You'll see."

The creak of the door let her know that he'd opened it, and they stepped through, the boards of the porch under her bare feet.

Julian's breath was at her ear. "Okay, open your eyes."

The entire courtyard was full of mason jars filled with candles, their flickering flames like stars in the night sky. It took her a minute to realize that everyone was there. Nick,

Rainy, Randolph, Hazel, and Zelda. Behind them, scattered among the trees and manicured yard were easels holding canvases.

Julian led her through the mason jars to the first easel. The canvas was covered with pages from Nick's math notebook. They'd been decoupaged onto the surface of the canvas. The zigzag of the numbers on the pages was artistic in its own way.

"Julian helped me do this," Nick said. "I made it for you, but I want to put it up in my room."

His honesty gave her a punch of amusement. Nick handed her an envelope. She lifted the flap and pulled out a card that simply said "Love."

"I love you," Nick said.

His words floated around her like feathers—she'd never heard him say he loved her before. Tears sprang to her eyes. Nick had shown his affection for her many times, but this direct approach was something she'd remember forever.

"I love you too," she said, barely able to get the words out.

Then Nick showed her to the next canvas while Julian followed. It was a watercolor of the Gulf, the soft grays and creams mixing with vibrant sapphire and turquoise.

Hazel stepped forward.

"Thank you for showing me a piece of myself I'd forgotten and for giving me so much more." She gestured to her sister and then to Josie, reaching out and giving Josie a big squeeze of a hug. Then she held out another envelope. The card inside read "Will."

"You have the will to succeed, and you've shown us all that we can too, and that, no matter what, we *will* be okay." Hazel's lips pressed into a caring smile, and she gestured to the third canvas.

Josie walked over to it. An incredibly intricate sketch of Josie's compass was pinned to the surface, and Zelda stepped forward. She handed Josie another envelope. The card inside read "Guide."

"You were the guide to lead me here. I followed you and found more than I ever thought I could. Not only do I finally have my daughter, but I have a sister too."

Josie swallowed the rising emotion in her throat. She'd always wished for a connection with Zelda and now she had it. She wanted to spend every single day getting to know her better.

Zelda put her arm around Josie. "While we love ya and all, and everything we've said is true, we're really here for this guy." She eyed Julian.

He stepped up and took Josie's hand once more, leading her to the fourth canvas. This one was blank. Julian handed her another envelope. She guessed what word was inside, but pulled out the card anyway and placed the four side by side on the final easel.

"Love Will Guide You."

"My card is 'You' because that's all I've ever wanted," Julian said. He waved his arm across the yard. "All those other canvases are your past and what has led you here, but this one is for you to determine. And I hope you'd like to spend it with me."

He pulled a small box from his pocket, got down on one knee in front of her whole family, and opened it. Cushioned in the white satin was a stunning emerald-cut diamond ring.

"Will you marry me?"

This was the moment that everything changed—her golden hour. She threw her arms around him, nearly knocking him off his knee.

"Yes!"

With a chuckle, he pulled back, slipped the ring on her finger—a perfect fit—and then pressed his lips to hers while her family cheered. Josie knew the hardest moments were behind her now, and with her loved ones around her, anything was possible. She looked up at the golden sky and sent a silent thank-you to her parents, knowing without a doubt that *all* her family was with her.

A LETTER FROM JENNY

Hello!

Thank you so much for picking up my novel, *The Golden Hour*. I hope it brought you warm feelings of togetherness and had you running for your loved ones.

If you'd like to know when my next book is coming out, you can **sign up for my newsletter here:**

https://www.itsjennyhale.com/email-signup

I won't share your information with anyone else, and I'll only email you once a month with my newsletter and when new books are released. It's the best way to keep tabs on what's going on with my books, and you'll get tons of surprises along the way like giveaways, recipes, and more.

If you enjoyed *The Golden Hour*, I'd be very grateful if you'd write a review online on the retailer's website. Feedback from readers helps persuade others to pick up one of my books for the first time. It's one of the biggest gifts you could give me.

If you would like to read a few more happy endings, check out my other novels at www.itsjennyhale.com and www. harpethroad.com.

Until next time,
    Jenny xo

ACKNOWLEDGMENTS

I will never publish a book without a nod of thanks to Oliver Rhodes who literally laid the road map for my career. He saw my raw talent, fostered it, and set the bar for everything I do with Harpeth Road today.

I could not bring this book to readers without my fantastic editors who always manage my tight deadlines: Megan McKeever, who swept in and saved the day right when I needed her; the fabulous Jodi Hughes, who I truly believe is one of the best in the business; Lauren Finger, my copyeditor extraordinaire, who I absolutely adore; and the most wonderful proofreader, Charlotte Hayes-Clemens. Another thank-you goes out to Harpeth Road's intern, Olivia Winston, who weighed in with a few of her own ideas that made it to the page. I couldn't have had a better team help me get this story ready than these women.

This book in particular also required the skills of someone very important: Amy Nielsen. Amy's expertise on autism and her explanations during her sensitivity read were invaluable. I am so very thankful for her kindness, candor, and her willingness to read the novel.

The amazingly talented Kristen Ingebretson, my cover designer, is the best of the best. Working with her on concepts is one of my favorite parts of the process. I'm so very thankful to have her for cover direction. There's no one better.

And most importantly, thank you to my husband, Justin, who is always cheering me on and letting me lead the way with every crazy idea I have. I couldn't do it without him.